CHILDREN OF CHICAGO

CHILDREN OF CHICAGO

Cynthia Pelayo

Cover and jacket design by Mimi Bark

ISBN 978-1-951709-20-4
eISBN: 978-1-951709-43-3
Library of Congress Control Number: available upon request

First hardcover edition February 2021 by Agora Books
an imprint of Polis Books, LLC
44 Brookview Lane
Aberdeen, NJ
www.PolisBooks.com

To my sons -

Once upon a time there was a mommy who ruled over a fairy tale kingdom, and there she lived with her king and their little princes for eternity, and they were happy.

The Rose

There was once a poor woman who had two children. The youngest had to go every day into the forest to fetch wood. Once when she had gone a long way to seek it, a little child, who was quite strong, came and helped her industriously to pick up the wood and carry it home, and then before a moment had passed the strange child disappeared. The child told her mother this, but at first she would not believe it. At length she brought a rose home, and told her mother that the beautiful child had given her this rose, and had told her that when it was in full bloom, he would return. The mother put the rose in water. One morning her child could not get out of bed. The mother went to the bed and found her dead, but she lay looking very happy. On the same morning, the rose was in full bloom.

—Jacob Ludwig Carl Grimm and Wilhelm Carl Grimm,
The Complete Grimm's Fairy Tales

CHAPTER 1

"You're going to get blood in your coffee, Detective."

"Hasn't happened yet, Officer Guerrero," Lauren said, digging her free hand in her black canvas messenger bag searching for her gloves. She brushed her fingers against the key to her father's office she made sure was locked before she left the house. "Lauren is fine, by the way."

He smiled, shook his head and lifted the yellow tape, POLICE LINE DO NOT CROSS.

"A little late for coffee?"

It had been a few minutes past seven o'clock when she'd received the call. "It's never too late for coffee." She waved him away. "Thanks, I got it," she said stepping onto the crime scene. The yellow tape separated her from the people gathering at the edges, watching her every movement as if she were on display. Others peeked out from house and apartment windows. The brave stepped outside of their homes, standing on their porches or taking a seat on their front steps covered in golden brown leaves. The chill did not bother them. A bite in the air never troubled Chicagoans.

Lauren finally pulled out a pair of plastic gloves from her bag, making a mental note to hide the key somewhere she would not touch it again. She slipped one glove on the fingertips of her left hand and pulled the opening back with her teeth. Even though she had been on the force a short time compared to her colleagues, she had been assigned enough homicide cases to make her feel seasoned. Her father had been training her to do this her entire life.

Officer Guerrero gave a single dry laugh as he observed her balancing her coffee. She switched the cup to the other hand and pulled on the other glove.

"I'm going to pretend I didn't see that," he said.

It was not sanitary, Lauren thought, but it was effective. "Didn't even spill a drop."

She stood over a white sheet on the concrete, crimson stains in the fabric around the head created a bloody halo. Red and blue flashing lights reflected on the canvas, adding to the glow from the streetlights that had just flickered on overhead. Calls to Humboldt Park had increased in recent weeks. Trouble was brewing.

"The hell happened here?" She asked.

"Male, seventeen-years-old. Wounded in the foot. Taken to University of Chicago Hospital. The other, sixteen-year-old female. Shot in the hip. Taken to Stroger."

"And this one?" Lauren squatted down beside the body. "Let's see who the ambulance is taking for a ride. No sirens needed." With her thumb and forefinger, she pinched the edge of the sheet. She lifted it just a few inches so the crowd behind her could not see.

"You were the first one here?" She sensed him hovering.

"Me and my partner."

"Who's your partner?"

"Rutkowski."

"Where's he?"

"Trying to keep the crowd away from you."

She looked up at him and nodded. That was fair. A lot of people were mad at her. She was used to it.

She returned to the silent figure. The girl wore a gray long-sleeved sweater and a red lightweight jacket. Blue jeans. Black gym shoes. A gray backpack was tossed a few feet away on the ground.

Screams erupted from the crowd.

"Get her outta here!"

Lauren did not know if they were talking about her or the girl. She did not turn around. There was no need to upset them any further.

"Just kids playing at the park," she said beneath her breath. She hated knowing that children risked their lives by being children in this city.

"One shot from what I could see," Officer Guerrero said.

"One shot is all it takes."

The bullet had torn through the girl's neck. The blood on the ground congealed into dark clumps that looked like tar.

"Age? Name? Gang affiliation? Anything?" She asked.

"Nothing confirmed yet, but..."

"But what?"

"A lot of activity around here lately."

"I can see that," she said. "What's going on?"

"There's been complaints. Calls. Kids hanging out too late. Fights."

Lauren looked back to the girl on the ground. Her unseeing eyes looked up towards something Lauren could not see.

"Witnesses?"

"Across the street. Behind you. Guy in the Bears jersey. Says his kid was looking out the window when it happened."

The air smelled of gun smoke and iron, and something else she could not place. Lauren's eyes stopped at the girl's hands. The concrete beneath her glimmered, silver and gold.

"That look like paint to you?"

Guerrero stepped forward, pulled out a small flashlight and aimed the light.

Lauren stood up and backed away, taking in the position of the body, a single orange and yellow leaf floated from above and came to rest on the sheet.

"That's spray paint. It's fresh." She took another step back, and now she saw the colored markings that stretched beyond the position of the girl.

"They're tagging the sidewalk now?" Officer Guerrero shrugged.

"Billboards and garage doors aren't enough for them, I guess," Lauren said.

"That her backpack? Check it for spray cans," Lauren said. "Ask her friends if they were out here tagging." Lauren could easily see if these kids had been out here marking this park it could have upset another gang or neighborhood crew.

"What are witnesses saying?" She asked Guerrero.

"Just that a group of kids was on the swings tonight when shots rang out. They ran. They were hit."

She raised her coffee cup to her lips. Her sixth cup that day. She took in the crowd. More people had gathered outside of the police barrier. The man in faded blue sweatpants and a Bears jersey stood beside who looked like his son, a boy younger than him, taller than him, wearing a white t-shirt, basketball shorts, socks, and black sandals. He was skinny, all arms and thin legs.

"That our witness?" She motioned in their direction with her cup.

Guerrero nodded. "Lauren," he hesitated "...you should probably wait for Washington."

"Why?"

"People...they're upset."

"They should be," she said and then moved towards the crowd. Someone immediately recognized her and began screaming "Killer!" But they were quickly approached by several other officers on the scene.

Lauren ducked under the police tape and approached the witnesses. Before she could ask anything, the man stared her down.

"Folks out here aren't real happy with you right now. A cop who's a little too loose with the trigger. You should've been fired."

Lauren pulled down the collar of her shirt, exposing a pink-white scar that ran from her left collar bone toward her shoulder. Though she did not need to say anything—her words had been quoted in the local and national news for months—she told him exactly what she told everyone else. “I feared for my life. The suspect lunged at me with a knife. I engaged my weapon as I had been trained.”

The man took a deep breath and motioned towards the boy. “I want him to see what happens out here,” he said.

“Did you see any of them?” She addressed both.

The young man shook his head no first.

“I walk my son to and from school every day. If he’s not at school, he’s in the house.”

Lauren removed a small black notebook and pencil from her bag. “Were any of them in school with you?”

The boy shook his head. “I couldn’t tell who it was. It was getting dark.”

Lauren looked out the corner of her eye. There were people on either side of her now. The crowd was growing. Officers Guerrero and Rutkowski stood at either end of the perimeter.

In the distance, the rising and fading wail of emergency vehicles approached, the city’s mourning song. Two more police cruisers appeared.

“Did you want to give me your name?”

The boy looked to his father.

“Johnny Sharkey. My son’s Johnny as well. Junior.” He pointed at the swings. “They were out there. Swinging. I saw them when I looked out the window.”

“Why’d you look out the window?”

“It was getting late. I heard a bunch of kids outside. I looked to see if there was any trouble. I saw them just hanging out and told Junior I was going to bed.”

“Where were you?” Lauren asked Junior.

"Living room. I was doing homework. I heard the shots. Waited a few minutes and then looked outside."

"Did you hear anything before the gunfire?" She asked. "Shouting? People fighting?"

He shook his head. "They were just laughing, and then I heard shooting."

"When you looked outside, what did you see?"

"Kids running and then some on the ground. Then I yelled for dad."

She looked at the words she had written and hoped they would carry some meaning later, something to unlock what had happened here tonight. Lauren put her notebook and pencil away. "I'm sorry you and your son had to see this."

Johnny Sr. placed an arm around his son.

Lauren handed him her card and told him to call if they remembered anything else.

As she turned her back to return to the park Johnny Sr. shouted, "I'm sorry any of us have to see this, day after day, after day!"

There was nothing she could offer. There were no reassurances that this would end tonight or any night soon. There was no saying, "This will never happen again," because this story would happen again, like it did last week and the week before that in this city.

Would they catch the shooter? She hoped, and that is what kept her up at night, sipping on cold, bitter coffee so much so her doctor warned if she did not take a break from it she would burn a hole through her esophagus. She imagined her stomach acid eating away at her, consuming her until there was nothing left, as if she had never been.

"Kids can't even play out in a damn park." A gruff voice said just behind her.

She spun around.

"Shouldn't you be planning your retirement party?" She asked.

"Shouldn't you be planning a funeral?"

"Everything's ready, Washington," she took another sip. "Just be on time."

"Your dad was my partner for twenty-six years. The least I can do is be on time for him."

"I've been your partner for a year, and you've never once been on time."

He shook a finger. "Trainee. Not partner."

"Whatever gets you through the night."

Washington looked tired. He wore the years of this job on his face, and she hated knowing that it was almost time for him to go.

"I worry about you. You didn't have to come out here. You know that," he said.

"I told you. Everything's ready, and I'm not taking any time off. There's just too much going on."

"You can't save everyone," he said, and to that she did not answer, because in her own way, she believed she had to save everyone.

"And when did you have time to plan a funeral?" He asked. "You've been working fourteen-hour days."

"Bobby took care of a lot."

"That's a nice husband you've got there."

"*Ex*-husband."

"Real nice husband."

She ignored him.

"I'm going to tell you again," he pointed at her coffee, "all that coffee can't be good for you."

"It's not good for you if you load it up with sugar and cream and all that crap. Real coffee doesn't need that junk. It just masks the flavor of the bean."

"What about Cuban coffee? That's pretty sweet?"

"Café con leche? Fine," she shrugged. "Depends where you get it."

"I know you don't want to hear this..." he started.

"I don't want to hear it." She knew what he was going to say, and she didn't want to hear him say it.

If Lauren could cover her ears and shut everyone out right now, she would. Their commander had just told her Washington would be retiring this upcoming Friday. He had put off his retirement an entire year to train her.

"You'll be fine," he said.

Lauren laughed to herself. "I'm not exactly everyone's favorite around here."

"Not true."

"Really?" She raised an eyebrow. "I found my chair out in the parking lot this morning."

"They did that again? Look, fine." He placed a hand on his hip. "You're not exactly a lot of people's favorite around here. They don't like you because you're young. They think you got this job because of your dad, and because..."

"I've made mistakes."

He hung his head, and then looked up at her. "Yeah, that you have. Maybe you just had some bad luck. Maybe you just did what you had to do."

"And Van?"

"Now," Washington put a hand up. "You've got to let that go. He asked you about your sister *one* time..."

Lauren did not want to be asked about her sister, ever. Lauren did not even want to think about her sister, because every time her sister came up it was a bad omen. The beginning of the end of something. "And if he asks again?" She rubbed the back of her neck.

"Ignore him, Medina. The case is cold."

"Detectives..."

Alderman Suarez approached, nostrils flared and eyes wild. "What's going on in my ward?" It sounded like an attack.

"Alderman, you and your community would be best to answer that," Washington said.

"That's bullshit, and you know that." Suarez removed his glasses and wiped them on the bottom of his shirt.

"I know you're concerned and all, but this is an active crime scene," Washington said.

"Four," Suarez flashed four fingers inches from Washington's face. "Four shootings this past week. Now a dead teen in the park. How are you going to fix this?"

"Fix this?" Lauren interrupted. "We're going to do everything we can to solve this, and the others, but community policing is the answer. Your people have to be proactive."

"That's what you said at the last few shootings."

"It's what I told you before," Washington said. "Community policing. Block clubs. Neighbors talking to neighbors. We've got a gang tactical team already assigned to this ward, but if the community is not talking, if people aren't telling us what's going on, then you're going to keep seeing us. Well, not us, her and her new partner because starting Saturday I'm retired."

"Washington, congratulations. I'm happy for you, really, but you've worked in our ward for years. We need someone who knows our community."

"Medina lives and works here. You'll be fine."

"Figure this out," he said to Lauren as he pointed to the body on the ground and then stomped off towards a collection of news cameras.

"He's an asshole," she said. "And I don't forgive you for leaving me alone to deal with all of this."

"Oh, you won't be alone. You'll have Van," Washington laughed.

"Van hates me."

"Van hates everybody."

Lauren watched as paramedics wheeled a stretcher over to the young woman. As she was lifted and placed on the padding, Lauren got a better look at the graffiti on the ground where the body had just been.

"What does that say?" As she started to read the words aloud, her breath became trapped in her throat. It had been a long time since she had seen those two words. She backed away. "Pied Piper." She forced herself to say it.

"Who is that?" Washington asked.

She coughed, took a sip of her coffee to clear her throat and then said what she thought would make sense. "Don't know. Maybe some new tagger's name?"

The back door of the ambulance slammed shut, and the driver gave her a wave, signaling their departure. The crowd began to thin, moving back into their homes, except Junior who remained standing alone in the same spot.

They walked back to the car. Lauren slowed her pace to match Washington's.

"I should've asked sooner," she said before opening the car door, "but I think you should say something at his funeral."

Inside, Lauren pulled on her seat belt and waited to start the engine until Washington eased into his seat.

"I'll tell people how great it was to work with your dad. He was the best partner I could ask for."

"You don't have to lie. *I'm* the greatest partner you've had." She took a deep breath. "I'm only going to say it once—and I don't want to be reminded that I'm saying this—but I may even miss you, a little bit."

Washington laughed. "Medina! Look at you showing emotion and everything," he wiped his eyes. "I promised your dad I'd watch after you. Make sure you got settled into the job."

The dashboard illuminated when she turned the car key. The radio blared a weather report warning of early morning snow showers sure to jam rush hour traffic. Chicago in the fall would never please

Goldilocks, the weather was either too hot or too cold, and rarely, if ever, just right.

Washington reached over and changed the station. Spanish lyrics filled the car. A high tempo followed by a brilliant chorus.

"You're serious about learning Spanish, then?" She asked, imagining him retired and settled in a little Mexican beachfront town away from all of this murder and mayhem.

"I'll even order my coffee in Spanish the next time you take me to that Puerto Rican place you like so much."

"I'm going to hold you to that."

As Lauren placed the car in drive, she took one more look towards the park. Junior still stood beside the police caution tape, taking in the graffiti. She wondered why a tagger would choose that name: Pied Piper. She hoped it was just a coincidence, but within, she could feel the growing branches of dread braiding around her heart.

It would not be a coincidence.

Either way, she had a feeling she would find out soon.

It was as if Junior knew she was watching. He raised his head and looked directly at her. Their eyes met.

He smiled.

She felt her throat close. His smile told her all she needed to know. At that moment, and with that look, she finally allowed herself to really believe the Pied Piper had returned.

Lauren closed her eyes tight. There in the darkness behind her eyelids was her little sister, Marie, clearly, in her school uniform, a khaki-colored skirt and a white Polo shirt.

Little Marie. So sweet. So innocent. So long dead. Missing, then murdered. A case so long forgotten it was no longer cold, it was iced.

In Lauren's mind she could so clearly see her, and that wide-eyed smile. Her cheeks, once rosy, turned cracked and gray. Her lips, once red, twisted up in rage, and when her mouth opened from it erupted black and brackish water. Lauren gasped, catching her breath.

She coughed and for a moment she could smell the rotten, stagnant water.

"You alright?" Washington pat her on her back.

"Yes," she lied, knowing very well dead things and wicked things drew near.

CHAPTER 2

The air this morning had a sting to it, maybe because it was Monday. Maybe because a sheet of frost covered the ground. Lauren slammed her car door and walked across snow-dusted leaves, coffee cup in hand, to the nondescript building. Her car was one of just two parked here this early. She thought of the girl who had bled out on the sidewalk last night and how everyone had heard gunfire, but no one had seen the shooter. The girl's name was Hadiya. This would have been her final year at DePaul College Prep, where Lauren herself attended high school not that many years ago.

There were no leads, but there was some chatter. Lauren had spent her night chasing suspicions and social media gossip. All she could verify was Hadiya was an honor student on her way to college in the fall. A classmate, Jordan, had arrived at the park after Lauren had left with Washington. Jordan was supposed to meet Hadiya there. The injured kids were her cousins, in town from Indiana for the weekend. The cousins had given willing interviews to the police and would be released from the hospital today. Their injuries were minor.

Jordan, however, refused to speak. Officer Guerrero told her that Jordan had screamed when he saw the graffiti of the Pied Piper's name. Jordan was who she needed to speak with, but he was already avoiding her calls.

An icy wind blew, and Lauren pulled up the collar of her black trench coat. She could feel the city's demons laughing, cheering, taunting her that they claimed yet another beloved child. Lauren took a sip of coffee. She had stopped at Intelligentsia, a coffee shop just a few doors down, before coming here. A shot of espresso there, and a black pour over of their El Diablo blend to go.

Her phone vibrated. She pulled it out of her pocket to find another text from Van. He had texted four times since last night, and each time she'd ignored his message. She did not want to accept the fact that he was going to be her new partner.

There was no one at the security desk. She turned her phone off and pressed the button to call the elevator. A part of her dreaded coming here, but a part of her enjoyed the illusion of progress. There was no one here who would look at her accusingly. There was no one here who would ask if she should have taken an alternative path.

"Why didn't you use pepper spray?"

"He stabbed me in my chest. There was no time to think."

She could still hear the knife plunging into her as it hit her collar bone. It sounded hollow. Like when you carve a turkey on Thanksgiving.

"And the others?"

"There isn't much time to think when you're going to be killed."

The elevator opened to a dark hallway. The worst part of coming here was how empty and silent she always found this building. Lauren did not trust the quiet. At the end of the hallway she found suite 1337. Inside, there was no receptionist to greet her. This office did not work that way. Her appointments were pre-set, pre-booked—everything managed via email, anonymous behind a digital veil.

It was dim. An essential oil mist of lavender hung in the air. As soon as Lauren took a seat a door opened, and a woman with large, long golden curls smiled.

"Ready?"

Lauren followed Stephanie down a short hallway and into a small room with a bright blue sofa on one side, and a gray plush chair across. A large window looked out over Millennium Park and Lake Michigan.

"How was work last week?" Stephanie asked, and Lauren responded "Good."

Both took their seats, and sat still for a moment, gathering their thoughts.

The word was a reflex. Good. It meant nothing—a pleasant, non-threatening exchange. Work was never good. There was nothing good about uncovering charred and decomposing bodies in moldy, abandoned buildings. There was nothing good about investigating a beheaded, nude body on the banks of Goose Island. There was nothing good about the pink and bloated body of a toddler found in a bathtub of scalding water. There was nothing inherently good about her actual job. The only thing *good* about her career was the level of effort she gave these people who could no longer speak for themselves. She served as the eyes and the voice of the dead, walking with her victims and Father Death, to find their killers.

Lauren noticed a fresh box of tissues set out on the corner table beside the sofa.

"How have you been sleeping?" Stephanie asked.

"Last night was hard," Lauren forced herself to say. Hard meant she had not slept.

Stephanie nodded, leaned forward, and remained silent. She was allowing time for Lauren to elaborate.

Lauren felt as if she sunk deeper into the sofa each time Stephanie leaned forward. Stephanie's eyes zoomed in, analyzing, maybe over-analyzing, Lauren's movements. But that was why Lauren was here. The only place she allowed herself and the trauma she carried to be examined.

Lauren carried many scars. She was raised by a police officer and a musician, two people who knew a lot about the city and its people. She was groomed to absorb the city's tragedies, but not necessarily allow them to affect her. To Diana's disappointment, she had no musical skill. Diana tried exposing her to every instrument she could: violin, guitar, saxophone, but there was no talent there. Lauren's gift resided in reading people and things and constructing a story from whatever puzzle pieces were exposed. Her father steered her into a career in law enforcement, first becoming an officer and then a detective, just like him.

"The funeral..." Stephanie started.

"It's tomorrow morning."

"How do you feel about that?"

Even though his body had been removed from the house days ago, her father had been dead for months. It was no longer Armando Medina who lived in that skin. She had lived with an angry, confused stranger; one who spent many nights outside in their backyard, staring up at the stars, muttering curses and accusations that this world had been tainted with magic so black it was driving him mad.

"I don't feel anything."

Stephanie nodded.

Lauren had been attending therapy in one form or another since she was fourteen. At first, her sessions were mandated by her doctor, the courts, and her parents. Later, when they were no longer required, her father still encouraged her to attend.

"Maybe you will remember something," her father had said.

Lauren did not want to remember.

During college, and her first few years on the job, she was lax about attending therapy. But given the recent attention she was getting from her actions on the force, and her father's death, Commander McCarthy stressed she attend counseling.

"And he will be buried at?"

"Rosehill Cemetery," Lauren answered. "Next to my mother..."

"And sister?"

"Yes." Lauren felt her chest tighten, those branches strangling her heart. She reached for her coffee and when her eyes scanned across the window she thought she saw a small figure with long dark hair standing at the edge of Lake Michigan in the distance. As she focused her gaze the figure waved both arms overhead, signaling she was watching.

"Is it a family plot?"

Lauren looked back to Stephanie. "I guess, but there's no space for me. I want to be cremated and scattered across Lincoln Park."

"The zoo?"

"No, the actual park. It used to be a cemetery. The first city cemetery—the Chicago City Cemetery in the 1840s, right along the lakefront. When the city grew," Lauren made quote signals in the air "they removed the bodies." She reached for a bottle of water in her bag, unscrewed the cap and took a drink. "The bodies, at least for those families who could afford it, were moved to the newer cemeteries away from the city center, Rosehill, Graceland..." She screwed the cap back on and put it back in her bag. "I want my ashes to be scattered there in that park, alongside the rest of the forgotten."

Stephanie took a deep breath and leaned back into her chair. "People who are a mystery?"

"I guess."

"You live for mystery, and your death will be a part of a mystery, Detective."

"Yes." It wasn't a question, but Lauren acknowledged what Stephanie had connected.

"There was this girl last night. She was just seventeen. She and her friends were in Humboldt Park, just playing and being kids. On the swings. I don't believe she was the intended target," Lauren looked down at her fingernails, bitten and broken. "She went to my old high school."

Stephanie nodded and allowed the silence to settle for a moment before asking "How does that make you feel?"

"It makes me angry. This girl wasn't in a gang, from what I can tell. She wasn't affiliated with any of that, and even if she was, so what? She was just a kid. No one deserves to bleed out on the concrete."

Lauren could feel the muscles in her neck tighten. She looked out of the window. The small figure now gone, Lauren followed the outline of Lake Michigan until it disappeared from her sight. "I'll find who did this," she said.

"Does it bother you..." Stephanie started and then continued. "I mean, does this one bother you more because of where it happened?"

"I didn't want to think about it, but it's there. It's something that won't go away. I can't drive through that park without thinking of Marie. I wonder, is that where she went? The playground? Was it there someone snatched her up and dragged her to the lagoon? It messes with me every time I think of it, and I'm not going to let go of that pain. I deserve that pain because I messed up. I let her wander off."

"You were just a kid yourself," Stephanie came to Lauren's defense.

"A stupid kid, whose stupid decision cost her sister's life," her voice wavered.

"Is that why what you do means so much to you? Like you're trying to fix something? Undo something?"

Lauren nodded. "Maybe. Prevent something."

"What do you mean?"

"I don't know. I'm just tired." She made to reach for the box of tissues, but then stopped herself. She was not going to allow herself to do this, to feel more anguish than she should. All she breathed in was guilt.

"You mentioned last week the anniversary of Marie's death was approaching."

"Yes, I like to visit my mom's favorite place on that day..."

"Which one?"

Lauren did not want to talk about these things, to excite entombed ghosts, but she needed to speak to someone, and that is why she was here. With silence, these memories could lay still, but the present was rattling them free. Even when her father was alive, she could not speak with him about her mother or Marie. Concerned friends…there were no friends. Her job pushed away any of her friends who held on after high school and college.

"Rosas. The jazz club close to our house."

"You still don't talk about either much, especially your mother," Stephanie said.

Lauren nodded.

"What are you feeling, Lauren?"

"I'm angry. This was her fault."

"You mentioned last week at the end of our meeting that the anger gets you into trouble? How?"

Lauren removed the lid from her coffee cup and drank the remaining liquid. She set the cup back on the stand. "A suspect was brought in, related to a shooting off the I-290 that struck a car. He died a short time later. When the suspect was brought in, I slipped on another detective's ID and went into the interrogation room and started beating him."

Stephanie held back any judgement. "You were angry because of Diana that day?"

"Yes, and because that's how it goes, right? You're happy, and you're looking forward to your day, your life, the moment that you're living in, and then all of that comfort and stability is ripped away from you because you think back on why your life is so shitty."

Lauren reached over to the cup but remembered it was empty and instead lay her hands on her lap. "People think I killed those other people because I was angry. That's not true. If I discharged my weapon, it was either because I was in danger or another person was in danger."

"Did you ever talk to Robert about any of this?"

Lauren laughed and wiped away at tears that formed in the corner of her eyes.

"I don't even know why I bothered."

"With what?"

"With him," Lauren said. "With believing in the lie of happily ever after, in believing that I could ever be happy."

"Were you happy with him?"

She was, very much so, at one time. It was the only point in her life where she felt she could think clearly. "Yes, and it fell apart."

"You'll be seeing him at the funeral?"

Lauren said yes and that she did not want to think about that right now, about seeing Bobby. She just wanted to make sure her father's memory was honored appropriately for all of his service. Lauren did not know how she was going to return to work and concentrate after this. The sense of heaviness and agitation that dug into her chest and shoulders when she arrived here only intensified the more she spoke.

Stephanie leaned forward, her long curls, the comforting hair of Rapunzel, cascading down around her face. "You blame Diana for what happened to your sister, but not your father?"

"No." Lauren straightened herself up. She knew this would happen. She knew the spirit of Marie would join them and confuse things. That's what the spirits of tricksters did.

"It wasn't his fault. It was Diana's fault. Diana was busy in her stupid room, working on music. Dad sent me a message to pick up Marie from school since Diana couldn't. Marie didn't wait for me. She just left school and tried to walk home on her own, alone, and no one knows what happened between the time she left the building to when she was found in the water." Lauren closed her eyes tightly. Tears ran down her cheeks. "Dammit," she muttered under her breath. Quickly, and silently she brushed them away.

"Lauren, you were lost and eventually found that night. That was a lot of responsibility for a fourteen-year-old. It's not your fault. Not your sister. Not your mother..."

"Diana..." Lauren said.

Lauren looked at the small clock on the table beneath the window. There were four more minutes left in their session. Four minutes was not enough time to unravel how she felt, and how she thought she should feel. A lot of people's lives were destroyed the day Marie did not return home. Some people's lives were damaged immediately, while others collapsed into their sorrow. That's what was happening to Lauren in many ways; she was wasting away along the edges of her own life.

Her nine-year-old sister was dead, found floating in the Humboldt Park lagoon. Then, a few weeks later, Lauren discovered Diana drowned in their bathtub at home. One death ruled a suspicious drowning. The other ruled a suicide.

Lauren knew there was more to the story of Marie's drowning, enough that the spirit of her tortured sister had come to her frequently in dreams and waking nightmares. The ghost of a dead girl demanding justice, but like all stories, there was more to be told. Marie's murder turned up no leads. Yet, someone, or something, had lured Marie out to the lagoon that day. Known, or unknown, there was a villain to every story.

It had been a long time since Lauren had seen the ghost of Marie, and now that Marie had returned to haunt her, Lauren knew the children of this city were not safe.

It was 8:02 a.m. Their session was over, but she needed a moment to process this flash of heat, this sinking, sickening feeling. Graveyard dirt was shifting and turning, and Marie was clawing at the inside of her casket, because she wanted out.

"I'll be thinking of you this week. I hope your father's funeral goes smoothly. I know he would be very proud of you," Stephanie said as she stood up and escorted Lauren to the exit. "It may be good for you to write some of this down. If you get to a place you don't remember, that's fine. Just leave it and write what you do know, what you do feel, and of course what you remember. I think it will be helpful for you."

Lauren had been told that in the past, to sit down in a quiet place and write, to journal, to write letters to people who were no longer active in her life. Perhaps some people thought of it as a sort of exorcism, closing the book on those who have tormented you by writing it all down. She had a bin in her house full of half-started notebooks. Each time she sat down to start another journal she grew frustrated, angry and panicked. Too afraid to disturb the past and conjure evil with her words.

She rode the elevator down and sat for some time in her car, alone there in the parking lot. The sun shone bright, and the thin layer of snow from just an hour ago was melting. Birds fluttered above, singing their warning song, another day, another murder lay ahead.

Lauren turned on the car, but before she pressed the radio button music blared through the speakers, a whining, clanging beat erupted that then dropped into a sparkling flute. She turned the dial, but the music level would not reduce. The loud, harsh beats returned, stinging her ears and then something tapped on the glass beside her, and the music stopped. Lauren shook her head, as if telling herself she would not look.

She knew what that music called.

Another tap on the window, and then a pound.

The sound of glass cracking.

Without moving, Lauren turned her eyes to the passenger side window. Someone's face pressed against the glass, a twisted grin spread across their mouth. Strands of dark wet dripping hair plastered against the surface. A palm faced her, pressing further and further into the cracked glass, cutting into pale, blue skin; black blood dripping down.

Lauren slammed on the gas and pulled out of the parking lot, racing down the residential street, not turning to look until she hit a major intersection, State Street and Congress Parkway. Her heart beat wildly inside of her, she could feel her pulse racing in her neck. At the red light she looked at her cracked passenger side window. It was smudged with dirt, water, and blood.

Lauren knew what this was. This was a warning, and a call.

Her thoughts raced back to that night long ago. To the park, those gnarled, winding trees, a forest within a city—the feeling of the damp grass beneath her feet. The rain pelting down on her face. A long-forgotten moon above, and the man in the black suit watching over her.

She found herself wheezing, trying to find her breath.

She hit the gas once more, driving in the direction of the police station. Her hands trembled on the steering wheel. She had to get in touch with Jordan because maybe he did not know it, but he was in danger. If he knew something about that spray-painted name, about its meaning or its maker, he had to tell her *now*.

Otherwise, it was unlikely he would live through the week.

CHAPTER 3

"Hey, Evie!" Daniel arrived out of breath at the bus stop, holding onto the strap of his backpack hanging from his left shoulder. "How'd you do on your paper?"

Evie tucked a strand of dark brown hair behind her ears. Her earbuds dangled in her other hand. She wondered if it would be too rude to shove them in her ears with someone talking to her, especially given that someone was Daniel. She had been trying to avoid this meeting at the bus stop for the past few weeks.

"Good, I guess." She forced a smile and then wrapped the earbuds around her hand. She looked down the street searching for the bus, hoping and willing it to arrive quickly. Daniel mimicked her moves, standing behind her shoulder and looking down the street for a bus en route.

"It's late," she said to herself and dug in her back pocket and pulled out her cell phone. She tapped on the black screen, waking it to her screensaver, and the glittering skyline at dusk appeared; black and silver pillars shooting into the heavens, like the towers of a magical castle. The Chicago Transit Authority bus tracking app told her the bus would be there in four minutes; four long minutes of standing outside on the corner, being forced to speak with Daniel.

"Oh, yeah. My paper was good too," Daniel offered. "How are your parents?"

"Good," she said, hoping he would not continue, but he did anyway.

"It must be so sad to be alone all of the time. My parents still think it sucks your parents are never there. I mean, it's like you live on your own practically."

Evie had known Daniel since kindergarten. They both attended the same Catholic elementary school, St. Sylvester in Palmer Square, a pocket neighborhood within the greater Logan Square community, surrounded by large homes built in the early 1900s along a green space once a popular raceway for carriage drivers. The plain park was gone, the upgrade included a running track that circled around the edges, and a playground inspired by *The Velveteen Rabbit* by Margery Williams. Evie had spent a lot of time at the children's park of Palmer Square before starting her freshman year at DePaul College Prep. Sometimes she would spend time walking the trail that linked each of the four sections of the children's park, thinking of the Velveteen Rabbit, how he was the wisest and oldest toy in the nursery, loved so much by his little boy, and then how one day after he was no longer of use to the boy a fairy took him into the forest and made him a real rabbit. Forests in fairy tales held that strange sort of magic, and while there were no forests nearby there were the city parks, and their trees, and within these parks Evie could pretend that real magic lived.

At the beginning of each school year when the teacher asked the class if they knew anyone Daniel was always first to raise his hand and say that he and Evie had grown up together. For years, he and his family had lived next door in a bungalow. Growing up, Evie's dad would often give Daniel a ride to school in the morning if both his parents were busy. Daniel moved out of the neighborhood beginning of summer. Evie was not sure why, but she suspected the increase in crime in their neighborhood was a factor.

One evening late summer, before the start of the school year there was some shouting outside of their window. Evie's dad had gotten up from the dining room, a glass of water still in his hand. He made his way towards the large picture window. Evie's mother warned that it was not a safe idea. Maybe it was something about her mother's intuition that kicked on because right then they heard the blasts, one, two, three. Her father released his hold. Bits of glass and ice scattered across their hardwood floor.

That sound of gunfire would go on to repeat itself several times throughout the summer. Each time it was as if the shots drew closer, death searching for their front steps. Her father installed a security camera at their front and back doors, followed by an alarm system in hopes of deterring people from gathering near their house. The cameras did not slow the action outside.

It was mere days before she was to start high school that her parents decided to change where she would attend. One evening, while her father was watching the news in the living room and she was seated in the nearby dining room finishing dinner, the image on the television screen that appeared was that of the side doors to her new high school. The news anchor stood in front of a gray SUV parked on the curb. A nineteen-year-old woman had shot and killed a fifteen-year-old boy for bullying her brother, the reporter said into the camera. A teenager killing another teenager—children killing children, the reporter stressed.

Evie's dad had muted the television and turned to face her. "How do you feel about Catholic School?"

She did not care. They were not Catholic. They were not anything. DePaul College Prep was a good school, affiliated with the nearby Chicago university of the same name. Attending Catholic School was no guarantee that she would be immune from Chicago's violence. Still, it made her parents feel like they were doing something to protect her.

The first day of school she ran into Daniel in the hallway. His family had moved to the safer North Center neighborhood, trading in their historic red brick bungalow whose design was plucked from a

Sears & Roebuck catalogue in the 1920s by his great-grandfather, for a small, newly-constructed condo. They traded history for comfort, to be close to their jobs and Daniel to be close to his school, and for perceived safety. Yet, no part of this city was really safe from violence.

"Evie!" He had stepped towards her, arms outstretched on that first day seeing each other again at the beginning of the school year. Evie took a step back and coughed. A cold, she warned, to avoid his hug.

He smiled awkwardly and patted her on her back. "I'm happy to see you."

When he had asked if he could look at her schedule, Daniel gave a thumbs up when he saw that they shared English at the end of the school day. That would come to be a significant inconvenience as both of them rushed to the bus after class. She learned to get to the bus stop faster to avoid him, but today that did not work.

Daniel did not mean to her as much as she meant to him. Perhaps she offered him some level of comfort, some aspect of familiarity in an unfamiliar place. To her, he was just something that always seemed to be there, like a piece of furniture.

Now, standing next to him, four minutes seemed an eternity.

"I wrote about comics..." He said.

When she did not offer anything else, he clarified. "For my paper on fairy tales..."

She looked down at the app. The bus was still no closer.

They were stuck there waiting, and so she asked: "Comics, like, what kind of comics?"

"I mentioned *The Sandman*," he bounced on the balls of his feet. "That's probably one of the best. The main character in it is called Dream. He's one of the seven Endless. The other Endless are," he rattled them off quickly: "Destiny, Death, Desire, Despair, and Delirium. It gets a little complicated there but..."

"What's the actual story about?" She rolled her eyes.

"How Dream," he scratched his head "learns change is inevitable."

Evie looked down the street once more, searching for the bus. She tightened the earbud cord around her wrist, her flesh turning pink. She needed to get home. "Things don't change. They repeat themselves differently."

Daniel again made as if he were looking for the bus, but Evie knew he was just copying her.

"What did you write about?" he asked.

"Fairy tales. People don't realize there are two main elements to fairy tales, transmission and significance. Some things just keep coming up over and over again. That's transmission. People think life changes, and it does in a way, but so much keeps repeating itself. A variation of the original thing."

Daniel's face was blank.

Evie sighed. "Think of the way these stories used to be told, 'Little Red Riding Hood,' or 'Goldilocks and the Three Bears,' she said. "First, these stories were shared by mouth. Maybe around a campfire told to kids at night, and then in books. Now they're on the internet. People are still telling those same stories, but today they're told differently. Then there's significance, and that's really about the meaning these stories hold for people. Sometimes what becomes important to people about fairy tales is not the *actual* fairy tale, but the representation of that fairy tale. Like, the Disney cartoon character Cinderella, it's not the actual fairy tale that is important to most people, but Cinderella herself, the promise she represents that happily ever after is possible. Or, it might not be the actual stories in a book that are important to someone, but the physical book because that's the book that was read to them by their parent. So, it's the *thing* that represents the story that becomes important, sometimes."

Evie stopped, sure he was lost.

"Comics are kinda like fairy tales, in a way," he said.

"How?"

"Mr. Sylvan said that fairy tales sometimes have supernatural elements, and their characters go through a change. You see that in comics all the time."

She nodded in silence and then dug her hands in her pockets. She felt the cord of her earbuds and regretted again not putting them on. Talking to people, trying to hold a conversation and fake interest was exhausting. No matter how well she knew someone, or how long she had known them, she felt uncomfortable speaking. It made her feel like she was being forced to exist outside of her skin by socializing with people. Right now, all she wanted was to be in her room, even though she was talking about her favorite subject in the world.

"What's your favorite fairy tale?" He asked, struggling to keep the conversation going.

"Guess I don't have one." This was a lie, but Evie did not want to share something so special with anyone. Her favorite fairy tale was all hers to know and no one else. Most of her favorites came from a book her mother had given her, *Grimm's Grimmest*. The cover was beautiful, a red jacket, with the word Grimm's in gold and Grimmest in old English lowercase and in red. It was the illustrations at the beginning of each of the stories that gave a glimpse into the terror of the tale that lay within. Stories like "The Robber Bridegroom," "The Crows," "The Willful Child," and "The Story of the Youth Who Went Forth to Learn How to Shudder." These stories were not about singing fish and dancing snowmen. These stories were brutal and shocking, and something about that made them feel much more real to her, much more possible to her than "The Frog Prince." These were tales told to children, but their warning was apparent; there were witches who lived in cabins who lured children to roast them for dinner, there were men who kept mangled corpses of their former brides in locked chambers, monsters who lurked in forests, and mothers and fathers who abandoned their children to worldly and other-worldly dangers. And like the beautiful words she had memorized from "The Juniper

Tree," *my mother she killed me, my father he ate me*, Evie believed something horrible lived and breathed, tucked within the pages, of the most magical of children's tales.

"Which did you mention in your paper?"

"*Snow White* and *Little Red Riding Hood.* Those aren't my favorites though."

"Why?"

She hesitated then reluctantly offered. "I like the darker ones."

The bus finally approached.

"There are some pretty messed up ones," he said to her surprise.

"Like?" She raised an eyebrow.

"What Mr. Sylvan said today, about the Pied Piper," he laughed once. "That was kinda messed up if you think about it."

"What? About that spray paint across the doors this morning? Pay the Piper? What idiot even wastes their time coming to school early in the morning before everyone arrives to do that? I mean, it must have been someone taking Mr. Sylvan's class, because that's just a weird coincidence."

"No, I didn't mean the spray paint, but yeah, that was dumb. I was talking about the actual story we read in class, about him, the Pied Piper. It's messed up, isn't it?"

She shrugged. "It's a story about a guy who exterminates rats."

"Yeah, but then he took those kids away when the town's people didn't pay him for exterminating the rats," he said. "Now, that's messed up."

The bus stopped in front of them. In the reflection of the glass, Evie saw her, a girl in a red jacket and blue jeans, a chunk of her neck gaping open, exposing bloodied, tangled tissue and bone. When the girl opened her mouth wide to say something, blood spurting from the wound, the bus door slid open. Evie spun around. A boy and a girl in DePaul College Prep uniforms, dark blue Polos, her in a pleated khaki skirt above the knee, and him in khaki slacks and a black belt, rushed past them. The vision in the red jacket disappeared.

The girl with the khaki skirt rubbed her pink and puffed eyes as she scanned her bus card. Her cheeks were streaked with tears. She lowered the hood of her jacket and ran her fingers through cropped blonde hair.

"He probably just killed all those kids," Daniel said from behind Evie as they boarded the bus.

"Funny how that never registered before," Evie said, scanning her card. "You always read how the kids followed him, but I never thought about what happened after. I guess you're right. The insinuation is there. He killed those kids."

Evie looked down the aisle of the bus, packed with people standing, scrolling through their mobile devices, asleep or staring outside of the window. There were practically no empty seats left.

"Hey," a small voice called to her right. It was the girl with the short blonde hair. She was wiping her eyes with the palms of her hands. "You can sit here if you want?" She motioned to the empty seat beside her.

More people boarded, pushing Daniel towards the rear of the bus where he was bunched in with other standing passengers.

Evie took a deep breath. As she sat down, she could feel the tension release from her jaw and shoulders. She pulled out a book from her bag, opened it, and tried to focus on the words on the page. It was difficult to concentrate, but something about the black letters across the page gave her comfort. These stories had been here long before her and would continue to be here long after she was gone. The bus began to move, and she heard the girl laugh as the boy next to her leaned in and whispered something into her ear.

"I had to pretend to care, didn't I?" The girl said, and she laughed again. "You'll see things will be good. They'll be great. I doubt he'll come back for a while."

At the next bus stop, the girl with the short blonde hair leaned toward Evie and said: "Glad to be rid of him?" The girl flashed her eyes toward the rear of the bus where Daniel was standing, looking down at his phone.

Evie could smell the strawberry-flavored gum on her breath.

The tears were gone, like they had never been there.

"Are you okay?" Evie asked.

"Yeah," the girl pulled out her phone, unlocked the screen and pointed the camera at her face. She patted around her eyes with the pads of her index and middle finger.

"Some girl in our class got killed."

Evie gasped. "I'm sorry."

"It's fine," the girl put her phone away.

"What happened?" Evie asked.

"She was shot in the neck in Humboldt Park. Probably some gang something. Who cares?"

The boy sitting next to the girl leaned in. "No one really knows what happened," he said.

"This is Mo."

"Mohammed," he said and waved hello. "Mo's fine though."

"I'm Finley...but Fin's fine."

"Did you know her?"

"Hadiya? Yeah. She was probably on track to be valedictorian. Smart." Fin shrugged. "Sad, I guess."

Fin's eyes widened when she looked down to the book in Evie's hands. "Ah, you're probably in Mr. Sylvan's English class. Which explains this." Fin reached for Evie's book, taking it out of her hands. "*Grimm's Fairy Tales*. He starts off the first few days of class pretty boring, but then gets into fairy tales, and that's where things start to have meaning." She flipped through the pages of Evie's book. "Weird, right?"

"We've already started on that part."

"Did you guys go on the field trip yet? To Newberry Library?"

Evie nodded. “Last week.”

Fin laughed. “He’s been teaching the same class for decades. My aunt had his class years ago.”

“He just came back out of retirement last year,” Mo interrupted. “He retired to Germany and then came back.”

Evie reached for her book, but Fin did not offer it back.

“Does he still do that thing where the class goes into the big conference room, and he tells you to stand in front of a covered book. Then it’s your job to unveil the book and title to the class and present it?”

Evie nodded.

“I knew it,” Fin said into Mo’s shoulder, a bright smile on her face.

“Nice,” he nodded.

“Very nice,” Fin agreed.

It was as if they were saying something without really saying anything at all.

“I had a feeling about you, as soon as I saw you with this book. Let me guess?” Fin looked from Mo and then to Evie. “Your pick at Newberry Library was an especially rare copy of the *Grimm’s Fairy Tales*?”

Evie’s mouth opened. Her eyes widened. “How’d you know...”

“A good guess. We got the same book during our field trip of Newberry Library too, and I could just tell there was something special about you. You flipped through the pages then?”

Evie nodded.

“And you found the black page?”

Evie stared. “I don’t understand.”

“I’m psychic,” Fin laughed. “No, not really, but I just knew you found it. See. We were meant to sit next to each other today.”

“It’s not real, though?”

What Evie had read on that black page, in that aged book could not have been real. What she had seen in the library later that day, and what she had seen later that night outside of her bedroom window could also not possibly be real. That page, a single black page in a book of aged, yellow paper did not make sense. Its shimmering golden text in beautiful looped script did not make sense. Because of that, she had ripped the page out of the book when no one was looking and tucked it away in her backpack. She *had* to have that page. She had to have those words.

Fin looked to Mo, and they both broke out in laughter. Mo applauded. "We are not alone," he said.

"Oh, it's real," Fin said. The bus sped along the street now. "It's very real."

That was impossible, Evie thought. For so long she had hoped for fairy tales to be real, but they could not be real, could they?

"You're joking," Evie said. She was sure that this was some mean joke on a freshman by upperclassmen. She was waiting for them to laugh in her face and spread the story about her throughout the school the next day, about how gullible and insane she was.

Fin shook her head. Mo smiled.

"I'm not joking," Fin said.

"Prove it," Evie said looking at her *Grimm's Fairy Tale* book resting on Fin's lap.

"Hadiya is dead, isn't she?"

CHAPTER 4

A floorboard creaked in another room. Lauren dropped her suitcase on the floor with a thud, and listened. It was quiet in her father's house—now her house. This suitcase contained the last of her things from the condo she and Bobby had shared. After he left, she'd lived there alone for some time. She came to live out of both homes, nearing the end of her father's life. She did not expect that she would take on the role of caretaker so early on.

It started while she and Bobby were still married a year ago, and it all happened so fast. Her father called her in the middle of the night and said: "Your mother wants to talk to you." He must have held up the phone to an unseen specter because Lauren heard nothing.

"Dad, mom's been dead for years. Did you have a bad dream?"

"No!" He shouted into the phone. "She's here with Marie."

That's when Lauren kicked off the blankets, signaled to Bobby that she was leaving and stayed on the phone with her father until she arrived at his house. She found him sitting outside on the front steps shivering in his pajamas waiting for her.

"Shh." He held a shaky finger to his lips.

She did not hear anything.

"The music is everywhere," he said. "It's outside. It's inside."

"Dad, let's go in the house," she said as she took him by his arm and led him inside.

"It's everywhere. The donkey. The dog. The cat. The rooster," he said as he shuffled slowly towards his bedroom. "They were so mistreated by their masters, they set out and left their homes and became musicians, and now they are here, and now they are playing for me. They are playing for you too, Lauren. They are playing in Bremen, because here they have their freedom and to live without owners and to become musicians is something better than death we can find anywhere."

None of his ramblings made any sense. He must still be in that in between place, between dream and awake she thought. She set him down on his bed. "Dad, please. I don't know what you're talking about. You need rest. I'll be asleep on the sofa if you need anything."

"And why don't you just sleep in your bedroom?" His eyes wide. "Marie is there."

Lauren sighed, tucked her father into bed, kissed his forehead and turned off the lights. Bobby called her to make sure everything was all right. On the phone she asked him:

"This might sound strange, but does this mean anything to you, a donkey, dog, cat, and a rooster and music and Bremen..."

"What? Umm...yes, the *Town Musicians of Bremen*. Why are we talking *Grimm's Fairy Tales* at one in the morning?"

She rubbed her eyes. "It's nothing. I don't know. Maybe dad was up late reading or watching TV and his brain got all jumbled, and he had a nightmare. He's fine now. I'll see you in the morning. I'm going to stay here with him to make sure he sleeps through the night."

She sat up in the living room all night that night, hoping to hear what her father heard, but she never heard the music.

Standing in the living room today, she almost thought she could hear a soft, repetitive cheerful melody. Maybe it was coming from a neighbor's house, their loud music seeping through their walls. It was still early enough, just shortly past 7 p.m. People had every right to play music outside at this time. Was this what her father heard that night many months ago?

It was just sounds of the neighborhood and nothing more. He was not well then and deteriorated from there, speaking of ghosts and witches, gnomes that lived in the walls, animals he spotted in the yard who begged him to come closer, so they could share secrets with him, and fairies who would float and dance above his bed, speaking of promises and curses. In those final days, her father was tormented by a world she could not save him from.

Lauren reached down and slipped off her black ankle length boots and set them beside the door. She hung her jacket in the coat closet. When she looked down the hallway, she thought she saw the wisp of a shadow floating across the kitchen. She rubbed her eyes. It was the lack of sleep, she reasoned with herself. Her eyes were tired. Lauren walked into the kitchen, opened a cabinet and reached for a bag of coffee—her father's favorite—Café Bustelo. The familiar yellow and red packaging was welcoming. Here in this kitchen is where he spent most of his time, or in his office, reading and drinking coffee. She looked to the right of the coffee can and made sure the key was there, and it was, gold and glistening and taunting her all the same. It belonged here and not in her bag. With it here, she would be able to watch it closely, and if the time ever came to use it she knew where to find it. Keys unlocked more than just doors and this one, she suspected, would give her answers to questions that she was not yet ready to have revealed.

Lauren shut the cabinet, spooned two heaping spoonful's of ground coffee into the French press, boiled water and poured it over the grounds. She poured herself a cup of black coffee into her Chicago Police Department coffee mug.

Hearing music in this house now was strange and conjured a memory of the way things once were. This had been a quiet home since Marie and Diana's death. When Diana was alive the house was filled with music. The living room was imprinted with the memories of Chicago blues players singing their sad, soulful song. When Diana was alive, the turntable in the living room seemed to always be on. The soundtrack of their home: Muddy Waters, Willie Dixon, Louis Armstrong, or her mother's favorite Buddy Guy…

My songs do not sound the same
There's so much heartache and pain
When it's all taken, I will not be blue anymore

The spare bedroom on the first floor had once been Diana's music room. There, Diana wrote, practiced and listened to music. It was a sanctuary of sound, a place where Lauren and her sister Marie would very often run off to when no one was looking. They would look through the books of music, sheets with cryptic symbols which were overwhelming to review, but it was all so exciting. Their curious script seemed secretive but intriguing—a mysterious clue to decode. They fought the urge to press the keys on Diana's piano. Instead, they would brush their fingertips across the ivory keys.

A saxophone, clarinet, and a guitar rested safely in their enclosed cases, but the sisters knew they were there, and still, sometimes they would open those cases just to look at the instruments their mother played. Then there were the harmonicas, so many shiny, brassy, leather and metal covered harmonicas. Lauren's favorites were those harmonicas in silver and metal finishes.

Diana would not necessarily be angry when she found the little girls in her music room, annoyed perhaps. Diana would laugh this dazzling laugh and cover her mouth as if surprised to see them there. An exaggerated look of shock to find the girls playing in her room.

"What are you two doing in here?" Diana would wrap her arms around Marie and give Lauren that forced smile she often gave her. By this point, Lauren's wish of having any skill at the piano had fizzled, and so it was very often little Marie whom Diana would sit at the piano, guiding her tiny fingers against the ivory keys, pressing them down and playing music. Amazing, beautiful, radiant music would fill the house, created without the help of Lauren of course. After Diana's death, Armando sold all of the instruments and turned Diana's music sanctuary into a guest room no one ever slept in. Music was never played in this house again.

Lauren dragged her suitcase upstairs, to the main bedroom that would now be hers. She set the bag beside the closet. It was unlikely she would unpack what was in it today or tomorrow, or ever. Exhausted, Lauren relaxed back onto the bed and closed her eyes. She wondered what it would be like to have her father still alive and healthy. She wondered what it would be like to have her mother still here, and finally, her thoughts drifted to Marie.

Marie. So sweet. So trusting.

Lauren had learned a lot about what happens to someone when they drown. She knew holding her breath was a conscious act. She knew if she were forced to hold her breath the desire to breathe would increase with intensity and burn. When someone holds their breath carbon dioxide levels accumulate in their blood. While underwater, when someone can no longer hold their breath they naturally, forcefully breathe, water rushing in. As the liquid flows in through their nostrils, and into their lungs, their vocal cords spasm. Their vocal cords close. When their body fills with water, they violently—and noiselessly—cough. Movements slow. Consciousness is lost. And as their heart struggles to work against the onslaught of water, it reaches a point where it can no longer effectively pump blood, too full of liquid. When awareness is lost, the body succumbs to the water. That's what Marie experienced when she drowned, according to the coroner's report.

Sweet little Marie.

Thump.

Lauren sprang up and listened. She closed her eyes and strained to hear the noise again, but there was nothing. Even the faint music from moments before was gone. All was silent. It did not escape her that this house held more than just mystery; it held the ghosts of people long dead and secrets that should stay hidden. Like Bluebeard's castle, or the murderous Chicago fortress created by America's first serial killer H.H. Holmes who filled dozens of rooms with bloody secrets, her father's mind too was full of rooms filled with blood. And this is why Lauren kept that key close, but never used, because she was not yet ready to unlock her father's office.

She checked her phone. There were no messages. She had spent the afternoon knocking on doors, asking people if anyone had seen anything before the shooting at Humboldt Park. People did what they often do in Chicago; they did not open the door, or they refused to provide any information. The unsaid "no snitch" policy was in full effect, not because of some loyalty to some gang, crew, or person: People did not want to talk about things that could potentially get them killed. It could have been a completely random shooting. Those were not unheard of in the city. What made this different was that spray paint on the concrete. That name gnawed at brain: Pied Piper.

Taggers got creative with their aliases around here, making their mark with not only their names but with color and characters. This name, however, seemed different. It stood out from the other famous Chicago street artists—JC Rivera, Hebru Brantley, Sentrock and the others. It also stood out from any common street tagger name. People around here often did not pick their names from books, legends, myth and fairy tales.

Thump.

Lauren walked to the stairway. Maybe it was a rat, or rats. If you saw one rat that meant there were dozens nearby. Her hand moved to her waistband. A 9mm semi-automatic Smith & Wesson on her hip. She slowly moved downstairs, listening. It was quiet. The refrigerator was old. It could be the ice maker. The ice maker at the condo always rumbled in the night.

She took a seat on the sofa in the living room and kicked her legs up on a footstool. She pulled out her phone and looked at the blank screen. It rang in her hand, as if she had willed it to ring.

"Hello," she answered.

"Hello, is this Detective Medina? This is Sara Crowe from Newberry Library."

"Yes, thank you so much for calling," Lauren removed her feet from the footstool and planted them on the floor.

"Sorry I missed your messages," Sara laughed to herself, a nervous laugh. "I have to tell you, Ms. Medina, I've never had a detective call requesting a book. Is this for official business?"

Lauren did not know how to answer. How could she explain that a rare book of fairy tales was needed in a murder investigation? She still did not want to revisit what happened that night. For years, it had gone without a name. Her childhood therapists had kept much of the scientific reasoning behind her condition out of their sessions. It was Stephanie, her therapist today, who helped finally give it a name.

"Dissociative amnesia, Lauren. That's what you have, and it's not your fault," Stephanie told her in one of their first sessions.

"Will I ever remember?" Lauren recalled asking.

"Maybe. Maybe not? There's no way to know right now," Stephanie said in that calm, soothing voice of hers. "Those memories still exist, and maybe they'll resurface on their own when you are ready. Sometimes a trigger is needed to recall them, but you can't worry about it. You can't obsess about that hole in your life. For whatever reason, your mind is protecting you from retrieving those memories. If it's something you think you would like to try to tap into, then I can refer you to someone who can probably help."

"Another therapist?"

"Yes, there are some who claim to use some techniques, hypnosis, for example, to try to unlock what the brain has stored away."

At that time, Lauren was not ready to dig into the depths of her mind. Instead, she asked for some reading recommendations on dissociative amnesia. She wanted to know why she had blacked out a space and time in her life.

Memories came flooding back over the years, at times like droplets of rain and at others, torrents. At first, all she knew was what she was told: that she was found wandering Humboldt Park hours after Marie was discovered floating in the lagoon. Lauren was told she was found barefoot. Her jacket was missing, and she was trembling, cold and soaked from a thunderstorm that had passed. Marie was found still in her school clothes, and her backpack was tossed onto the sidewalk. A copy of *Grimm's Fairy Tales* was found resting in the sand at Chicago's only inland beach. Lauren was questioned at her father's police station by Commander McCarthy before he was Commander McCarthy—Detective McCarthy then. After being questioned, Lauren was sent home.

When Lauren became an officer, she checked in the evidence archives for the book, but it was gone. All evidence related to Marie's disappearance and death disappeared. Misplaced, Washington suggested. That book was lost among the thousands of cardboard boxes, plastic bags and evidence files locked away and forgotten in storage, yearning for their clues to be lifted and a killer to be found.

"You said that you're looking for the earliest edition of *Grimm's Fairy Tales* that we have?" Sara asked.

"Right, I actually have seen the book before. I'm not sure if you've acquired any older editions since I saw this last one, but it's that one particular edition that I'm looking for."

"When were you last here?"

Lauren thought back to when she was a high school freshman. "It must have been eleven, twelve years ago..."

"Oh...that is a while back, but you are right, I don't think we've acquired anything new in that area for quite some time. I think what you are looking for is an 1823 copy of *German Popular Storie*s that we have that was translated from *Kinder-und Hausmärchen*. It's a first edition, second issue."

Lauren wanted to shout, "That's it!" but she restrained herself. "I feel like that has to be the one."

"The problem is..." Sara began, and Lauren's heart started to race. She needed to get ahold of that book now. "It's actually on display in an exhibit that's due to conclude next week. It's a short exhibit. I can certainly reserve it for you for next week."

Next week was too late. Someone else would be dead by then.

"Is there any way to access the book for a private viewing beforehand?"

Sara chuckled. "I don't think so. The curator would be quite displeased if we move anything, considering there was a recent robbery attempt of another rare book after hours. If you provide us with a warrant we will certainly comply, but otherwise it will have to be until next week, unfortunately."

Of course Lauren could not get a warrant. How was she supposed to explain any of this to Commander McCarthy? It was Monday afternoon. She could not wait another day. After seeing the graffiti in Humboldt Park, she had a feeling, a horrible, suffocating, sinking feeling that more young people were going to die this week in this city. There was no lawful reason she could present to the librarian for needing this book now. She could not say that this antique book in a rare collection was connected to a greater evil blanketing this city. That book had already destroyed so many lives and would never tire of destroying more.

"What's wrong, Lauren? Did you forget to pay the piper?" Sara said on the other line.

But it no longer sounded like Sara.

Lauren pulled the phone away from her ear as the woman started growling. A long drawn out laugh pierced through the speaker.

Lauren flung the phone across the room. It hit the wall with a crash. The dent in the wall was apparent. The screen remained intact.

Thump.

Thump.

Thump.

Thump.

The sound was coming from the guest room mere feet away. Lauren stood up and removed her weapon. She listened as the floorboards moaned under her weight. The slow, repetitive knocking continued.

"Police! Stay where you are!" she shouted.

Thump.

Thump.

Thump.

Thump.

It was a single, rhythmic weight. It was not a rat. A rat would scurry and claw across the floorboards as soon as it heard her voice. This sounded heavier.

Lauren pushed the door to the guest room that no one had ever slept it. It did not open into the never disturbed, plain room. Instead, she found herself staring at Diana's music room, perfectly intact the way Lauren remembered it on the last day. The small piano. The cases of musical instruments Diana had shooed her away from so many times. The dozens of harmonicas that Diana had collected over the years were all opened and tossed beneath what was making that thumping sound.

The body of her sister hung from the ceiling fan in the middle of the room. A rope tied around her neck. Eyes bulging. Hair dripping wet. Her white Polo shirt and khaki skirt—the school uniform she drowned in. Soaked.

Thump.

Thump.

Thump.

Thump.

The ceiling fan's blades beat as Marie swayed. Water rolled down her blue face. Large sheets of water fell from above, over her, and into the large pile of harmonicas gathered beneath her. All of Diana's harmonicas were collected beneath Marie as if it were some grotesque variation of a bonfire.

Instead of fire, metal.

Marie's body continued to sway, the fan blades struggling to turn, but unable to against the weight, so it just continued to click away.

Thump.

Thump.

Thump.

Thump.

Lauren fell back.

Marie's arm shot up. Her eyes wider now, bulging and black. One finger pointed to Lauren as water rushed down Marie's contorted and grotesque face.

Lauren aimed her weapon, closed her eyes and fired. She pulled the trigger over, and over, and over again. Unloading the weapon into all that she feared. When the gun emptied, and the room smelled of smoke, she opened her eyes and found herself looking at the empty guest room and a bullet-ridden wall.

There were no musical instruments. There was no piano. There were no harmonicas, and there was no Marie.

Just a plain bed, a nightstand, and a ravaged wall and the smell of gun smoke remained.

Lauren hoped she had finally exorcised the ghost of her sister from her mind, but she knew the specter of death was still there. It was that book. It had always been that book.

She should not have ignored it for so long, because now it had been opened.

Now she needed to find it and destroy the message within.

CHAPTER 5

"Everyone is bringing you food," Washington said, standing beside Lauren, both of them staring off into the crowd. "Hell, your freezer will likely be full by the time everyone's gone, and you won't have to worry about what to eat for weeks."

Lauren did not say anything. She just nodded and held the double whiskey she had poured herself. Each time she tried to take a sip it seemed as though someone stopped to tell her just how sorry they were.

The ice cubes melted. Lauren wondered now if this made her whiskey neat. Funny, that is how her dad drank his; no ice, no water, not chilled, just straight from the bottle—neat.

It was odd seeing so many people in her father's home. For a moment she became overwhelmed with the thought of all those shoes in her house, walking up and down on her hardwood floors. She wondered if any of those shoes had walked across a murder scene, fragments of blood and brain matter embedded in their rubber soles, and now dragged through her house.

"I'm so sorry." A woman she did not recognize pulled her into a tight embrace. "If you need anything please reach out to me and my husband."

"Okay, I will," Lauren said. She was not even going to pretend to know the woman's name.

The woman gave her a somber, tight-lipped smile and walked out the open front door where many mourners were making their way.

"You have no idea who that was," Washington laughed to himself, stirring his drink in a clear plastic cup. Rum and Coke.

"Not a clue, Washington. Not a damn clue."

"The commander's new wife."

"His third?"

"Fourth." He downed his drink.

The house was stuffed with the smells of the pork shoulder Officer Nieves had roasted the night before, a cheese and guava tart baked by the head of the Office of Emergency Management and Communications, and the dozens of other dishes that covered the living room table, kitchen table, buffet, kitchen counters, and end tables. Food covered every surface. Lauren had never seen so many people in her house.

"Whatever's in the oven smells like apple pie," she said softly. "Dad was obsessed with all things apple, apple tarts, apple turnovers, apple pie. I'll miss apple picking with him in the fall," she laughed to herself, years of memories of driving up to an apple orchard in Wisconsin to pick Honey Crisp, Pink Lady, Granny Smith, Jonagold, and more, all of those moments were packaged into a single thought of childhood joy.

"It's okay to cry, you know," Washington said.

Lauren gave him a side-eyed look "I don't cry," she said.

"That's not good for you, holding everything in all the time."

"If you cry, they can't rest," she took a sip of her drink. "There's this story, 'The Burial Shirt,' of a mother who cried so much over her dead child he kept coming to her in visions, telling her he could not rest because his shirt was wet with her tears. I don't know, I don't believe in ghosts or anything, but I just don't want to risk the possibility that he is somewhere else, and he can see me and if I'm suffering then he can't rest. He deserves to rest after everything..."

"Where'd you hear that story from?" He faced her.

"My mother."

He nodded silently and turned back shoulder to shoulder with her, watching those in the house talk amongst themselves, eating, or sitting in quiet contemplation.

It was as if all the city's first responders came to mourn with her because they too had lost one of their own. Lauren tipped the whiskey back. The sting was missing. The water had taken that away.

"What are you going to do with the house?"

Lauren stared at her empty glass. "Keep it, I guess. We sold our condo. Bobby's living in some apartment somewhere."

"I'm sorry. I forgot to ask how that's going. Wait," Washington looked around. "Where did he go?"

"He left," Lauren set her empty glass down on a side table. "He likes to do that."

"Really? Didn't you leave him?"

"It's complicated."

She did not want to talk about Bobby anymore, so she let the conversation drop. She scanned the room and found herself staring at the American flag set in the middle of the living room table in a triangle-shaped display case.

"Each fold symbolizes something," Washington said. "There are thirteen folds. The first fold symbolizes life. I think that your father would have wanted for you to live your life as fully as you can. He was very proud of you."

"Funny, he never said anything like that to me. Plus, it's partly because of him that things have been so difficult."

"You need to stop beating yourself up. The other officers don't hate you because your dad was a detective. You're new. It's just a bit of hazing. It'll die down soon."

Both of them knew that it was more than just hazing. Lauren *was* hated. All of her colleagues thought she was too young, didn't have enough experience, and only got where she was because of her dad. Chicago nepotism at its best. It also did not help that she had discharged her weapon more than once.

"Medina," Commander McCarthy patted her on her shoulder. "Take as much time off as you need."

She did not want to take any time. The thought of being away from work, alone and in this house made her worry. There was so much to do. Hadiya's death had set off protests in the community, marches and vigils. Alderman Suarez hinted at police incompetence, steering blame away from him and his community. Someone had to know who fired that gun, yet no one was talking.

"Sir..." she caught him at the door. "I want to come back to work. Tomorrow. A lot is going on right now. The Humboldt Park shooting has people upset."

"Van can take care of that."

"It's not that..."

"What then?" He cut her off.

"It's odd. The graffiti at the crime scene."

"There's graffiti everywhere."

"Yes," she stood in front of the doorway, blocking his exit. "But I feel like I've seen this signature before."

"Medina," he lowered his voice. "You're tired. You've been through a lot. You're going to need some time. When my father died, some things needed to be done. His things needed to be taken care of. For that alone, take some time. The work will always be here."

Commander McCarthy gave her another pat on the back, that awkward pat a coach gives you right before you go into a game both of you know you cannot win. He stepped through the doorway and was gone.

Before she could say anything to get his attention Washington stopped her.

"Look, he's right you know. You don't have to worry about proving yourself right now. You can give yourself some time to mourn. Then, when you're ready, you can come back on board and deal with all of this."

Lauren shook her head slowly, trying to put the pieces together, but she knew half the puzzle was missing. "There's just something not right about this."

"Hadiya's shooting could have been the wrong place, wrong time. It happens. I don't think she was the intended target either," Washington said.

Washington's wife Loretta appeared. She handed him his jacket.

"I made you a dish of breakfast sandwiches. They're wrapped up and in the freezer. Just take one out and microwave it for two minutes. If you need some more or anything just call me. I'm home and can help, honestly," she placed her hand on Lauren's shoulder. "I don't mind at all. Frank's busy with school. Earle's wrapping things up at work and I'm just at home dealing with this move."

Loretta had retired last year and now was happily planning their move to Mexico. She was ready to leave this city and was hoping Washington would be prepared to leave it too. They'd fulfilled their parental duty. Their son Frank had made it to college, a freshman studying music at Northwestern University. Washington reminded them at work every chance he got how his wife was counting down the days to his own retirement, and now that day was almost here.

"How's Frank doing?" Lauren asked.

Loretta smiled. "Really well. He will be performing this Friday in the school orchestra, 'The Earle King' by Schubert. It's a piece he has been practicing for a very long time. It's challenging. I'm very excited."

"I'm excited too, for him."

"I'm going to the restroom. Loretta said. "That should give you two enough time to finish talking about what you don't want me to hear."

When Loretta was out of earshot Lauren said, "My son, why do you hide your face in fear?"

"You're talking crazy again, Medina."

"It's from the Erlkönig poem."

"You know a lot of weird stuff," he said.

"You don't want to leave, admit it," she said.

Washington drew in a deep breath. "There's just so much I didn't get to finish. So much I was never able to set straight."

"I have to go back to work tomorrow. I can't let this get cold. Talk to him for me."

Washington had both hands on his hips and was doing that slow head-shaking-side-to-side-open-mouth-movement he did when he was so frustrated he did not know what to say.

"You need time off, Medina," he finally blurted. "You need to take care of yourself."

"I'm not going to let this go. I'm coming in to work later today. I can't let this be forgotten."

Loretta returned and was at Washington's side. "Ready?"

When he did not move, she said "Well, I'll leave you two. I'll be in the car." Loretta gave Lauren a hug and then whispered in her ear to be strong.

"You've got to talk to McCarthy for me. It's Tuesday. Hell, let me finish off this week, and I'll take a break afterward..."

"What's so special about this week?" He asked.

"I need to just figure this one out." She was working against a deadline she could not really share, but still, she could not imagine her life without working, without helping people, without putting the pieces back together. Worst of all, she could not imagine just sitting here and drowning in the thick grief that consumed this house. It had been brought in by everyone, dragged into this home on the soles of their shoes, and had been smeared across her living room, and dining room table, a pinch of sorrow added to each dish.

They had all smelled musty, from sitting in the church for over an hour. The sun came out as the casket was lowered into the ground at Rosehill Cemetery. The words of the priest had registered to her only as muffles. As the gravediggers stepped forward to fill the grave she stood there stunned with the realization that the last living member of her immediate family was gone.

Lauren had stood in front of her father's plot, covered with fresh dirt and could not cry, but when she turned to the plot to the far left of him, away from Marie and Diana she collapsed, and it was Bobby who had cradled her in his arms. "I just miss her so much,"

Bobby kissed her forehead and held her until her body could produce no more tears.

When she could finally stand on her own, Bobby had asked her for the keys to her father's house. He told her he would make sure the house would be ready for her guests. She told him the door was open. Perhaps he assumed she had been so distraught she had forgotten to lock the doors. That was not the case. She never locked her doors anymore. Unlocked doors meant she could run out of the house whenever the memories overcame her. She did not like sleeping in this house alone. Intranquil spirits lived here.

When Bobby had spoken to her, asking her for those keys, those were the most words they had exchanged in weeks. She had seen him in the house when they arrived from the cemetery, but he had disappeared at some point without a goodbye, slipping away in silence—just like he had when he left her the first time.

Washington shook his head. "You're your father's daughter, but you have to live for something besides yourself. What's done is done."

"I do live. I live for this job."

Washington pressed his lips together and reached for his jacket on the coat stand beside the door and put it on. He rubbed his chin and then said: "Now you know I've never brought this up, ever, but..."

"You really don't have to," Lauren shut her eyes tight, as if doing so would prevent him from saying what he was about to say.

“You don’t have to live like this. You can’t live with that much guilt. Don’t ever feel like you have to do this job, live this life. You don’t have to repay anything. You don’t have to redeem yourself. Having this job, this career, should not feel like penance.”

Lauren felt her throat tighten. This job was her absolution.

“Look,” Washington continued “I’m not saying that what we do isn’t important. It is, but you have to live for something else.”

“I need to talk to that kid, Hadiya’s friend.” She said. “Officer Guerrero said he started screaming and broke down in tears when he read the graffiti. He knows something about it, Washington.”

Washington laughed. “You didn’t listen to anything I said.”

“No,” she shook her head. “I didn’t because I need to do this.”

Lauren turned around and looked at the remnants of her father’s funeral. Detective Van was standing next to a near empty tray of flan. She could not help but watch Van for a moment, wondering how this new partner relationship was going to go considering he did not trust her and thought her inadequate for the job. She’d heard when Van complained to Commander McCarthy about being partnered with her.

“Lauren’s too young,” Van had shouted in McCarthy’s office. “She doesn’t know what she’s doing. She doesn’t belong here. And...”

“And what?” Commander McCarthy had snapped.

“You know...”

“I don’t listen to gossip. I listen to facts. This better be the last time I ever hear you utter anything questionable about one of our own.”

Now, Van was here in her father’s living room paying respects to the man whom he blamed for guiding her towards this life. Nearly everyone on the homicide team had a spouse, significant other, or children. These people had support. Both of Lauren’s parents were dead, and her husband had left her. Then there was the ghost of a sister she barely remembered. And the ghost of that memory was trying to not only break into the tragedy of the present but destroy Lauren's life as well. Lauren was not going to allow what she had built her entire life to be destroyed by the past.

"The boy was questioned. He said he went to visit Hadiya. Just a Sunday evening meet up with a bunch of kids," Washington said.

"I don't think that's all. I need to talk to him."

"He was already interviewed. There wasn't much he said, and I don't think he wants to talk about this again. There's not much we can do. He's not a suspect."

"Can you get him to talk me? I know you can."

Washington reached for a bottle of Bacardi on the side table and poured himself another drink."

"Weren't you leaving?"

"We parked down the block. I've got five minutes to finish this up before she comes looking for me." Washington knocked the drink back, closed his eyes and shook his head. "I knew you wouldn't let this go."

"I won't."

He placed the glass down on the table. "I did some digging and learned he spends some time at the Young Chicago Writer's writing program before school."

"Where you're on the board?" Lauren smiled. "Thank you!"

"Wait," he raised up a finger. "First, I'm no longer a board member since I'm retired and leaving this city. Second, he's not going to talk to you if you just walk in there and flash your badge."

"Why not?"

"He's a minor," he started counting fingers on a hand. "There's no reason we should be interviewing him. You can get sued, get the department sued. You have been walking a fine line already. Do I need to keep going?"

"Fine, what do I have to do?"

"Volunteer. I know the director there."

"*Volunteer*? Doing what?"

"Tutoring. Tutoring him early mornings before he goes to school. When I reached out to the director over there, Elizabeth, she said Jordan needs a new mentor."

Washington removed a faded brown leather wallet from his back pocket. It was stuffed beyond its intended capacity, slips of paper and business cards sticking out. He shuffled through a collection, mumbling to himself. "It's here somewhere...ah..."

He handed her a card with the name, Elizabeth Ryan, Center Manager.

"Please help me understand what I'm supposed to do. I'm not a writer. I'm not a tutor. I can't do either."

"If you want to talk to him this is probably your best way. Plus, you know a lot about literature and poems and all that. Look at Frank's performance this Friday. I couldn't even tell you what the name of that thing is, and you knew it right away. I didn't even know it was a poem. I just thought it was a composition, a piece of music Frank was going to play on piano this Friday. What's the poem even about?"

"A child is on horseback with his father at night on their way home. The boy reports seeing strange beings and the father just attributes it to the boy's imagination, that he's seeing fog or mist or shimmering willow trees or the swaying leaves. The boy shrieks. The father checks and discovers his son is dead."

"You see, I'm certain you're probably the only one in the department who even knows that. Look, just call Liz. Tell her I sent you. That you've got fancy degrees in English and Literature and you want to be a writing tutor for at-risk kids, but you can only tutor early mornings. That should lead you to him."

"Really good detective work. Thank you, Washington. I appreciate this."

"Don't worry about McCarthy. I'll take care of him. Now, what are you going to ask this Jordan kid when you see him?"

"I'm going to ask him why he's lying."

CHAPTER 6

On her way to her room, Evie stopped by the kitchen, grabbed a glass of water and a cereal bar. Her mother kept boxes of fruit and nut bars for when Evie got home from school. It was a small way her mother felt she was still actively parenting her teenager, making sure she had something to eat while she was away at work. She had stopped at the library a few blocks from her house to check something in the reference materials, and even getting home late from her usual time did not matter. No one was ever home when she got home from school. Normally, by the time Evie got home from school, her mother was starting her second job.

Evie pulled out her phone from her jacket pocket and tapped on the glass to check the time. Her father would still not be home for a while either. He was nearing the end of his day at his job downtown. Her father got home first, around 6 p.m. and then her mother would get home a few hours after. Evie would see them in the morning for a few minutes, pouring coffee as they complained about how tired they were and how the house needed another repair they could not afford. Evie knew that money was tight because they had to pay for her school tuition.

In her room, Evie hung her jacket in her closet and set her backpack on the floor with a thud. "Dammit," she winced as she pulled out a notebook and her tablet. Evie set both on her writing desk.

She thought about what Daniel said, about comic books being modern folklore. She also wanted to reread the Pied Piper story, and so she stood in front of her bookcase searching. It took her a moment to find it, but then she plucked out her copy of *Grimm's Grimmest*, containing nineteen of the darkest of fairy tales, fiendishly illustrated.

Evie spent as much time with the fairy tales as she did with their history. The brothers Grimm, Jacob and Wilhelm started collecting fairy tales in their youth, and many of these folktales, legends, and myths were told to them by Henriette Dorothea Wild who would years later go on to marry Wilhelm and live with the Grimm brothers for the rest of their lives. Evie loved their history, magic, mystery, and even the horror spun fantastically into those words. She flipped the pages, looking at the gory illustrations. First, seeing "The Robber Bridegroom," where thieves dragged a young woman to their underground hideout, forced her to drink wine until her heart burst open, and then stripped her naked before hacking her body into pieces. She turned another page, the "Six-Swans," where a wicked mother-in-law was burned at the stake. She turned yet another page, and there was "The Juniper Tree" where a mother decapitated her stepson and fed him to his unknowing father. Then dear "Cinderella" in which the evil stepsisters chopped off their toes and heels, and forced their mutilated feet into a glass slipper to try to gain the love of a prince. Finally, she turned to the last story in this short collection of violent Grimm's tales where, in "Snow White," the evil queen was forced to dance in red-hot iron shoes until she died, all for attempting to poison her stepdaughter with an apple. Stepchildren, stepmothers, distant fathers, and heartbroken and lonely children always figured prominently in these tales.

She turned more pages, searching for "The Pied Piper," the story of the mysterious man dressed in a suit of pied who whisked an entire town of children away as revenge for not receiving payment for exterminating the town's rats. Evie flipped back to the table of contents but did not find the title there. She was sure if it would be anywhere it would be in this collection of blood-soaked tales. She took a seat at her desk, turned to her tablet and searched The Pied Piper. The first search entry that came up was "The Pied Piper of Hamelin," but nothing appeared immediately associated with the Grimms brothers. The further down she looked she found that many had written about the Pied Piper; Johann Wolfgang von Goethe, Robert Browning and more.

She reached for her phone in her backpack and texted Fin. She and Fin had exchanged numbers on the bus and Fin made Evie promise that she would text her this evening. Fin said she wanted to reveal to Evie all that she knew about him, the man whom she had read about and now the man that she had seen. Fin told Evie on the bus as Evie got up to leave "You'll see him too. You'll see, and when you do that means it's starting."

"What's starting?"

"Your new life. Everything you've ever wanted and more."

But life did not work that way, could not work that way, could it? Magical and enchanted keys, snow, glass, apples and mirrors? Strange creatures and beings that lurked in the woods, animals that talked and witches who blessed and cursed? Could it be true? And if there was an ounce in the power of this magic, what would Evie do with it?

"Hey," Evie started crafting her text message. "You mentioned Mr. Sylvan's class and the Pied Piper. Didn't the Grimm brothers write it?" She hit send and imagined not hearing back from Fin tonight, or ever.

Evie's phone vibrated in her hand. Fin responded.

"There are tons of variations. Robert Browning's is popular. It's a poem. Read that one."

"Tons of variations of a guy who killed rats?" Evie responded.

"Haha. He killed more than that. He killed all of the town's kids. Read the poem."

Evie set her phone down and searched. It did not take more than a few clicks to find Browning's version, a fifteen-stanza poem online.

"Found it yet?"

Evie looked at the text. She could feel Fin's excitement radiating through her messages.

"Looking at it now."

"Cool. Read it. Do it now."

A nervous laugh escaped Evie's mouth. It felt almost like Fin was standing behind her, encouraging her to look at something, read something forbidden.

Evie grabbed her phone and turned the screen face down on her desk forcing herself to concentrate on the words on her computer.

In Browning's version, he introduces the town of Hamelin, a place so overrun by rats that the townspeople demand their mayor and officials put a stop to the public nuisance. During a council meeting to discuss the rodent problem, a stranger appears. He is tall, gangly, wearing a suit of pied—multicolored—with a flute hanging around his neck. He says he would rid them of their troubles.

"Please your honors," said he, "I'm able,
By means of a secret charm, to draw
All creatures living beneath the sun,
That creep or swim or fly or run,
After me so as you never saw!
And I chiefly use my charm,
On creatures that do people harm

After a payment amount was agreed upon, the Pied Piper stepped outside and began to play his flute. Immediately, the rats came from everywhere, following him down streets as he played and danced. He led them to the river, and the rats continued moving forward, on into the water, not caring that they went deeper and deeper into the water, not caring that they had no need or want to reemerge to the surface. And there, they drowned.

When the piper went to collect his payment, the townspeople dismissed him, saying they would never pay a vagrant, breaking their verbal contract. With that, the piper left, only to appear early the next morning, when he again played his flute. But this time, it was not rats that appeared by his side. It was all of the town's children who walked towards him, and silently stood beside him, hypnotized by the music. The adults were frozen in place, unable to interfere, and watched in horror as the stranger led all of their children away; kidnapped during the day, as the sun shone down on them, and under the watchful eyes of their loved ones.

Evie reached for her phone.

"What does that mean?" Evie text Fin. "*I chiefly use my charm on creatures that do people harm*?" She sighed as soon as she sent that. She felt silly for doing so. It was a story, that's all it was. So why did any of this matter?

While she waited on a response, she finally located the Brothers Grimm version, "The Children of Hamelin." Evie read quickly. This version read more like a news article than a fairy tale, about a small town in Germany who had lost its soul in losing its children.

Evie looked at her phone again. A sinking feeling grew in her stomach. What if Fin was at home right now laughing at her? What if Fin was texting, or was with, Mo telling him how stupid Evie was to be taking such a deep interest in fairy tales? She stood up, tossed her phone on her bed and did all that she could do—pace her room.

Browning's poem was beautiful and lyrical, but still, it told a story of what happened. The Grimm's version felt very real, reading like it was pulled from a newspaper or official account. There was something here. Evie wanted to believe in it so much she balled her hands into fists and willed for this to be true. The brothers had themselves said that the meanings of the tales had been lost long ago, but that one could still feel their substance because these stories were not insubstantial fantasy.

Evie stopped and stood in front of her bookcase and the titles at the top row were all screaming at her; *The Uses of Enchantment: The Meaning and Importance of Fairy Tales*, *Off With Their Heads! Fairy Tales and the Culture of Childhood*, *The Hard Facts of the Grimms' Fairy Tales*, *The Irresistible Rise of the Fairy Tale* and more, so many more. Some people spent hours playing video games, on social media scrolling and buying into the culture of content and consumption, but this is what Evie did, she poured over the historical fact and fictions of fairy tales. She knew more than Mr. Sylvan could ever teach her. Folktales and fairy tales exist on the same line, but folktales bend towards the naturalistic while fairy tales bend towards the supernatural. Yet, Evie knew that the stories collected by the Grimms ran the gamut from folklore to literature. Evie also knew words were edited, with Wilhelm in particular editing them again and again, trying to improve upon the source material, but why? And how? The Grimms brothers altered the telling of these tales by their very presence, being present to have the stories told to them so they could be recorded. The stories were then edited, and then the stories were edited again for younger audiences. What was omitted or changed will never truly be known, but this was a game of telephone across generations, cultures and languages, a game Evie felt was still being played. She believed that fact and fantasy were blurred on these pages.

Still, hundreds of years had passed and the real meaning of all of these fairy tales it seemed had still not been unearthed. This process seemed exhaustive, as exhaustive as the Aarne-Thompson-Uther-Index, a system like the Dewey Decimal System but with wolves. This massive catalogue includes classifications for over 2,000 fairy tale plot types across seven categories; animal tales, tales of magic, religious tales, realistic tales, tales of the ogre, anecdotes and jokes, and formula tales. This was not something Evie could look up online. She had to actually go to the library and sift through the catalogue in order to find it, ATU 570, The Rat-Catcher.

The phone vibrated on top of the comforter. She reached for it, and there was Fin with another message.

"You found the story then?!"

"It's crazy. I wonder if that's what he wanted all along. The kids?"

Evie covered her eyes with both hands. "Ugh, this is so dumb," she said to herself as she hit send on the message, but as soon as she sent it, Fin responded.

"He did that because the town's people failed to meet their obligation. They wanted someone to come in and solve their troubles. The Pied Piper appeared and promised to get rid of their problem. For that, they promised to pay him. They did not. He took payment in another form. Their kids. You always have to settle your debts. You always have to pay the piper."

Evie stared at those last three words. The same as the graffiti on the doors outside of school this morning—pay the piper. Evie was beginning to wonder if Fin was hinting at something else. Was she missing a greater point? Evie turned back to her tablet, this time bringing up her notes from the library, ATU 570:

The earliest known record of the story of the rat-catcher is in a depiction in a stained-glass window created for the church of Hamelin, which is dated to around 1300...

Fin sent another message.

"Do you always pay your debts?"

Evie did not have any debts. How could she possibly have any debts? She did not even have a part-time job. Her parents would not let her look for part-time work until she was at least a senior in high school. She was only a freshman. There was a long way to go before she had any financial independence.

"I don't even have money. No way I'm even going to get into something where I owe someone money."

"Right, I get that, but if you make a promise to someone, do you tend to keep it?"

"Yes, always."

"I've got an odd question for you," Fin text. "You don't really like Daniel, do you?"

Evie could feel her nostrils flare. She hoped that Daniel did not put Fin up to this.

"Totally not interested in dating Daniel," Evie responded quickly as that is where she thought this was going.

"No. Right. Nothing like that. I mean like, you just can't stand him at all, right?"

Fin was right. That was an odd question. Maybe Evie seemed especially annoyed when she started talking to Fin on the bus. She was flustered that Daniel kept asking her questions. She just wished he left her alone.

Fin added to her message. "What if I told you I knew of an easy way to get rid of people you didn't like. People who were a problem. You could get rid of Daniel."

Evie laughed aloud to herself. "Nice, but I've tried everything you can imagine."

"Not everything," Fin quickly responded.

Evie stepped back to her bed and sat down, crossing her legs beneath her, and scanning her books on fairy tales and lore. It was in them that she read the hero generally enters a fairy tale world in order to escape their conditions at home but is very often exposed to more perilous situations where they have gone to seek refuge. Evie considered herself the hero of her own story and those from her old world, her mother, father, and people like Daniel were her monstrous adversaries. She was intrigued and wanted to know more. If there was a way to get rid of Daniel, then she was open to listening.

"The Pied Piper could get rid of him for you. No one would need to know."

Evie felt like throwing the phone across the room and covering her face while at the same time screaming "yes" and charging forward with whatever quest this would lead her on. Yet, how could she know she could trust Fin? A girl who seemed to fall out of the sky with a wondrous tale? What if Fin and Mo were at the other end of that phone laughing their asses off? What if this was all a lie? Evie could feel tears in her eyes pooling. This is why she did not have friends, because all the kids she thought were interesting and smart thought her odd, and easy to make fun of. The only people who ever wanted to talk to her were her teachers, or Daniel: people who knew how alone she was all of the time since her parents were never home. Evie had practically raised herself, learning to cook on her own, learning to take the train and the bus on her own. Her parents were occasional tenants of this house who slept here, showered and left. Evie lived here in isolation, with her thoughts.

"Evie..." Fin texted again. "I'm serious. Meet us at Humboldt Park after 7. Bring Daniel. I can show you. Promise."

Evie did her homework, then spent too much time online looking through people's pictures and feeling like she was standing at the edge of her own life. She rechecked the clock, and it seemed like no time passed at all. Eventually, she made her way to the chair beside her window, curled up with a copy of *The Bloody Chamber* by Angela Carter, and as she read about the vampire shuffling her tarot cards Evie's eyes closed. She was awakened what felt like just a few minutes later by her father's knock on the door "Hey, you okay?"

"Yes," she said from her chair.

"Did you eat? Need anything?" He said from the other side of the door.

"I'm good. I ate. Just going to work on a few things and then step out to meet some friends," she said.

"Alright, be home before nine."

Evie picked the book up again but forgot where exactly she left off with the vampiress alone in her crumbling castle. She closed the book on her lap and turned to the window and watched as the sky turned a golden red, then violet before shifting black. She sent Daniel a text asking him to meet her at Humboldt Park at seven, and within seconds he responded that he would be there. She closed her eyes again and awoke at the sound of rumbling.

Evie sat up, scanned her dark room and noticed a light flashing from the floor just next to where she was seated. Her phone must have slipped and fallen on the floor at some point during her sleep. She leaned over, picked it up, and turned off the silent alarm.

Evie stared at her phone and wondered if she should text Fin, but what would she say? She had no idea what Fin was planning. Yes, Daniel was annoying, and yes, Evie wanted him out of her life. Evie now wondered, how wrong was his presence and what would she be willing to do to remove him entirely? He had occupied this space in her life since kindergarten. He was there since she was five years old, and beyond, and had inserted himself in nearly any conversation he could and served as a constant reminder of how alone she was, and how her parents were never really there. Birthdays and Christmases were rushed celebrations because there was always work—they were always having to get back to work— and she was left alone to attend to the birthday cake leftovers and decorations that needed to be put away by someone, which always seemed to be her. Maybe Daniel was just lonely, like her. Perhaps he genuinely thought that there was a chance that their association could become romantic. Or, maybe he just really wanted to be her friend. Whatever it was Daniel felt for Evie she felt nothing for him other than distaste and hatred.

It was getting close to time. Evie looked under her bed and retrieved the black page she had taken from Newberry Library on that school trip not long ago. She stood up and moved over to the window to pull aside the curtains and unveil the reason why even though her parents were never home she always felt she needed to be. It was then that she noticed movement across the street. It was as if he materialized from the shadows. While her parents were never there, at least he was.

She looked down at the bright, shimmering golden script against the black page, and knew this was the same man the words spoke of. He stepped out from the darkness and took several steps forward, standing beside the streetlight. The man in the black suit looked up at her bedroom window. He extended an arm up into the sky and waved hello. Evie could not see his face as it was mostly obscured by a massive black hat.

He tilted his head just slightly back, and that still did not help her make out the blurred features of his face, but she could make out that chilling smile bathed in shadow.

He waved again, and again, slowly, back and forth, back and forth, letting her know, like always, he was here watching, waiting.

She was not alone as long as she had him.

She pressed her face against the cold glass and waved back.

He pressed a hand to his heart, and dipped his head in a bow, as if to say at your service.

CHAPTER 7

She ran with her gun.

Her father had warned her against it. A gun made people nervous. Yes, she was an officer. Yes, Illinois was a concealed carry state, and that applied to the city of Chicago. But, if someone saw a bulge on your waistband, followed by the metallic handle of a gun, their mind did not automatically register you as law enforcement. You were the villain.

Lauren had told her father not to worry. Still, as fathers do, he worried.

"Where are you going?" He'd shouted from his office, the door was opened halfway. She saw through the crack in the doorway that his reading glasses rested on his face as he read something on his computer screen. A mug of coffee in one hand. It was a coffee mug she had made for him when she was in middle school, years ago. It bore the Chicago flag—two horizontal blue stripes on a white background, and across the white center, there were four six-pointed red stars. When she'd made it, Lauren did not know the meaning of the stripes or stars. The top white stripe represents the North Side, middle stripe the West Side, and lower white stripe the South Side. The top blue bar represents Lake Michigan and the north branch of the Chicago River. The bottom blue bar represents the Great Canal and the South Branch of the river. Four red stars are situated across the Chicago flag. The first for Fort Dearborn, then the Chicago Fire, The World's Columbian Exposition, and the Century of Progress. Beyond that, each point of those stars represented something else. That was Chicago, every layer held significance, everything held meaning, and if you looked away too quickly you could miss history.

He did not wait for a response. He continued. "It's too early."

"Dad..." She opened the door completely, standing just outside of the office. She did not like entering. There were too many files in here, too many names ended in tragedy. Too much clutter and too much detective work centered on death. His office was like a morgue, but the dead here were stored in pages, in files, on notepads. His office was his own personal catalogue of cases he had worked on, interviews and notes, police reports and complaints. The stories of people and their lives unraveled and ended in this space. While the room felt overwhelming, with towering stacks of documents across his desk and every surface, there was a system here, and he could retrieve information within minutes. She had seen it herself when Washington called or McCarthy or another detective who was now working one of the many cases Armando handed off after retirement. No detective ever retired with a fully cleared desk. Most remained forever tethered to those they were meant to protect or find.

"You should be in bed."

"I'm not sleepy," he said.

"It's 4 a.m. You should be sleeping."

"So should you," he countered. "It's still dark out there."

"I'm going for a run, Dad. The sun will be up by the time I get to the lake."

"Don't take your gun," he said as he stood up and shuffled toward her. She took him by the arm and walked with him to his bedroom. He sat down on the bed. "Retirement, it's lonely," he said, and she wished she could tell him something to make him not feel so lonely.

"Once I get settled in, I promise, we'll catch a Cubs game or something."

He laughed to himself.

"What?"

"Washington's going to keep you busy. There's no settling into this job. This job rips you away from your friends and family." He had said it jokingly, but he choked on the last word. "There's a lot of things I regret, and a lot of things I miss. I miss them, all of them. I tried all that I could to find her…"

"Me too," was all Lauren could say.

Retirement had given him time to think, time to mourn again, and with mourning again, came renewed suffering.

"I just want you to be safe," he said as he lay down.

"I have my gun on me, for exactly that reason; so I can be safe." She gave him a kiss on his forehead. "Don't worry. I'll be fine. I'll be back by the time you wake up."

Her father closed his eyes. She turned off the light, shut the door, and hoped he would have a restful sleep without the nightmares.

"I'm proud of you, Lauren," she heard him say softly from the room as he drifted to sleep. It was the first time he said anything like that in a very long time. He did not tell her that he was proud of her at her undergraduate graduation or at her master's graduation. In fact, she was surprised he showed up to each of them because he was always busy, always working. He did not even tell her that he was proud of her when she was accepted into the academy or when she graduated as an officer. Maybe his illness was allowing him to finally say things he should have said long ago.

She had parked her car at 31st Street Harbor. This is where she started her run, mostly because there were no businesses nearby. It was just her and the lakefront running path that took her toward the city skyline. Running towards those buildings that stretched into the sky gave her encouragement. Like if she was focused enough, ran fast enough then maybe she could catch up to those skyscrapers and their fairy lights that illuminated the heavens. The run from 31st Street Harbor took her through Museum Campus that held The Field Museum of Natural History, The Shedd Aquarium, and the Adler Planetarium. Then, she ran through Millennium Park, and to her destination, Lincoln Park Zoo. One way it was 6.2 miles, and the round trip gave her more than enough practice for the upcoming Chicago Half Marathon.

Lincoln Park Zoo opened at 10 a.m., but she had made it there shortly after 6 a.m. Her father called. He said he could not sleep. So, he got out of bed, made another cup of coffee and was reading the news.

"Don't be too long. You have work," he reminded.

She told him she would be home before 9 a.m. She was meeting with Washington after 10 a.m. After working as a police officer for a few years and passing the written exam and two months of detective training, her trainer had conveniently become her father's previous partner, Earle Washington. There were cries throughout the department that reached her, people accusing her of not having to have worked as hard as others, and of getting by quickly. The system was rigged, they said, to make it easier. Just look who was training her? Washington assured critics and Lauren that there was to be nothing easy about her training after the academy. She would have to do the work. She would have to read the case files, interview witnesses, the coroner, paramedics, and whoever else seemed critical to any pending investigations.

Reaching Lincoln Park Zoo was one of the highlights of her run. She did not run through the zoo, like many joggers in the early morning hours. She had preferred to walk and enjoy the place to herself. The city's zoo was free and set within the more massive Lincoln Park that spanned thirty-five acres.

Like many of the city's neighborhoods, the Lincoln Park neighborhood held a wealth of history. When tourists visited Chicago, they were often curious about the city's criminal present and past. Of course, the city's most famous crime boss was Al Capone, who many believed orchestrated the infamous St. Valentine's Day Massacre of 1929. The murders happened just a short walk from where she had found herself, where seven members of the North Side gang were gunned down, suspected murdered by Al Capone's South Side gang. No evidence ever connected Capone to the crime, but everyone knew he did it. In Chicago, criminals very often got away with it.

Chicago was a graveyard. Even Lincoln Park itself was a literal graveyard, once holding the Chicago City Cemetery, where the first recorded burial was in 1843. Maybe that is why Lauren had visited the zoo frequently. Thousands of bodies were exhumed there and relocated to several new cemeteries throughout the city beginning around the 1860s, or so people thought. In many cases, they moved the headstones but not the bodies. To this day, during construction in the area, bodies were still being found. It saddened Lauren to think that beneath her footsteps lay the bones of a forgotten someone. Like the horrors of Chicago's past, some things remained the same in this city; crime and how quickly the dead were forgotten.

Lauren entered at the main entrance off Fullerton Avenue. She noticed a handful of cars parked in the lot, likely belonging to other runners like her who ran through the park or along the lakefront path. At the East Gate a sculpture of beloved African lion Adelor who had prowled the Kovler Lion House from 1995 to 2012 greeted her. She rubbed the bronze statue's nose for good luck and entered. Just beyond the entrance gates was the actual lion's enclosure. No animals would be outside for some time, still. She continued up past the enclosure towards the lion house. Lauren stopped, and walked up the steps and looked inside. She placed her hand on the door, not thinking that it would open but it did. Lauren stepped inside the damp hall, with vaulted ceilings. Inside there was an information board that welcomed visitors to the historic landmark built in 1912.

"It's not open yet," a male voice said.

She searched and spotted a man standing in front of one of the empty animal housings.

"I know that," she said.

"Then why are you here?"

Lauren searched his shirt for the insignia of the zoo or anything to indicate he worked here, but there was nothing. He was in a leather jacket, faded jeans, black shoes, and wearing dark sunglasses. Not an early morning jogger.

"I can ask you the same," she said.

"You a cop?" He looked her over.

For a moment Lauren's mind raced. Why would he ask that question? And just when she was going to ask him why he would ask something like that he pointed to her navy-blue sweatshirt. CPD emblazoned across. Chicago Police Department.

"I see the new recruits jogging in those same clothes in the morning outside my house."

"You're a South Sider hanging out way up north at," she considered her watch "6:22 a.m.?"

"Yes," he nodded. "You have a gun on you and everything?"

He caught her completely off guard. She collected her thoughts, looking down the long hall. When she looked back, he was smiling.

"I think I should go," and she took off, walking briskly towards the exit.

"Here," he jogged ahead of her, pushing the sunglasses up over his forehead. He reached for the door, but Lauren beat him to it and opened the door for herself.

She walked back toward the entrance gates. It was time to start heading back home. She had that meeting with Washington she could not miss, and her father was waiting for her.

He continued following her. "My name's Robert by the way. Bobby."

"Didn't ask for your name, but now that I have it I can ask Bobby, why are you here so early?"

"I can ask you the same."

She eyed him and then said "Running." Motioning to her clothes, and then wiping a film of sweat from her forehead.

"That's very attractive," he said. "And your name?"

"I'm not going to give you my name. You could be a serial killer."

"I gave you my name. I'll give you my full name, Roberto Garcia. I'll even give you permission to look up if I have any tickets or outstanding warrants."

"Do you?"

"Maybe a parking ticket for leaving my car double parked to pick up a pizza."

"Lauren. No nickname."

"No nickname? Everyone needs a nickname."

"How do you even find a nickname for Lauren?"

"How's Lore?"

She liked the sound of that, but she did not want to admit it.

"Do I have a choice?"

"No," he smiled.

"I told you what I'm doing here. What are you doing here?"

"Taking pictures," he motioned to the SLR camera hanging from his neck.

"I don't know if you noticed this, but there are no animals out yet. They don't release them until the zoo opens."

"I'm not taking pictures of the animals. I'm taking pictures of statues," he motioned her over to look at the viewing window of his camera. She hesitated, but he encouraged her. Plus, she had her gun on her, so she felt comfortable enough to approach.

"Statues?" she questioned.

"Here," he held out the camera. "Just look. I'm not crazy. It's just easier to take pictures when there aren't people swarming around them."

She took the camera in her hands and looked at the image. It was of Adelor, the lion. “Yup, that’s a statue, and probably the most obvious one to take a photo of here.”

“That’s a nice attitude you have there.” He took the camera from her hands.

“I guess I should say thank you?” She said.

“Here, maybe you’ll like this one.”

On the screen, there was an image of a winged statue leaning over the figures of two small children.

“I volunteered some time to take pictures for the Statue Stories Chicago project. It’s kind of cool, really. The Richard H. Driehaus Foundation is funding the project. When completed, you’ll be able to visit any of these statues throughout the city. Scan the nearby QR code with your phone, and you’ll get a callback...”

“From the statue?”

He nodded. “And they’ll give you a short history lesson about themselves.”

“This is what you do for a living?”

He laughed. “I’m a volunteer. I just wrapped up my Ph.D. at the University of Chicago and start teaching there next term.”

They were walking now, and she did not know why she continued to talk to him. Maybe it was because the extent of her social life beyond work involved only talking to her father. Lauren had no one else, really. After so many deaths in her family no one wanted to remain close. Yes, there were those who came around immediately afterward, with plates of food and pity. People liked to hover around times of tragedy, but no one remained around for long. She was lonely, and it felt nice to talk to someone, and for someone to genuinely want to talk to her.

They walked past the Endangered Species Carousel, featuring forty-eight endangered animals, from elephants to rhinoceroses, hand carved by artisans. The song of the cicadas played this morning, their rhythmic chirping rising and falling. She looked down at her feet. The sun washed the cement in an orange glow, and when Bobby told her to look up, the fairy appeared.

"That's the Dream Lady, Lore."

It was the same statue from the image he showed her just moments before. The Dream Lady was more beautiful in person.

On the ground right at her feet were the words EUGENE FIELD. Before Lauren could ask Bobby who Eugene Field was he told her.

"Eugene was a Chicago author and a journalist who died in 1895. He wrote a humor column for the *Chicago Daily News*. He was famous for writing poems for children. He was called the poet of childhood. This monument was erected in 1922. It was funded mostly by kids. They collected money, pennies, whatever they could at school to build this."

"Funny," she said. "it's been here this entire time, and I never noticed it."

"Sometimes you can't see something unless you're looking for it, you know?"

"It's lovely, but I honestly am not one for fairy tales."

"Really?" His eyes met hers. "Everyone likes fairy tales."

"Not me, or anyone over ten."

"Not true. I know a lot of adults who love fairy tales."

She raised an eyebrow. "What makes you an expert on fairy tales?" She crossed her arms in front of her chest.

He looked from side to side and then pointed to himself.

She laughed. "Wait, is that what you studied at your fancy school?"

"I have a Ph.D. in folklore, and yes, my dissertation was on fairy tales," he gave her an exaggerated bow. "I teach comparative fairy tales, my queen."

"Wow," she covered her mouth, genuinely shocked and a little bit flattered, and for the first time, self-conscious that she was covered in sweat and grime.

"Not everyone can save lives. Some of us save stories, making sure they are loved, studied, and never forgotten."

"I don't save lives," she said. "I'm a homicide detective."

"Oh," his face grew serious. "That must be really hard. It's great, but it must be hard. Things that you see that is."

Lauren did not answer, because it was hard, and there was nothing more to say about that.

They approached the bronze statue. The winged fairy held a flowered wand above the heads of two small sculptures of children, a girl and a boy leaning on one another asleep.

On the front left-hand side of the base it read:

Have you ever heard of the sugar plum tree
Tis a marvel of great renown
It blooms in the lollipop sea
In the garden of shut-eye town

On the right-hand side of the base it read:

Wynken, Blinken, and Nod one night
Sailed off in a wooden shoe
Sailed on a river of crystal light
Into a sea of dew

"You know fairy tales are in our blood as Chicagoans."

"Go on." She wanted to hear more.

He continued. "L. Frank Baum wrote parts of *The Wonderful Wizard of Oz* in Chicago. Walt Disney was born in a house in Hermosa, and he went on to create an empire based on fairy tales. Ray Bradbury is from the Chicago area, and he created his own fairy tales with stories like *The Halloween Tree* and *Something Wicked This Way Comes*, Carl Sandburg wrote the *Rootabaga* Stories here beyond his adult fiction works, Gwendolyn Brooks wrote *Bronzeville Boys and Girls* here, a collection of poems for and about children, Shel Silverstein who wrote *The Giving Tree* and more, and then there's Mo Willems with his stories of Elephant and Piggie, and more. Chicago has a long history of being the home of people who create whimsical and legendary stories. It's part of this city's history."

Lauren moved behind the sculpture. "Why is she called the Dream Lady?"

"She appears in a poem that Eugene Field wrote, 'The Rock-A-By-Lady.'"

Would you dream all these dreams that are tiny and fleet?
They'll come to you sleeping;
So shut the two eyes that are weary, my sweet,
For the Rock-a-By Lady from Hushaby street,
With poppies that hang from her head to her feet,
Comes stealing; comes creeping

"I'm impressed. Chicago authors. Obscure children's writers. Fairy tales. This sounds like it means a lot to you."

"What's wrong?" He asked.

"Isn't it sad, how there are people who lived and died and built this city and made magic here, and they're forgotten today? I didn't know anything about Eugene Field. That's what surprises me about Chicago, I'm always uncovering its history."

"I try not to think of it that way, that they've been forgotten. Their influences are still here. Their stories have evolved, adapted, Lore. Chicago's always going to be full of magic and mystery. It's just that kind of place."

"Is there anything else on the back?" Lauren asked as she walked behind the statue.

There she found an engraved image of a woman in bed with a hag hovering over her. Bobby stood closely behind Lauren.

"The folklore of the Germanic hag, the wise old woman and fairy goddess or witch of fairy tales," he pointed at the engraving of the hag and the woman asleep in bed. "This tells us a story of restless sleep. A woman who is being tormented by something unseen.

"Sleep disturbance seems like a common occurrence in fairy tales, Snow White, Briar Rose...other than that, I haven't been able to find much information about why they are included with this sculpture," he said. 'The Rock-A-By Lady' is a poem about a sweet fairy who put children to sleep."

"Because those wonderful things from your childhood can sometimes become monstrous in adulthood," Lauren said.

He knit his eyebrows together, reading into the engraving, forcing himself to see what Lauren saw. She stepped to the other side of the statue and found another engraving. This image was of the same girl from the hag scene. This time there was no hag hanging over her. She was seated on a horse, charging upward on onward.

"I like this one the most. It's hidden out of the way, and it feels like it's about a victory. Her conquering that darkness. She beat the hag, escaped it, and she can finally move on."

"I think you know more about fairy tales than you like to let on," he said.

"Maybe there are a few I know a little too much about."

CHAPTER 8

As the detectives drew closer, they could see the flashing lights of police cruisers. One ambulance remained of the three that had been called.

"Which hospital did they take her to?" Lauren asked.

"Masonic," Van said as he placed the car in park.

"Why not Lurie's?"

The sun was setting, a burst of orange dipping below the horizon, to slink off to other continents to make room for a new moon here, where nothing was really new. Nights came quicker this time of year, and tragedy had taken a liking to this park.

"Masonic is closer. They didn't have time to get her to the children's hospital." Van said. "Lots of bleeding."

He looked over to her and then back to the wheel. "Are you sure you're okay? I can handle this."

"I don't want to be home," she thought of the bullet holes in the dry wall she had started spackling before she received the call. A runner had found a bleeding girl in Humboldt Park.

"You buried your dad this morning, Medina."

"I did. "Lauren could feel her face growing cold as they drove closer to the lagoon. The pulsating emergency lights, red and blue illuminating the trees, and a single bright beacon marking their spot. Police cars were parked on the sidewalk. Yellow tape sectioned off the area. It was early enough that no media was present, but they, and Alderman Suarez, would be here soon demanding answers to questions none of them would know how to answer. Van parked behind a cruiser and both exited the car without a word. The trail of blood was easy to follow. It started in the prairie grass, and stretched down to the beach, which had closed weeks ago at the end of summer. Even with the thin sheet of frost on the ground, they could see the blood-soaked sand.

At the foot of the lagoon, Lauren scanned the dark water. She looked behind her and saw a backpack on the ground. A few inches away there was a clump of hair, with a flap of pink bloodied skin still attached. Torn from the scalp. Then, there was the book. It lay on the sidewalk, its pages open, begging someone to read it.

Van knelt, reached for a plastic glove in his back pocket, slipped it on and closed the cover. He shook grains of sand off the book. He read the cover to himself and then held it up to Lauren. "Look familiar?"

She did not know what to say. Van faced the lagoon. Several divers could be seen bobbing in and out of the dark and murky water. "I heard the city pumped hundreds of gallons of fresh water into the lagoon each day over the summer. They hoped it would bring down the bacteria level and make it safe for swimmers."

"It doesn't matter how much water they pump into the lagoon," Lauren said. "The water is stagnant. There's really no way to keep it clean with the constant flow of people."

"*Grimm's Fairy Tales*," he said slowly. "You read these as a kid, right?" He looked to the book in his hand.

"Some of them," she said. Inside she was screaming, screaming because here it was again. The questions and the accusations.

"Your dad said you majored in literature, undergrad and grad school, and then got into law enforcement? That's interesting."

Lauren pulled out gloves from her messenger bag and slipped them on. "What's interesting is that you're trying to say something without saying it and I'm going to call you out on your bullshit, Van, because I'm tired of it."

Van sighed, heavily. "Bag this up," he waved over to an officer passing him by carrying a small box.

"Sure thing, Detective."

"Thank you, Officer Torres," Lauren said

"I'll be over there at the bench getting some notes together."

"All kids read fairy tales," Lauren said as Officer Torres walked away. "Plus, we don't know who the book belongs to."

"If I had to bet," Van said. "I'd say it's the girl with multiple stab wounds in her body."

An officer walked past whom Lauren quickly recognized as Officer Pagan.

"Officer Pagan, any weapons found?" Lauren asked.

"Nothing," he shrugged. "Could be in the water. Officer Torres is going to go through the backpack also and check," he pointed toward a nearby bench where Officer Torres sat, hidden in the shadows of a nearby tree, jotting down notes.

"Witnesses?"

As she scanned the ground, she spotted the sprays of blood that led them all here like bloody breadcrumbs.

"Guy walking his dog. He said he'd give a statement but had to take his dog back home."

"You got his name and number?"

"Right here," Officer Pagan handed her the contact information. "Said to call him."

"And you just let him go?"

"The guy literally lives across the street, Medina," Officer Pagan pointed to a Greystone building. "He ain't going anywhere."

Lauren approached Office Torres and said she needed to review the contents of the backpack. "I haven't gotten to it yet, but here you go." Officer Torres did not ask any questions and left her to review the materials. Lauren took a deep breath, trying to control her anxiety and fear. This place held too many bad memories, and it continued to add to its history of tragedy. Lights flashed in the darkness. Shadows stretched across the sidewalk. Officers in uniform, detectives in street clothes, and paramedics all gathered here, trying to piece together a puzzle of tragedy, but none of them could comprehend what really happened here. Lauren's memory cut back to her past. Images appeared in her mind like pictures scattered across the floor, all ripped in two, and Lauren had to pull all of them together to make out a coherent scene, a coherent memory of what happened here because she knew that whatever had happened so long ago, no matter what it was, was happening again.

A horn blared. The fire department had just packed up and driven off, their taillights no longer visible.

She searched the bag's contents: two notebooks, the first blank and the second with clean, orderly writing in black ink. The owner of the notebook had written their name on the first page, Evie Baez. Lauren also found a couple of pens, a hair tie, and a cell phone. There was no knife or other instrument in the backpack that could stab a person. Lauren tapped on the phone. The screen came to life. A message appeared on screen from Mom.

"This isn't funny. Where are you? Call me now, or I'm calling the police."

The phone went into sleep mode. When Lauren tapped the screen again, the red battery indicator told her there was just a few seconds of life left.

"Ah! Dear shepherd, you are blowing your horn. With one of my bones, which night and morn. Lie still unburied, beneath the wave. Where I was thrown in a sandy grave. I killed the wild boar, and my brother slew me. And gained the princess by pretending 'twas he."

"Detective..."

Lauren heard the crunch of frozen leaves underfoot. "You okay, Detective?"

"Yeah, Officer Torres. Just...singing a song. It was in my head."

He looked at her strangely, and she was not surprised.

"It's nothing…"

He was holding an evidence box in his hands, still gathering items as they were found. "A song?"

"Yes, it's umm…" she gazed at the phone in her hands and wished it could tell her what happened here, like the words she had just recited from "The Singing Bone." The Grimm's tale about how a man was murdered by his brother. A shepherd, years later, found a singing bone, one from the murdered man. The shepherd rushed it to the king. When the king learned from the singing bone that the man who sought to marry his daughter was the killer he ordered the man drowned as punishment. All of the dead brother's bones were recovered and then buried in a beautiful grave. "It's a song...from a silly story."

"Can we get this charged?" She handed the phone to Officer Torres. "Have we contacted the parents yet?"

"We're about to." He placed the phone in the box. "She had her high school ID on her," he said.

"What school?"

"DePaul. Freshman."

Students at DePaul College Prep had been busy, Lauren thought. "Good, because her mom's freaking out, as she should be."

Lauren could imagine Evie's parents getting a visit from police late this evening. A knock at the door. "Your daughter has been injured." Her parent's hearts crashing into their stomachs. Screams. Questions. Tears.

Officer Torres did not move.

"Is there something else?"

"Detective Van said you were going to look through this." Officer Torres handed her the book, still wrapped in plastic. The word EVIDENCE in black bold letters from the bag hung just above the title. Those stories were indeed evidence of a lot of our history, and they had been left to fade away, their meaning disintegrate across the ages into bedtime stories and bright, bold and colorful theatrical animated features. But Lauren knew their essence never really left us. True crime and true criminals slumbered between these pages and awakened on a whim, because that is how all horrific things happen, like a summer noontime breeze, unexpected, but not impossible. Of course, Van was going to push that book on her, and she was sure he was watching her right now, waiting to read her face, her body language. She was not going to give him the satisfaction of having anything to interpret. Like always, she remained calm and still.

"Thanks," she took the book in her hands.

Officer Torres' walkie crackled. "Excuse me, Detective," he said and then walked away to take his call.

It had been many years since she had actually read a fairy tale. Why did she need to read them now? Many had been committed to memory and for many more Lauren had at least memorized some major plot points. There were plenty of nights, after Marie, that she came out here, reading these stories aloud hoping to rattle her mind, to brush away the cobwebs and cast light on what happened here. But nothing ever happened, and so she read, she memorized, and she learned the wandering and twisting accounts of two brothers scouring rural areas of Germany for fables and myths from country people to pull into a scholarly text of traditional folktales. And it was a text intended for academics, the first edition of *Nursery and Household Tales*, weighted down by an extensive introduction and lengthy annotations.

This was not a book originally intended for wide reaching audiences. Yet, by 1815, all 900 copies of the first edition sold. Wilhelm Grimm became obsessed with developing a second edition because of the intense demand, and Jacob Grimm too realized that the tales could be a great source of income. In the second edition, the preface and notes were eliminated. Illustrations were added of mothers and grandmothers reading to children, and anything that hinted at scholarship was omitted. Wilhelm fleshed out and polished the texts, in many cases doubling their original length. And the brothers both admitted that they had taken great pains to remove any and every phrase unsuitable for children. So, if they claimed to have rid the stories of content they deemed unsuitable for children, then why was violence all allowed to remain, and in some cases intensified?

The brothers claimed that the more Hansel or Gretel or Cinderella were victimized, the more audiences would sympathize with them. Still, even though the brothers edited version two and ramped up the violence, it was still tame by comparison to the original version dictated to them by country people. Maybe the stories the Grimm brothers recorded were not really so unusual. They were not entirely uncommon at the time; the impoverished mother and father who drove their children away from the home, leaving them to starve in the woods, the cold-hearted stepmother, a fierce expert in child abuse who made her husband and his children's life unbearable—none of these stories were fairy tales then, or now. With, or without Bobby, Lauren knew all of this. He may have his doctorate, but she had spent her life since Marie's death researching and analyzing, and she knew that in all of those stories, as in life, the outcome was either happily ever after, or suffering and death. There was no inbetween.

Lauren stared at the book wrapped in plastic and felt no need to open it. This was not the edition she needed. She took a deep breath and told herself she just needed to get through this. Displaying a false sense of calm, she stood up and scanned the black water in front of her.

Van was pointing out over the lagoon. Lauren could not hear what he or the other officers standing at his side were saying from this distance, but their tones sounded urgent. Van's mouth moved rapidly. His hands waved and pushed into the sky, and they nodded. What worried Lauren most about Van was that he did his research. He had even done his research on her—and not just the cases she had been assigned to, but the one she and her father were directly involved in.

The one they had lived.

“That case drove me nuts,” Van had told her the first time they ever went out for coffee. They were standing in line at Cafe Mustache. “You know, your dad was the first one on the scene. Later on, that made some people question things, but then you know, he was called out there by the dispatcher, and there was no way for anyone to know at the time what he was walking into. It was just a coincidence. A bad coincidence. Still, people were bothered by that, for a lot of reasons. No father should have to pull his kid out of the water like that.”

Lauren handed the cashier some money. The extra change was dropped into a tip jar, and she took hold of her coffee and stepped aside as Van reached for his.

“The coffee here’s strong. Fair warning.”

“Must’ve been horrible what you all dealt with,” he said. “It must still be horrible knowing there hasn’t been movement on it.” Van reached for several napkins, pulled away the lid and poured two sugars in and stirred. “And you were out there too, huh? Found way out on the other side of the park? Mile away. And you still don’t remember anything?”

“No,” she answered it quickly and with conviction and took a sip from her coffee cup. The liquid burned the tip of her tongue, but still, she drank.

Van was right. There were no signs of struggle anywhere on the body. Lauren had memorized the coroner’s report. It was as if someone Marie trusted had carried her out there to the lagoon, laid her in the water to float, and the nine-year-old girl who did not know how to swim drowned, submerged in a lagoon during the day and no one saw anything.

Marie’s body was found a few hours after school let out. A missing person’s alert had gone out for Lauren who could not be found. Divers searched the lagoon, but nothing, and then hours before the sun rose the next day Lauren was found trembling, barefoot and in another part of the park where Marie had died. She was found standing in front of the statue of Alexander von Humboldt, the German naturalist and geographer who lived from 1769-1859, and for whom the park was named. The statue of a man thousands of Chicagoans drove, ran, and walked past each day, but knew very little about, likely just his name.

Lauren could not talk for a very long time afterward.

With coffees in hand, both walked out to their car. Lauren had remained silent. There was nothing more to tell Van other than what she had told him in the cafe.

"I'm sorry," he said getting in the passenger seat. "I know it was your sister, and that your mom...well, I'd just like the case solved like I assume you'd like it solved as well."

He was wrong. Lauren did not want her sister's case solved. She wanted this cold case lost among the stacks of dusty boxes in some nondescript facility, sitting alone, frozen and forgotten like thousands of others of unsolved crimes.

Lauren had placed her coffee in the cup holder and turned on the car.

"You really don't remember anything?" Van pressed.

"I don't remember anything. It's dissociative amnesia. Repressed memory syndrome. Basically, whatever I witnessed was too horrific for my childhood mind to hold on to. I mentally sliced it out. That memory's gone, and it's not coming back."

Van shouted, bringing her back to the dark park, with divers splashing into the lagoon. "We've got something!"

The shouts of confusion all came crashing together. A knot tugged at Lauren's chest. Two more people in dive gear plunged into the water. She gasped for breath. Van was swallowed by a swarm of people, and when she saw him emerge again, he was carrying a large, dripping bundle. A person. A boy. Arms limp at either side, his right arm had been hacked away at, and it was held together only by bits of meat and bone. Eyes wide open following the second quarter moon above. Cheeks blue.

The paramedics appeared, two of them covering the boy with blankets. Their movements frantic. Checking his pulse. Blowing breath into this mouth. Pumping his chest, all as he was lifted and placed onto a stretcher and wheeled into the ambulance.

Lauren knew this was her only moment of distraction to check. No one would be looking at her, or for her, at least not for a few seconds. She rushed down past the lagoon. It was here somewhere, watching, listening. Lauren turned off her flashlight and allowed the park lights above to guide her, because it was here. She walked down the paved pathway towards a section of tall prairie grass. She brushed against five-petaled bursting orange wild columbines, twisted green jack-in-the pulpit leaves, bottle brush grass, and oak leaf hydrangeas. Two small piercing golden orbs flashed at the bridge, and Lauren knew it had been there the entire time, a dreadful thing lurking and waiting, licking its teeth just as the Big Bad Wolf sat in wait for Little Red Riding Hood. Little Red Riding Hood, like so many of the others, based in truth but wrapped in the lie that it could never happen, that a little girl could never be snatched up in the woods by a stranger and broken. Greek traveler Pausanias who lived from 110 to 180 AD recorded the local legend of how a virgin girl would be offered to a malevolent spirit each year, dressed in the skin of a wolf, who would then rape and kill the girl. Then one year, boxing champion Euthymos slew the spirit and married the girl who had been offered up as that year's sacrifice. Legends, myths, and lore all came from somewhere, and, as Lauren discovered, all came back.

Lauren scanned the sidewalk benches and listened as the leaves rustled in the wind. She walked over to a small concrete bridge over a creek that overlooked the lagoon. She dug in her pocket and dropped a coin into the water before stepping foot on the bridge. There, on the bridge lay a dark mass. Lauren knelt down beside it, the only sound the trickling water of the creek beneath her, and bugs. Flies and gnats buzzed around the mound of blood, flesh and fur. A freshly skinned gray wolf pelt. Lauren dug her gloved fingers into the remains of the animal and pushed, its head appeared, eyes torn from it sockets and instead placed inside its open mouth. Lauren pushed harder, forcing the stinking, rotting mass into the water, where it fell with a splash. She removed her bloodied gloves and shoved them into her messenger bag.

It was taunting her.

"Where are you?" She called out to the darkness. She removed her flashlight and scanned the trees, back and forth and right when she was ready to turn back her light captured something. A splash of color.

Gold and white. Multicolored. Pied. Spray painted across the trunk of an old tree overlooking the lagoon were those familiar words:

Pay the Piper

Lauren took a step back, trying to hide her fear and her pain. She leaned over the bridge railing, heaving and vomiting sour coffee and stomach acid, all that she held inside.

It was no longer a coincidence.

The book.

The body.

And now its calling card.

There was no denying it any longer. The Pied Piper wanted his payment, and he needed it now.

CHAPTER 9

“I’m thirsty. How much longer?” Mo asked between gasps of air as he jogged ahead to catch up with Fin who was speed walking with no intention of slowing down.

“Not much,” Fin answered keeping her eyes forward, fixed to a point Mo could not see.

“Feels like we’ve been walking forever.” The sidewalk seemed to stretch out in front of him into eternity.

“I told you, we are not stopping until we get there.”

The light at the crosswalk changed just as they approached. They continued onward. After a few minutes of silence, Mo said: “My hands feel gross.” His skin felt tacky. There was pressure beneath his fingernails where dirt and debris had caked. Mo had the overpowering need to wash them. He had done a poor job back at the lagoon, quickly rinsing off, and then rubbing his hands back and forth in the grass. That did not work. The residue remained thick and sticky on his palms.

Fin glanced over at him, still keeping in step. “Your hands look clean.”

“They don’t feel clean.”

“Forget about it,” Fin said as she dug her hands into her hoodie pocket.

“How?”

She did not answer, and they continued on. The only noise they made was of their gym shoes hitting the sidewalk.

Mo's clothes were damp from the struggle, but he did not mention that. He shivered as they walked. The cold, wet fabric rubbed against his skin, but what pained him the most was his left foot. He was sure a toe had been severed. But water, if he could just get some water to drink and wash his hands then maybe he could think about what to do next.

"After we see him, we'll go home and wash up. We just have to actually *see* him to know it worked."

"Fin, when are we going to see him?"

Fin stopped and faced him. Her eyes manic. Her short hair wet and flattened around her head. She removed her hands from her pocket and curled them into tight fists.

Mo was sure she was going to strike him.

"You said that he was going to take care of it!" Mo blurted. He waved around at the empty sidewalk and street they found themselves on. "We're in so much trouble right now."

"He's going to make this right." She punctuated each word.

"It wasn't supposed to go this far!"

"You," Fin shoved a finger in his face "have no idea how any of this works. It's fine. We're fine. We'll find him, and then we'll go home."

He felt they did not have a clear direction as to where they were going. They were wandering a part of the city they had never been before. They might as well have been abandoned in a forest, searching for shelter.

"Are you sure we're even going the right way?" He asked.

"I told you already, Mo!" She raised her voice but looked around the street and quieted her next words. "He's not going to let us down. We will find him. He will appear."

Mo laughed to himself. "We've already been let down."

"It shouldn't be much longer now."

They continued on, deeper into parts of their city they had never walked before. Familiar neighborhoods had given way to brownstone buildings with cracked and broken yellowed mini blinds, faded by the sun and time. Lawns were strewn with weather-worn frayed plastic bags and empty water bottles and food cartons. Water, all Mo longed for right now was water for his dry throat, so he could think clearly.

Evie caught his eye staring at an empty water bottle in the street. "They walked the whole day over meadows, fields, and rocky expanses; and when it rained little sister said: 'Heaven and our hearts are weeping together.'"

"Where's that from?"

"'Brother and Sister' by the Grimms."

"The sister in that dies," he said.

"But she comes back to life," she said. "Nothing ever really stays dead."

The people who passed them on the street at first did not seem to give them notice. As they ventured farther and farther into the West Side people stopped, stared, asked them if they needed any help, but not in the way that indicated they were really ready to offer assistance.

Fin moved with confident steps, but Mo was unsure. The scene at the beach played back in screams, scratches, pleas, and blood. He did not know what they had accomplished other than something gruesome.

"My foot hurts," he said, reminding her of his injury.

"It'll feel better once we get there and see him," she added. "He'll fix it. He fixes everything."

He wondered how Fin could know where *there* was. He also wondered how all of this could potentially be fixed.

Mo rubbed his fingers together and felt the dried bits of blood crusting over. It felt as though hours passed and yet nothing was happening. His foot burned, first throbbing for some time but now the hot, sharp needles of numbness were spreading. His calf ached as he put more pressure there to keep his leg moving. He reached for his phone. He wanted to do a quick search to tell him how he could make it through this pain, but as he placed his hand on his back pocket, he remembered that his phone had fallen out in the water. Mo did not tell her that he had brought his phone with him to the lagoon, and worse, that it was lost during the struggle.

He did not think anyone would search the lagoon, at least not right away. It would be drained in a few months anyway when the park district would clean and prepare it for spring. By then he would come up with a clear explanation as to why his phone was there if it were traced back to him. People stole people's cell phones all the time in Chicago. He had even seen it himself, sitting on the red line train one Saturday morning with his father heading to Wrigley Field for a Cubs game. The train was packed, steaming from the July summer heat and people standing down the aisles and in front of the doorways, holding on to railings and avoiding crashing into each other at each stop. A woman had been texting, and as the doors opened at the Clark and Lake stop, a guy snatched the phone right out of her hand and dashed out of the doors, down the platform, and up the stairs towards the connecting brown, orange, pink and blue line trains. Mo would say something similar happened to him. He would brush it off being found as no big deal in the lagoon, if it were even found. He knew horrible things were left behind at the lagoon all the time anyway. His older brother Jamal told him how limbs, torsos, heads, and bodies were tossed in that same lagoon in the 1980s through to the early 2000s during a wave of increased gang violence. Just recently, a toddler's foot had been found in the cattail reeds. No one had yet come forward to identify the dismembered remains or say they had a missing child. So, no one would be surprised with what was left there tonight. Drowned bodies and body parts were not an unusual find in Chicago's lake, river or lagoons.

"Maybe around here?" Fin said softly.

The sign at the corner of the park read Garfield Park. Mo had been here once before, visiting the Garfield Park Conservatory, one of the largest conservatories in the country. The city once had three West Side conservatories, one in Humboldt Park, Douglas Park and the other in Garfield Park. The conservatories in Humboldt Park and Douglas Park were demolished, but many of the original plantings that started the large Garfield Park collection came from the three earlier conservatories. Opened in 1908, the conservatory was often called landscape art under glass, as it is encased in a large glass dome. He did not remember any of the names of the plants or trees his biology teacher walked them through. He did remember the Fern Room, a glass-domed covered room with a koi pond, streams, and ferns that lead you around a moss-covered path. What he also remembered was a small gallery set away from the main showroom. There, black and white photos lined a concrete block wall, images that spanned the early years of the conservatory, the early 1910s through the 1960s in Chicago. What haunted him most about those images was a grainy picture of the conservatory workers from the 1910s dressed in black suits and top hats, their blank eyes looking at the camera. They were lined up in three rows, like a class picture, a backdrop of gigantic palm leaves behind them. It was as if they could see him across decades and time. It was as if they had never left, in some ways. Something in those black eyes, pools of emptiness, stretched across the years and pulled him into their darkness. One of the men in that photo in particular still haunted Mo, one of the tallest men, set furthest back, cast in dark shadow. Mo was certain he had seen that same man before.

A car horn blared.

The driver side window rolled down just a few inches, not enough to see a face.

“Y’all lost?” A rough voice asked from within.

Neither of them responded.

There was a laugh from inside the car, and then it sped away.

“I feel like we’re out here, exposed,” he said.

“We are,” Fin said. “We’ve always been.”

He began to wonder if Fin really knew what she was doing. He even began to wonder if he should have listened to her. Now, out here, with the cold and the pain, it was the first time he began to really think of what they did, and if it was worth it. Could they really be rid of their problems like this? Was it really this easy? And if it was, why did Fin have to do it again, and so soon? Guilt washed over Mo. He never thought of himself capable of hurting anyone, all for the hopes of what a grim genie in a bottle promised.

"I'm tired. I'm thirsty. I can't feel my foot. We can at least sit at a bench for a few minutes."

"There," she pointed to a copse of trees deep within the park. "He's right there."

"I don't see anyone."

Her face beamed. "He's right there!"

Fin started walking, hearing the call of something deep within the park. Mo reached for her forearm.

"Fin, there's no one there."

Fin moved towards the park, searching the darkness. "Shh," she said, her back turned. "I hear him. I hear the music."

Across the street, an orange and red sign at a corner store that read LIQUORS flickered, except the letter U which was dimmer than the other letters and pulsating. Next to it was a funeral home that did not appear as though it had hosted a wake in years. The bars over the windows were rusted over with time. The windows were streaked over with age. A man in black, the man in black from the photo at the Garfield Park Conservatory, stood in the alley and sneered at Mo. Gaping black pits were where his eyes should be. A gray hand reached up and touched the rim of his hat with two long, thin fingers.

Mo closed his eyes, shutting them tight. His heart pounding in his chest. Nothing was there, he told himself. He was tired. He was cold. He was in pain. Nothing and no one was there. When he opened his eyes terror stood before him. The man was inches from his face.

The man snarled. "Of the Devil's power and wickedness, here, I will tell you a story. I gnawed on their bones..." The man in the black suit produced a bloodied toe with a flourish with his right hand, and then he dropped the toe onto his black tongue and crunched.

Mo collapsed in pain, looked down at his shoe and found it soaked in blood. "Fin!" He screamed.

The man in the black suit was gone.

Fin pulled him up to his feet.

"We need to go..." The words in his brain were a tangle of sharp thorns. He did not know what he had seen, but he knew what he felt, hot pain that shot up his leg into his jaw.

"Fin..." His whole body shook. This felt wrong. It felt sick.

"Dammit, Mo! What is wrong with you?"

"This isn't right. There's this guy, over there," Mo raised a shaky hand. "Looking at us. My foot…" Mo fought to catch his breath. His words failed in his mouth. He wanted to leave. He wanted to go home.

Fin looked back into the dark cluster of trees and across the street at the abandoned funeral home. "It's part of the test," she pleaded. "To see if we're worthy. We just have to go to him and this, this can all be over, and we can go back. No one will know. No one needs to know what we did."

It sounded like she was trying to convince herself. And for the first time, he felt like there was something she had failed to tell him. A chill ran through him.

The fluorescent letter U in the LIQUORS sign burst on as the other letters brightened with intensity. With more light shining on them, Mo could see Fin's face. Now, standing in front of her and looking at her closely for the first time in hours, he spotted the flecks of dried blood sprinkled across the bridge of her nose. They looked like freckles, born with the markings of death. Mo's eyes shifted down Fin's shoulders, her arms, and then to her hands and he saw it; the dried red, brown smears that had been absorbed into the cuffs of her hoodie. Then there was the blue spray paint that she tried to scrub off her fingertips but could not.

"What if we're missing something? What if we did something wrong? What if he forgot about us? Is mad at us? What if what we did was for nothing and..." Mo felt like he was gasping for air.

"Just stop!" Fin threw her arms toward the sky and screamed. She lunged at him, grabbing him by his shoulders. "You can't doubt! If you doubt it, it won't work! You'll ruin this! Ruin me! Us!" She looked back toward the trees and lowered her voice. "He can't hear you talking like this." Her trembling hand motioned over to the park. "He'll get mad if you talk like this. We just need to go there," she raised a finger to her lips and lowered her voice. "Listen to the music. He's right there," Fin reached for Mo's hand, and he realized then that it was the first time she had ever taken hold of his hand, and he smiled, under her spell.

A movement drew their eyes upward. Blue and red lights swept across the tops of trees. A horn blared. The police cruiser stopped right in front of them. Fin released his hand with such force he thought she was going to push him next. She was angry, and at that moment he saw something sinister in her face that unsettled him.

"We're both dead," Fin whispered.

An officer exited the passenger side, followed by the driver.

"Guys," the officer addressed them as she slammed her door shut.

Neither Fin nor Mo offered words.

Mo searched Fin's face for something, anything that could help them get out of this, but she did not say a thing.

"Mohammed Ramsen and Finley Wills?"

Both officers stood in front of them. "I'm Officer Bauer," one said and pointed to her partner "Officer Doyle."

Officer Bauer repeated the names. "Mohammed Ramsen and Finely Wills," being careful to make eye contact with each.

"Yes," Mo stammered.

Fin remained silent. Her gaze fixed toward the darkness where she was sure they were supposed to go. Tears welled up in her eyes.

Officer Bauer looked down. "What happened there?"

"Stray dog bit me," Mo said.

"Dog bit you?" Officer Bauer said slowly and then turned to Fin. "And you, your hands?"

"Painting," Fin said as she shoved her hands into her hoodie pocket.

"Dog bit you and you've been painting? Okay. Let's get you two to your parents and figure out what you have been up to tonight."

The officers flanked them, escorting them to their police cruiser. Droplets of cold rain proceeded to fall, running down Mo's forehead, and rolling down his temples.

"Shit, I know I left my back porch windows open," Officer Bauer said to no one in particular.

"Not trying to make you feel bad," Officer Doyle said as he sat in the driver's seat, pulled on his seat belt and shut the car door. "It's going to pour all night."

Officer Bauer opened the back door, and Mo went inside first, sitting behind the driver's seat.

Mo sucked in air between his teeth, wincing in pain as his legs, cramped and pained, finally settled to rest. He could no longer feel his foot.

Lightning flashed, and then the sky roared, angry and hungry.

"Where are your other two friends? Evie and Daniel?" Officer Bauer asked, but Mo looked over to Fin who was standing outside the rear passenger door.

Fin shook her head back and forth slowly, as if debating with herself on what to do next.

Officer Bauer closed Mo's door and walked over to where Fin was standing and opened the rear passenger door for her. "Ah, covering for your buddies after curfew. I get it. We'll find 'em." She pointed inside the car, directing Fin to sit down.

Fin took a deep breath. Her nostrils flared. For a moment Mo thought she was going to do it, that she was going to run off into the darkness in search of her promise. Perhaps Officer Bauer sensed something off about them. She placed her hand firmly on Fin's shoulder, directing her to enter the car.

Officer Bauer told Fin to be careful, not to bump her head as she eased onto the seat. Mo knew Fin was furious that it had ended this way. Her eyes narrowed in on him. Her lips twisted. It was then that he heard something fall to the ground with a metallic clang.

Officer Bauer looked down to the object that had fallen, water splashing around her feet. She moved her hand to her hip fast, inches above her holster. Her eyes met Mo's. Officer Bauer took one step back, her eyes locked on Mo.

"Out of the car! Both of you!" Officer Bauer ordered.

Officer Doyle scrambled out of the car, without question or hesitation and drew his weapon. "Out!" He commanded and opened the car door.

Mo rushed out of the car. "I didn't do anything!" Furiously wiping the rain out of his eyes.

"Stop moving!" Officer Doyle shouted. "Hands above your head!" Officer Doyle directed Mo to turn around and face the car.

Fin slowly got out of her seat. She faced the car with a smile. Rainwater pouring down her hair and face. She stood still, not affected at all.

Officer Doyle looked to Officer Bauer for an explanation.

"Knife," she said.

Officer Doyle pulled down Mo's hands. Cold metal dug into his wrists, squeezing and tightening around his skin.

"What'd we do?!" Mo shouted.

"That's what we want to know," Officer Doyle said. "Where're your friends?"

Fin laughed as Officer Bauer placed handcuffs on her as well.

With both of them handcuffed and the doors locked, Officer Bauer bent down to retrieve the object. She raised the knife and exposed the red streaks of blood and strips of hair clinging to the blade.

Inside the car, it sounded like thousands of frozen peas falling onto the roof of the vehicle. Fin's eyes fixed on the knife outside the window. She burst into laughter, rocking back and forth in her seat.

The laughter was piercing. Mo wanted to tell her to be quiet, to stop, but he was too afraid.

"Want to tell us where your friends are now?" Officer Bauer asked.

Nothing. Fin continued to laugh, a loud, earsplitting laugher that rattled Mo's insides.

"Call it in Doyle. Something happened."

Officer Doyle pressed a call button and spoke. "Car 3232 here. We found Mohammed Ramsen and Finley Wills." The walkie-talkie crackled. "Taking them to Grand and Central." Officer Doyle looked to Officer Bauer who took over.

"We have a knife. Looks suspicious."

There was an electric squeal from the radio and then a flash: "Medina here. We're at Humboldt Park now. We found the other two. I'll meet you at the station."

As the car drove away, Mo looked over to Fin who seemed to be watching something or someone outside of the window. She raised a hand up to the glass and waved goodbye in the direction of the park.

CHAPTER 10

"If you want me to help you, you have to tell me what happened," Lauren said as she set a plastic cup of water in front of the young man.

"Do you go by Mohammed or Mo? I heard your friend shout out to you and she called you Mo."

The interrogation room was small. It was cold. There were only two chairs and a small folding table. There was nothing comfortable about this room. It was not supposed to offer any comforts.

The boy started hyperventilating again. His cheeks grew red as he puffed air in and out of his mouth.

"You're going to make yourself pass out again, and if you pass out again guess what? That just extends your time here with me."

"Mo," his voice sounded like sandpaper against drywall.

"Mo, good. That's how this works, Mo. I ask you questions. You answer those questions."

He lowered his head between his legs. She could hear him wheezing. Lauren rolled her eyes and took a sip of water.

When Van saw her filling up two cups of water earlier, he stopped.

"Those both for you?" He asked her.

"One's for the kid," she said. "He just had a toe ripped off."

"Yeah, and he got patched up at the hospital. He's doing better than the kid that's never going home." He shook his head. "They're murderers, Medina."

"Suspected. Plus, they're still children," she said.

"Children found with a knife and blood all over their clothes."

Van's face grew red, and he muttered something under his breath before entering Interrogation Room 2. He had his method. She had hers.

Still, Lauren knew Mo had good reason to worry. This was not looking good for him, or his friend.

"It's scary. I know, but if you want me to help you, you're going to have to start talking to me."

Mo raised his head and pressed the palms of his hands into his eyes and let out a wail.

"Talk to me. What happened out there?"

She fought the urge to yawn. The need for sleep washed over her. How many hours had she been awake? Twenty-four? Thirty-two? She was functioning in a state of twilight and exhaustion. Pushing the limits of sleeplessness had worried Commander McCarthy so much he'd nearly demanded she go home, but she refused. Not now with another murder investigation, she argued.

"Fine Medina. Don't sleep. You're questioning Mohammed." Commander McCarthy had handed her a sheet of paper when she arrived at the station. "Van, you interview Finley." He shoved a sheet of paper into Van's hand resting at his side.

"Wait, why am I interviewing the girl?" He'd snapped.

"Because last time Medina interviewed a girl she broke her jaw."

"That was a long time ago," Lauren said under her breath.

"Five weeks ago," Commander McCarthy responded. "You've

got no friends on the Chicago Police Board, Medina. They'd sure be happy if they had to investigate you again. You're a good officer. A better detective, but if you don't lock down your anger and these controversies that seem to just follow you around you'll be out on your ass."

"Controversies? I was attacked! Do you need to see the scar on my neck to prove it?"

"I'm not talking about the guy you killed last year. I'm talking about the girl you beat up five weeks ago, and the confidential informant you hit with your car last summer. And if you really wanted to go back, we can talk about your 'accidents' when you were a rookie. Reign it in, Medina, because your dad's not here to protect you, and Washington is on his way to retirement. Now move! Both of you."

"I have no idea what's going on," Van grabbed a notepad and pen and went off to interview Fin.

In the room with Mo, she promised herself she was not going to let anger consume her. She was not going to allow this to ruin her. Plus, this was beyond her job. She needed to know what happened out there for herself.

"Are my parents worried?" Mo asked.

"Very worried, but they know that you are here now speaking with us." Her throat was dry. Her eyes felt heavy. She took another drink of water and continued.

"Your father's on his way."

"Can I talk to him?" Mo's lips quivered, and he let out a sob. "He's just...he's not good right now."

"Yes, you can when he gets here. What's wrong?"

"He just got out of the hospital. A few days ago. He was robbed leaving his store. Attacked. Hit in the face with something sharp. He lost an eye." Mo brought his arm up and cried into his sleeve.

"You're worried about him?"

He nodded, pulling his face back, eyes and nose pink and wet. "I didn't want our store to get robbed anymore. I didn't want my dad to get hurt anymore. Or, my brother or sisters who work there sometimes alone. So, I had the guy who did it stopped..."

"Stopped? How? Daniel?"

"No! It wasn't him." He slapped himself. The sound ripped through the room with a crack. "Nothing!" He shouted. "Nothing!" He clenched his hands into fists and pressed them against his temples. He squeezed his eyes shut. "I didn't do anything. I didn't do anything. I didn't do anything. I just...couldn't give him what he wanted. I didn't know that was part of the deal."

"First, you need to calm down," Lauren raised her voice and held out a hand. "Hitting yourself and shouting is not going to make things any easier for you." Lauren looked down quickly at the few notes she had been handed by Commander McCarthy. There was no mention of a store, or a robbery, or an assault. "Does what happened in Humboldt Park have to do with your dad? Siblings? Your family's store?"

"No. Yes. I don't even know anymore. Nothing makes sense. Everything is water." He glanced around the room as if the concrete walls would give him an answer.

"Back up," Lauren dropped her pen on the pad of paper and crossed her arms in front of her chest. None of this was making any sense. It could be because he was trying to write the lie as he spoke, but lying now was not going to help him. As far as she understood it, Mo was here suspected of murder and attempted murder. He would be tried as an adult. Maybe this was the girl's idea, Fin. Perhaps this was an accident. Self-defense. Maybe there was someone else involved. Or maybe, this was entirely his idea, and he intended very well to kill those kids and get away with it. Right now, what Lauren needed was the full picture.

"Let's start where all stories start, at the beginning."

Mo looked from the door to the table, to his hands. There was nowhere to go, so he might as well start talking.

"There was this book at the library..."

Lauren reached for her pen then stopped. "Library?"

Mo lowered his head into his hands. "It's stupid."

The book. He mentioned the book.

He knew.

"What's stupid is if you don't start telling me exactly what happened."

"It was Fin's idea. All of it."

That did not take too long, pointing the finger to the other person.

A metallic bang rang down the hall. Mo looked towards the door. A look of fear burned across his face. "We messed up," he said. "And now here we are."

"Just stay right there," she held a hand out, motioning for him to stay in his seat as she moved to the door and looked out of the small window in it. There was no one in the hallway. She texted Van:

"The hell?"

"I fell."

She rolled her eyes as she shoved her phone back in the pocket of her jacket. She turned back to face the table and Mo.

He was giving her a look that she could not quite read. Was it a scowl? Was it a smile? "Your mother liked music, didn't she? Wait," he closed his eyes. His eyeballs moved rapidly from side to side. "She wasn't your *real* mother. Your stepmother, a woman who could see through her eyelids. Stepmothers who cast spells on forest streams. Children are swept away too far and too fast by their angry feelings. Ever since mother died, we haven't had a single happy hour, and those who fail to move are banished into exile."

The lightbulbs above them exploded and sharp shards of glass rained down on Lauren. She could feel the grass beneath her toes, and the sounds of outside things. Crickets and chirping. The whooshing of leaves in the wind. The howling of wolves in the distance. The lapping of water somewhere close. She reached in front of her and felt the body of a tree trunk, rigid and rough beneath her fingers. She could smell the sharp scent of a wood burning fireplace, and then something else. Roasted meat? Pork?

"I will pick the remnants of your milky eyes from between my teeth with my claws if you don't pay me, Lauren."

She reached out into the darkness, feeling nothing but the night, and then the lights turned back on.

Lauren fumbled back into the door. Her heart erupted in her chest. She looked around, searching for answers. She could still feel the cool forest air on her flesh.

"What did you say?"

Mo looked from side to side. "I didn't say anything."

"You said my mother liked music."

"No," he raised his hands in defense. "I didn't. I don't know your mother. I'm sorry. I didn't say anything." He hung his head and cried. "I just want to go home."

Lauren was tired. Last night she had stayed up all night going through some of her father's papers, literal stacks of newspapers that sat piled on the living room table, arranged in some order she could not decipher. She filled several large, black garbage bags full of them and when she walked past his office, she hesitated for a moment. She reached for the doorknob, turned and pushed, making sure the door was locked. She could handle what he left throughout the house. She could still not handle what was in his office, and she did not know if she would ever be able to reach for the key that sat in the cupboard.

"Tell me about this book, Mo."

"There was a nursery rhyme we found in the book."

She reached for her water but knocked it over. There were no napkins nearby with which to dry off the tabletop, so Lauren just grabbed her notepad and set it on her lap before it got wet. She breathed deeply, willing her heartbeat to slow and then cleared her throat. "Tell me more, Mo. I can't help you if you don't tell me what's going on."

"It was the Pied Piper. Not me. Not Fin. The Pied Piper. He did this."

Mo leaned his head back, resting it against the wall, tears filling his eyes. "I told Fin. This was stupid. It wasn't real, but she said we had to. She said we just needed to give the Pied Piper a name, a name of someone we wanted dead and that he would kill them for us. I didn't know he would come back and ask for more."

Lauren lowered her voice, all the while trying to control her breathing. She felt like she was suffocating, drowning. "You want me to believe that the Pied Piper, a real one, from the kid's story is behind what you and your girlfriend did?"

"She's not my girlfriend."

"I don't know, Mo. I don't know if I can believe anything you're telling me. I can tell you what I do know, everything coming out of your mouth is a goddamn lie!" She shouted.

Mo shook his head. "No. I'm not lying," his eyes wide. "It was Fin. She said we should do this."

"I thought you said it was the Pied Piper?"

"It is," he sat up straight. "I mean. It was. But it was Fin too. It was her idea. She found the page in the book. She wrote the words down, and…I don't know. She figured it out. She figured out that we had to say the words in front of a mirror, in the dark with a candle to call him."

"What?!" Lauren said. "The page in the Grimm's fairy tale book?"

Mo blinked rapidly. "I didn't tell you which book."

Lauren remained silent for a moment, chasing her thoughts. "We found a book, *Grimm's Fairy Tales*. It's in evidence. Whose book was it?" She said, changing the direction of the questioning.

"Evie's, but that's not the book I'm talking about, the one where we found the page."

"Where then?"

"At the Newberry Library. We were on a field trip there last year. We were shown an old copy of the Grimm's fairy tales. I forgot the exact name, but that wasn't it, the one you found. This one was really old. From the 1800s or something. There was a page, a black page with gold writing." Mo pressed the palms of his hands into his eyes. "I didn't think she really meant to do this."

"What did the page say?" Lauren asked. She needed the confirmation.

Mo dropped his hands. "A rhyme. I don't know. Fin had the copy, but she lost it in the lagoon."

"Where's the book now?"

"Back there, in the stacks."

Mo looked toward the door. His eyes widened. Lauren watched him. It was as if he saw something outside the window.

"Do you realize how this sounds? Is this what you're going to tell your lawyer? The judge? That you and Fin found a rhyme in a book of fairy tales and that it told you to kill your classmates?"

Lauren knew the interview was being recorded, so not only did she have to be cautious of what she said and how she said it, but of her body language as well. She could not show she was worried.

"I'm going to need a lot of coffee because your story is not making any sense."

"It's real!" He shouted. "You have to believe me."

"Mo, you really believe that the Pied Piper is a person, like you or I?"

"Yes," he said without hesitation. "Once you say those words, you have to go through with it. The Pied Piper gets rid of whoever you want."

"By get rid of you mean kill."

He nodded.

"That doesn't make any sense. Why not just kill them yourself?

Why fake that some fairy tale monster is doing this?"

"If you could kill whoever you wanted to kill without getting caught, wouldn't you?"

She did not answer.

"But then..." Mo ran his fingers through his hair. "Something went wrong."

"You think? Something went very wrong the moment you and your friend decided to try to kill two people!"

"*Try*? They're not both dead?"

"What? Are you disappointed she's not dead?"

"No. No." Mo's face grew pale. "This is bad," he shook his head. "This is very bad." He stood up and paced the room. "They're both not dead?!"

Lauren stood up slowly. Raising her hands up to show him her palms. She was not afraid, but she very well knew why he should be worried. "Sit down. Now." She ordered.

Mo sat down on top of his hands and proceeded to rock back and forth in the chair. The metal legs squeaking beneath his weight.

Lauren looked back down to her notes. She did not write down the information about Newberry Library. She hoped no one would review the recording and ask about it.

Mo looked down at his pant leg and winced as he adjusted his feet.

"We'll make sure your bandage gets changed."

"It doesn't matter. Nothing matters because he's coming for me."

It was now time to ask the next important series of questions. "Who stabbed who first?"

"Fin stabbed..."

"Stabbed who?"

"I don't know. It was dark. I don't know. She was getting impatient." He rubbed his shoulders. "It's cold in here."

"Little bit."

The squeaking from the metal chair stopped. "You really don't remember, do you?" He asked.

Lauren paused, looking up from her handwriting and noticed he stopped rocking back and forth in his seat. Mo was sitting perfectly still now.

"Remember what?" She glanced back at the page of notes.

Mo leaned in slightly. "You really don't remember anything, do you?"

"I don't think I'm following..."

"About yourself. You really don't remember?" Mo leaned in further, Lauren watched as he studied her face. "Oh," he said as if he found what he was looking for in the contours of her face, and the depths of brown in her eyes. "Sometimes we forget. It happens."

"Forget what?"

Mo said, "What do you mean?"

"You said 'sometimes we forget.' Forget what?"

Mo looked confused. "I didn't say that."

He started to rock back and forth in his seat again, slower this time. "My dad's going to be so mad."

Lauren rubbed her eyes. "You're not making any sense, Mo." She knew she had not misheard, but she did not want to ask him again, for fear of bringing too much attention to it in the recording.

"You said you learned how to call him last year, so why did you both wait until now to ask for the Pied Piper's help to kill someone?"

"Fin did call him last year."

"Are you telling me that Fin killed someone before?"

He nodded once.

"Why two people now?"

The smell of firewood filled the room.

"It doesn't matter. It's over for me." He looked up to the ceiling and screamed a harsh, jarring scream. His hands covered his ears, and he just yelled, the veins in his neck bulged. "Help me! I need help!"

Lauren rushed to the door, opened it and locked it behind her. She stood at the door, looking through the glass, watching as he screamed louder and louder for the kind of help he could never ever get. Mo slapped himself again, and again, screams echoing from the room. He picked up a chair and threw it at the door, and then turned and kicked over the folding table. He pressed his back against the wall, staring at Lauren, mouth open, a long continuous agonizing scream escaping his body, veins bulging in his neck. He banged his head once against the concrete wall, and then again, a spot of red staining the surface with no end in sight. She took out her phone and called in an ambulance.

People came rushing to the hallway, asking her if she needed assistance, and if he was all right. Neither of them were fine.

CHAPTER 11

"Did you guys talk about doing this beforehand?" Van asked as he wrote the date on the upper right-hand corner of the page like he was preparing to write out an assignment for school or a journal entry.

He needed immediate distraction. He understood that the coldness of this place could generate shock. He could not imagine what he would have felt if he were placed in a cruiser and driven to a police station, escorted past the main desk through a collection of locked doors into an interrogation room. He wondered how Medina felt, questioning someone, when she had once been questioned under similar circumstances.

The room was small. Claustrophobic. A camera in the upper corner of the room served as a watchful eye, recording all audio and video. The concrete walls in this room had recently been painted white. A lingering chemical scent of paint hung in the air. There were no windows, except for a strip of one in the metal door. A girl younger than Fin with pale blue skin and long dark ringlets pressed her face to the window and smiled. Fin raised her fingers to wave, but the girl disappeared.

Van spun around in his chair, but returned to his notes when he did not see anyone.

Fin sat cross-legged in front of him and seemed at ease, comfortable. Too relaxed for the situation she was in. Most people he brought back here were manic, angry, or anxious. Not Fin, she sat still, almost bored.

"It's cold," she said, pulling the hood from her large dark blue jacket up over her head. She pulled the sleeves down over her hands, just the cuffs of the sleeves showing. Her form seemed collapsed inside the giant material.

Several sheets of white paper lay face down on the table. It was reported to Van that during the ride to the Grand and Central police station Fin did not speak, but she did laugh incessantly the entire trip, howling each time the officers asked her to quiet down. When the arresting officers finally asked her what was so funny, she only laughed louder and kicked their seats.

When they arrived at the station, the knife was placed into evidence and Fin and Mo were separated. When Officer Bauer passed Van in the hallway after placing Fin in the interrogation room, she told him, "That was the most terrifying ride of my life. She just laughed. There's something wrong with her. Him. All of this."

"Mo told me we had to do it," Fin's voice was as soft as pages being flipped in a book.

Van wrote her exact words down on paper, a quote moving on to admission. Many questions ran through his head, but he remained focused. He wanted her to do most of the talking. This was how it was going to work. He was here to guide the conversation, ask tricky questions, and gather a clear picture of what had occurred. Like with all cases, a confession was the goal, but each time Van looked up at the girl he could not, or perhaps, did not want to, believe that she was involved in something so heinous. If a child so young could do something so terrible, then anyone was capable of anything.

"Why?" He asked looking directly at her, waiting for a response before starting to write down her answer.

Fin adjusted herself in the plastic chair. She folded her knees up to her chest and pushed out her hands from inside her sleeves. She crossed her arms on top of her knees, resting her chin on the back of her hands. She looked like a pile of clothes tossed on the chair with a head sticking out on top, her oversized sweatshirt stretched down past her knees.

"Because Mo said he'd kill our families."

Van felt his stomach twist.

"Mo would kill your families?"

"No, the man."

He felt uneasy about the way she coolly said that, but still, he wrote it down.

"What man?"

"A man," Fin scratched her nose. "I don't know him, but Mo knows him."

"Do you know the man's name?"

"The Pied Piper."

Van did not look up from his writing. "And who is the Pied Piper?" He thought it was someone's street name. A graffiti artist. A gangbanger. A guy from the neighborhood whom everyone knew by nickname only. Fin's response stunned him.

"The Pied Piper. From the fairy tale."

He stopped writing. Now he felt it, what Officer Bauer had mentioned. This felt wrong. This name and this crime. For the first time ever, he felt uneasy interviewing a suspect, and even though she was a teenager, a child, a streak of fear ran through him, and he wished he could excuse himself. The room seemed too small, too quiet, too cold. He wondered how Medina was doing.

Footsteps shuffled down the hallway, but he did not hear any doors open for someone to have access to this private area of the precinct. The door to access this area was a sturdy metal door which screeched as it opened and produced a loud slam when shut. Van looked through the corner of his eye, making sure not to add distraction to the questioning. A black and white form, flickering like an old television program, moved past the window.

His hand holding the pencil trembled.

A knock at the door, and then a face, the blue face of a girl with black pools for eyes. Dark ringlets hugging her face.

Van jumped to his feet. His chair fell behind him, landing on the concrete floor with a loud crash. He looked out the small window in the door, his heavy breathing casting fog on the glass. He looked left and then right. Nothing.

He opened the door and scanned the empty hallway. Nothing. Then he looked down at the floor.

One set of wet footprints stood right at the door, nowhere else in the hallway.

He slammed the door. He was seeing things he assured himself.

Fin sat still in her seat, staring ahead of her.

Van sat down. His phone vibrated in his pocket. He took it out and placed it on the desk. It was a text from Medina.

"The hell?"

"I fell," he typed the letters quickly and then turned off his phone and placed it back in his pocket.

The black and white streak was nothing, he told himself. Forget about it. Focus on questioning.

"Can you tell me more about him? Where is he from? Where does he live?" At this point, he hoped the girl was just confused, that there was really a person and not her imagination behind this story.

"Have you ever listened to the trees talk? The blades of grass sing? The rocks scatter across soil and laugh. The symphony of the forest. That's him. That's his music." Fin said. "He's everywhere. You just have to listen for his song."

Van felt his tongue sticking to the roof of his mouth. His throat was dry. He asked the only question he could think of. "How do you know?"

"I've read so many things about him."

"Where did you read these things about him?"

"The internet. Other places," she laughed softly to herself.

"Can you give me a list of websites?"

"Everything about him is on NeverSleep."

"NeverSleep?" He wrote down the words and underlined them.

"His story is on there. You just have to find it. He's hard to find. You find him only if he wants to be found. If he *chooses* you."

His shoulders felt tight. He wished he could get up and leave the room for a moment, to gather his thoughts, to get a drink of water. She sounded too confident in all of this.

"You've seen him before?"

"If he's interested in you then you will see him in your dreams. You can see him when no one else can see him. Sometimes I see him out of my window. He stands beneath the streetlight and waves to me. He plays his song. He tells me he is going to give me whatever I want. The other people did not pay him, and so he took them all away."

"He took all who away?"

"The children," she said plainly.

Van had managed interviews with people who were disturbed, but what struck him about Fin was how calm she was. There were no tears. There was no remorse. There was no anger. She was detached. Uninterested. The type of brutality that her and her friend had inflicted was shocking.

So many stab wounds were not easy on a moving, fighting individual. There was clothing to tear through, skin, and fat, and bone. Each plunge of the knife brought more damage, and fight, and an attack. How could they stab a classmate so many times, and why?

There was no regret. He had seen more remorse from teenagers when they had been called to the disciplinarian's office when he was working as an onsite police officer at Orr High School just a few miles away.

He looked back to his notepad and turned the page. The sound of the page flipping was the loudest thing in the room. Paper slicing through the air.

Fin raised her head slightly.

"Why do you need to know about him?" While she was reserved when she asked this, Van picked up a sense of defensiveness, almost protectiveness, for this person, this thing, this idea.

"Because I think that the Pied Piper might have something to do with what is going on with you today." He did not like saying the name, Pied Piper. It sounded archaic, and wrong. Maybe this was all just a kid's game gone too far?

She lowered her head back to her hands. "Oh, okay."

"Where did you get the knife?"

"Mo," she yawned.

"And where did Mo get it from?"

Fin placed her feet on the ground and sat up straight, stretching her arms above her head as she yawned again. "The kitchen. His house. Maybe his dad's job? I don't know, but it came from Mo."

"How did he pass it on to you?"

"He sort of just shoved it into my hands...and there it was." She waved a hand in the air. And then I don't know what I did. It sort of just happened. It didn't feel like anything really," she said making repeated stabbing motions with her right hand. "It was like air."

It was then that Van really noticed her hands, covered in dried blood, splashes of paint, black and purple. Her fingers and nails were blue.

"Been painting much?"

"I like to paint," was all she added, but nothing more.

Van continued. "Who attacked first?"

"I think Mo, and then I continued, and then Mo said, 'Fin make sure they don't escape.'"

"You were afraid they would escape?"

"If they escaped it wouldn't work," she shrugged.

"What wouldn't work?"

Fin shook her head.

"*What* wouldn't work?" He repeated his question.

She closed her eyes, stuck her index fingers in her ears and shook her head from side to side, shutting him out.

Minutes passed like this. When she finally lowered her hands and opened her eyes he asked her again.

"What wouldn't work?"

Fin looked at her fingers and picked at a flake of blue paint that had crusted over her fingernail. She refused to answer or to say anything.

Van placed his pen on the pad of paper, crossed his arms and asked her again. "What wouldn't work?" He needed this answer. What would not work? What was their motive?

Fin's voice was lower now. A rasp. "I want to be locked up so I can't hurt anyone anymore. I knew this would happen. I knew we would get in trouble."

Van tried reading her face, but there was nothing. She was blank. He repeated the question, but Fin offered nothing new. The questioning stalled. He could not yell at her. He wanted to stand up, toss his chair across the room and scream in her face, demand to know why. What the hell did you do? What the hell were you thinking?

But he could not do that. She was a minor, and the judge would be all over him if he tried to intimidate her.

"Are you going to lock me up forever and ever until I die?" Fin asked sweetly.

She was taunting him. She knew that. He knew that. Even though he had enough to take to the courts he still wanted to know precisely what occurred out in that park. He could only hope that Medina was able to get more information about why two children felt the need to sacrifice their classmates.

CHAPTER 12

"You should go home. Get some sleep." Detective Washington stood over her. "You're tutoring in the morning." Lauren had finished digesting the notebook, making copies and taking her own series of notes. When she looked at her watch, she had to check the time again. It was past midnight.

"I'll sleep on the sofa here. If I'm lucky, I can get a few hours."

"McCarthy's going to start charging you rent." He looked her up and down. "You're still in the clothes from the funeral, Medina. Go home. Shower. How are you supposed to meet with a kid in the morning like this? Smelling like a graveyard?"

Lauren rubbed her eyes and groaned. She was tired, but there was just so much to do and not enough time.

"I think it's time you get out of here. Sleep in your own bed. Make coffee in your own machine. You don't want to drink this Keurig shit they have in the break room. You have to take care of yourself. No one else is going to do it for you."

Lauren fought a yawn and waved him over to her desk. "Before you fly off into the sunset I need your help."

"You didn't listen to anything I said."

"I never do."

Washington eased down in the chair beside her desk. He moaned and his knees made soft popping noises as he stretched his legs out in front of him.

"Do you think Frank will answer some questions for me?" She pointed to her notebook and then to her tablet. "He's young, and everything I'm finding out online about this is that it's part of some kid's game."

"Kids' game?" He questioned.

"What Fin mentioned to Van, about the NeverSleep website. I did some searching and found a single story on the Pied Piper on the website. It's more like instructions, but missing the final step."

The instructions were there, but not the nursery rhyme. You needed the nursery rhyme to complete the process, Fin had told Van before he wrapped up his questioning. To Van, it sounded like insanity. To Lauren, she knew it was all connected to that book sitting in Newberry Library.

"It's like Bloody Mary. You stand in front of a mirror and say Bloody Mary three times. She's supposed to appear and..."

"Kill you," Washington laughed. "Kids have been doing that one for ages. Dumb isn't it? Call up the very thing that will kill you. Why do people think that's a good idea? I'm not saying I believe in any of it. I'm just saying I'm not going to risk it, that's all."

"Look at these," she grabbed her cellphone and brought up a folder of related pictures.

Washington took hold of her phone as Lauren pointed.

"It started at Hadiya's shooting..."

"Medina..." Washington started, but she cut him off.

"This graffiti was right beneath where her body was found."

"I remember. I was there." Washington said. "It's just street art."

"No, it's not just street art," she searched through her phone for another image and showed it to him. "Then, yesterday when I drove past DePaul High School there was this." She pulled up the graffiti scrawled across the entrance doors. "And then, last night there was this." She pulled up the graffiti written down the trunk of the tree in

Humboldt Park next to the bridge. "Pied Piper."

"It's a new tagger, Medina. That's all."

She put her hands on her forehead leaned back and stared at the ceiling. "No, it's not." She sat back up. "The writing is different in all of them. It's not the same person. These three were written by three different people. Maybe it was Fin and Mo..."

"Okay, I'll go with it. Who is the third person?" He folded his arms across his chest.

"I don't know. Maybe this Jordan kid who showed up to Humboldt Park after Hadiya was killed. There's something more."

Washington sighed. "You're reaching, Medina."

She ignored him, grabbed her tablet. "Here's what else I found..."

"Medina...I think you need to find your bed and get some sleep."

"No, Washington. Look at this." She pulled up the website NeverSleep. She searched for the Pied Piper, and there it appeared. A short story, so simple, but so terrible.

"This right here says if you light a candle, stand in front of a mirror in a dark room and say this nursery rhyme you can have whoever you want killed, by him."

Washington placed his hand on the tablet. "I want you to go home and get some sleep before I have to talk to McCarthy myself. Sleep deprivation is a very real thing, Medina. And you're not well right now. Your divorce. Your dad's funeral. It's a lot."

Lauren hung her head, shaking it from side to side. "No. This is real. I feel it. I just need someone else to tell me I'm not crazy."

"I can tell you, you're not crazy. You're not even running on fumes. You have no fumes to run on. You're tired. Take some time off."

"Can I talk to Frank?"

Washington closed his eyes and shook his head. His mouth open, unaware of what exactly to say.

"This specifically talks about kids in Chicago, in our city kids are conjuring up this thing to kill people."

"Why would kids even play this game, Medina?"

"For the hope that something will get rid of their problem. For the hope that something will kill the very person making their life difficult, and for the hope that they will never be connected to that death. If you could have a person making your life miserable killed and know for certain you'd get away with it, would you do it? Look, this isn't unheard of. Just follow me..."

"I wish I wasn't, but here I am diving in..."

"People have always played these sorts of games, at sleepovers, camping. I mean, they're more ritual than game, but people play them. They've gotten the instructions from siblings, friends or off in some dusty book somewhere. While people aren't necessarily convinced they will work, they still believe that there's a hint of a story there, an urban legend. Still, they play the game. They start the ritual. Set the candles, all because they want to look in that mirror they believe can become enchanted in that moment and see the shape of someone form. People want to believe, and maybe even them wanting to believe has driven them to act out what this ritual was intended to accomplish."

Washington drew in a breath of air, in through his mouth and exhaled, blowing the air out of his mouth. "Medina, you can talk to Frank if it will help you," he said. "I want to help you. You're the daughter of my best friend. I saw you grow up. You're like the daughter I never had, and never wanted really. But, all I've wanted to do is protect you, just like your dad protected me. It's late. Very late, but I'm sure we can wake him up." He held out his cell phone. It was on speaker and already ringing.

The phone rang three times before Frank picked up on the other end and mumbled "Everything alright?"

"Yeah, sorry for waking you..." Washington said. "Medina wants to talk to you."

"What!?" The grogginess was knocked out of the boy's voice.

"Hey, Frank, I was wondering if you could answer a few things for me."

"Sure, Medina. What's up? Look," he lowered his voice. "Did I do something?"

Washington interjected "Why? Something I should know about?"

Lauren ignored them and continued.

"You're on speaker, and no, you're not in trouble. I just need someone closer to high school age who may be able to give me some information. Or, let me know where I can get more information... because I'm..."

"Old..."

"Old?" Her mouth dropped. She was twenty-five. She did not think of herself as old but compared to a high schooler, or college freshman like Frank, she was ancient.

Frank tried to recover quickly. "I mean old*er*. It's cool. I get it. No problem. What's up?"

She was the youngest homicide detective the department had seen in recent memory, but that did not matter. To Frank, and many of the teenagers she questioned, and sometimes arrested, she was old. Her colleagues at work did not see her that way. They saw her as someone who did not deserve to be here because she was too young, too inexperienced. A kid who did things her way, who did not ask for permission and took chances, no matter how treacherous her way of getting there. Maybe that is why she did not sleep, forgot to eat, and had perfected the five-minute shower because each and every minute she could be working she was, and not to prove herself to them. She was not here for her peers. She was here for the bodies in the street who needed someone to speak for them. She was their medium in a way, and she would do whatever she could to do right by the people of her city. If that meant making a deal with a demon, like the little boy made in Grimm's "The Spirit in the Bottle," she would. That little boy had been gifted riches and the power to heal, all simply in exchange for letting the demon out of his bottle.

Sometimes one needed to risk danger in order to save.

"Pied Piper..." She brought herself back to her call with Frank.

He did not let her finish her thought.

"Whoa, you went there."

"I did. What do you know?"

"It's some game. Some, you know, Bloody Mary kinda game. You probably had that one when you were younger. Say her name three times in a mirror, and she appears and kills you. This one's a little different. You turn off the lights, stand in front of a mirror, light a candle, and you say this nursery rhyme. The Pied Piper appears, and instead of scaring the hell out of you or killing you like Bloody Mary he kills whoever you want him to kill."

It was the grim reaper as a genie, she thought.

"What's the nursery rhyme?"

He sighed. "That I don't know. Lots of people don't know, but it sounds like some people do know where to find it. I just didn't care enough about it to go looking for it, you know what I mean? But for sure you need that rhyme. If there's no rhyme, he won't show. He just doesn't show up by you saying his name in the mirror three or five times or whatever."

"How does he know who to kill?"

"When he appears in the mirror you tell him the name of the person. He prefers to kill people by water."

"Like the Humboldt Park Lagoon?"

"Exactly. Wherever there's water, and a park, people say he'll be more likely to appear. Say the nursery rhyme in the mirror, give him your target's name, if you got it. Then wait. He'll take care of the rest."

"What about the graffiti?"

"That, no one really knows about. Yeah, we've seen it. Kids have seen Pied Piper writing all over town, but no one really knows who's doing it. At least I don't know. A warning, I guess, that he's here, always watching."

"These kids are crazy nowadays," Washington muttered. "This is all nonsense."

"Do you know anyone who's ever played this game? "

"No, but even if I have, I'd never tell. I'm not getting mixed up with any of that," he laughed nervously.

Washington grumbled in the background. "Good."

"What are you trying to say?" Lauren asked Washington.

"It's crazy that you believe in this, Frank."

He laughed. "I'm not saying I believe in it. I'm not saying I don't believe in it. I do know there's some weird stuff going on, and I'd just rather stay away from it. Oh, and there's just one more thing..."

"What's that?" Lauren asked.

"If at any point you try to stop it, you're done for."

"What do you mean?" Lauren looked over to Washington who rolled his eyes, as if he could not believe she was entertaining this.

"Exactly that, if at any point you tell him that you're done, that you no longer want to participate, that you don't want that person dead anymore, then he comes for you, and kills *you*."

"And how do you know he's going to hold up his end of the bargain? Like, he's going to kill your target and then leave you alone?" Lauren asked.

"You don't," Frank said. "Sure, maybe he'll take out the person you named, but how do you know he's not going to turn it around on you and ask you to kill people for him instead? You can't trust these things, I say. Summoning spirits. Communicating with supernatural beings. I know people are curious, they want to see what's out there, but there's a reason why these are dangerous games."

"Thought you didn't believe in any of this?" Washington said from his seat.

"Again, I'm not saying I believe in it. I'm not saying I don't believe in it. I'm only saying that I've heard about it, and I'm not messing with any of it."

Lauren thanked Frank and ended the call.

"Fairy tales? A nursery rhyme to call up some villain to kill your enemies? I've heard it all. I tell you this, I'm glad I'm retiring. People around here have lost their damn minds, Medina."

"Kids, though?"

"Look, people do horrible things to one another," Washington said. "Young people are no different. They can most certainly do horrible things to each other. Last night, an eighteen-year old and a nineteen-year-old beat up a fifteen-year-old on the blue line train so bad they broke her nose. Her face was swollen so bad her eyes were shut. Why? Because they wanted her damn phone. They broke someone's nose and messed up her face for a phone. Think about that? This case of yours, it's violent. It's cruel. The case doesn't make any sense, but they confessed. Finley and Mohammed confessed to their crime. It's time to let it go. There's no reason to give it any more energy than you've already given it. You solved the case. Let the law play out how these kids will be punished. They'll serve their time. You did your job. A good job too."

Lauren removed her ponytail, running her fingers through her hair before retying her hair back up in a tight bun. "They confessed to what they did to Evie, but about Daniel, that's where things get cloudy. They're not sure what happened. They're blaming each other, and the Pied Piper."

"Is this why you want to talk to Jordan? You think he knows something about this Pied Piper mess?"

She knew it sounded crazy to him, but she nodded anyway.

Washington sighed. "Again, let it play out in the courts."

"I still need to talk to Jordan."

"Whatever, talk to the kid. Just don't let him think the rest of the police force believes in this nonsense."

"Fine," she raised a hand up, hoping he'd stop, but he didn't.

"You've got enough work to do out here. You got your bad guys. Anytime you get your bad guy it's a good day."

"Then why do I feel like I didn't?" Lauren asked.

"What do you mean?"

She propped her elbow on her desk and rested her head in her hand. "People are always so horrified when they hear about how bad Chicago is, but you know, it's always been bad. It's like this damn city is cursed. Our city was literally founded on a massacre site, Fort Dearborn in 1812. Then we held thousands of Confederate soldiers in a prisoner-of-war camp down south at Camp Dearborn where many died of cold and disease. Then the Eastland Disaster, Chicago's Titanic, where over 800 people drowned. Then there's just so much more," Lauren crossed her arms across her chest as if she were cold. "Chicago fire. Mafia crime bosses. Serial killers. Street gangs. Chicago has it. We have such a bloody past and present that it just makes you wonder."

"Wonder what, Medina? If Chicago was built on top of a cursed Native American burial ground?" He smirked.

"No, not like the movies, but in a way people have always been killed right on the site of this city since before it was a city," she rubbed her forehead. "I guess I don't know what I'm trying to say other than Chicago's always been the kind of place to breed and attract tragedy. It's not right, but something about this place seems to draw out the worst in people. And if kids are using some game, some nursery rhyme as a justification for killing people, well, that's all that is, an excuse. It plays into this darkness this city is founded on."

Van laughed. Lauren did not hear when he entered, but he was standing right behind her.

"Couldn't sleep either, Van?" Washington asked.

"No, just left some notes here and had to come to grab them, to reread for my report."

"When'd you learn to read?" Washington asked.

"Funny. Relax, Washington. This place isn't your worry anymore. See you guys later."

When he exited, Washington turned towards Lauren. "He's annoying."

"Thanks for leaving me with him."

"I had no say in that."

Lauren stood up and stretched her arms above her head. "I'm going to go home and try to get some sleep." She reached for her car keys on her desk and then asked "Should I be worried about him? He asked a lot of questions about Marie tonight."

Washington stood up and stretched out his back. "He thinks Marie's crime scene was tainted. A lot of people think that—or thought that. It was so long ago. Van's a boy scout. He's always got to get his nose in something to make sure things are being done the right way. Just ignore him. There's nothing he's going to turn up that your dad or I, or the dozens of people we had working on that case for years, didn't already find. He's convinced someone knows something more about Marie's death."

"Why didn't you tell me this before?"

"Because you were too busy worrying about your dying father and you didn't need this. Why worry?" He raised an eyebrow. "You don't remember anything different, do you?"

Lauren rubbed the side of her head with the base of her palm so hard it was as if she was hoping for some new information to spill out. "I remember leaving school, and I remember waking up at Humboldt Park. That's it."

"You were a kid. A bad thing happened. That's all. Ignore Van. He's an ass."

Lauren was already halfway to the door when Washington shouted. "You shouldn't believe in ghosts and monsters, Medina."

"Why not?" She smiled as she turned around. Fine, it sounded completely, utterly insane, but these kids believed it.

"Because we, people, we're the real monsters in this story."

She laughed because he was right.

"Good luck tomorrow, Medina. I hope you get the answers you're looking for."

CHAPTER 13

The simultaneous ringing and vibration of her phone woke her. It took a moment for Lauren to register where she was. The sky was a dark blue, with streaks of orange. The sun was rising. It was cold. The cuffs of her pants were wet. She was barefoot. The soles of her feet stung. Ice. Frost. Lauren looked down to her phone in her hand. She looked to the garage in front of her. Lauren was standing in her backyard, facing her garage. The house was behind her. Her mouth dropped. She stifled a scream. Her arms and legs trembled in the early morning chill. The ringing and the vibration fell away. Whoever was calling stopped.

It was 6:00 a.m.

She did not know how it was she came to be standing outside, or how long she had been standing here. Her last memory was entering the house, going upstairs and falling asleep face down on the bed. Maybe it was her active mind that willed her body out here. It had happened before, sleepwalking. Stephanie had told her about it and had urged her to get more sleep to prevent it from occurring again. It was called hypnagogia, a mental phenomenon that happened during the fine threshold between being awake and falling asleep. And in that in-between place is where lucid dreaming, sleep paralysis and hallucinations, could occur. The hag, she thought, and then she remembered the hag engraved on the sculpture of The Dream Lady in Lincoln Park. Hypnagogia, the name sounded like some mythological monster, because it was.

It was then that she realized she was still holding her phone in her hand, and just as she looked down at her hand the phone erupted again. Blinking and buzzing. Lauren dropped her cell to the grass. Fear settled over her. She could not remember stepping outside, but here she was. She allowed the phone to ring. She did not recognize the number and was afraid to touch it for fear of answering a call in this confused state.

When the caller finally gave up, she bent down and picked up her phone and held it at her side. She turned around and faced the house that she grew up in. The house that she inherited, a Chicago worker cottage. Worker's cottages were built in the city as early as 1830. These were modest, utilitarian buildings made of wood. Some later versions were built of brick, but not hers. The Chicago worker's cottage are either one or one and a half stories in height, with gabled roofs that faced the street. Their basic styles have remained the same, but they have varied over the decades in some accents, from Greek Revival to ornate Queen Anne. Yet, no matter how they have been adapted over time, their influence on this city remained. It mocked her. All of its windows were illuminated. Each and every light in the house appeared to have been turned on. She had no memory of turning on all of those lights. Lauren sucked in a breath, pulling in crisp morning air into her lungs. It was time to face to ghost within.

Lauren proceeded to walk toward the back porch that led up to the first floor door. Once she reached the wooden steps she counted in her head, up the number of each step —*one, two, three, four, five, six, seven, eight*. She shuffled across the small wooden deck and opened the back door. It had been unlocked, so she had no doubt that it was her, in her sleepwalking state, who had turned on all of the lights and walked to the backyard. She locked the door behind her, took a seat at the kitchen table, and slipped on her house shoes. She looked to the cabinet where she stored the coffee—and that now radiated energy from the key. She could hear it calling to her. It knew she was cold. It knew she did not want to return to this home, just like the poor little boy in "The Golden Key" who was forced to fetch wood in the deep snow, and who then did not want to go home. Instead, he wished he could light a fire and warm himself a little. As he scraped away at snow, he found a golden key. He felt what it opened must be nearby, and so he dug out more snow and found an iron chest and believed precious things would be found in that little box. He found the keyhole, turned, opened the lid, and the story—the very last story collected by the Grimms brothers—concluded with "and then we shall learn what wonderful things were lying in that box." A mystery that was agonizing. The brothers had left her and the world and all of history to wonder what curiosities, what secrets lay within. Now, she had her own version of the golden key and she feared discovering what lay within that room. Now was not yet the time.

It was then that she noticed how much colder it was inside the house than it was outside. She stood up, grabbed her faded navy-blue academy sweatshirt and pulled it on. She walked over to the thermostat and raised it. The house would warm soon. Then, she walked up the stairs to the second floor. She started in the main bedroom. She walked to the end of the bedroom, making sure nothing was out of place, and then she turned off the bedroom light before entering the main bathroom, looking it over, and then turning off the light there as well.

She proceeded down the stairs to the basement. There, she turned off the light to the laundry room, small bathroom, and then she stood in the middle of the open space for a moment. The finished basement was brightly painted white. Her father had installed drop lighting a few years back. He would hold Christmas parties here for his co-workers, and during the rest of the year, this was where he would come to watch the Bears, Bulls, Black Hawks, Chicago Cubs, or the White Sox play on his large screen television. Unlike many Chicagoans, her father held no allegiance to either the Chicago Cubs or the White Sox. "We have two baseball teams and that is an incredible thing," he would say as he watched their games and cheered both teams on. When the Cross Town Classic would roll around in summer—when the Cubs and Sox would play each other—her dad would just enjoy the game, content with either outcome.

The White Sox were as mythical as the Cubs. The Chicago Cubs were well-known for the Curse of the Billy Goat, when Billy Goat Tavern owner William Sianis was refused entry into a game with his pet goat, named Murphy, in 1945. He cursed the Cubs saying simply "Them Cubs, ain't gonna win no more." And they didn't win a World Series for seventy-one years, until the curse was lifted by his ancestor. Decades before Sianis, it was eight players of the White Sox, later nicknamed the Black Sox of 1919, who threw the World Series for money in a gambling syndicate. Even the most enjoyable and wholesome things can hold a history of wickedness.

On the first floor, she turned off the lights to the living room, dining room, and what had been her father's bedroom. She quickly turned off the lights in the guest bedroom, merely opening the door and sliding down the light switch. She did not want to look at the spots where she had patched up those bullet holes. Lauren would wait for another day to paint that room. She then walked up to her father's office door and looked down at the space between the floor and the door. The light was off. She breathed relief knowing she did not need to get the key out from the cupboard today.

Her phone rattled on the kitchen table. The screen illuminated with that unknown number again. It was probably someone from work she finally reasoned, or someone finally willing to give her answers to a case.

"Hello," she said with a croak. Her throat was dry. She needed water. She moved to the sink and poured herself a glass. It had been hours since she had spoken. Her own voice sounded foreign to her.

"Hi, Detective Lauren Medina?" The voice on the other end

waited for confirmation.

"Yeah," Lauren said after gulping down the glass of water and setting it on the counter. She could not quite place the voice, but that was not unusual. Her business card had been passed out all over the city.

"Detective Medina here." She took a seat at the kitchen table.

"It's Elizabeth, Liz Santos with Young Chicago Writers. I'm sorry for calling so early, but I know this has moved so quickly. We got your application, and I got your message and spoke with Earle. We're very happy to have you join us."

Lauren rubbed her forehead. "Right, yeah. Thanks for calling." She settled down at the kitchen table. Listening.

"Sorry for calling a few times. We have Jordan coming in at 7 a.m. and want to be sure you'll be here today. If not, we'll team him up with someone else for the day."

"No, I'll be there," Lauren looked at the time. She did not have much time to shower, get ready and make it over there.

"Great, do you have any questions?"

"No," Lauren lay her head on the table for a moment, and then she straightened herself up. "I mean, just not right now, but I'm sure I'll have some questions later this morning."

"We're always in need of mentors, and I'm happy you offered to help. It's such a difficult time for Jordan. He's bright. He's a wonderful writer, but with the recent loss of his friend I just don't want for things to..."

"Turn dark," Lauren ended her sentence. Whether or not she was going to use those same words, it did not matter. It is the essence of what Liz meant. Getting lost and allowing the streets to feast on your bones.

"Exactly."

"I understand." Lauren hesitated. "I actually spoke with him Sunday, the night of Hadiya's murder."

"Oh, I didn't know." Liz's voice grew softer.

"I was there taking witness statements. I was gone by the time he got there. An officer at the scene got his contact information, and I reached out..."

"Excuse, me Lauren, but would you mentoring him cross some sort of, I don't know, department line? Is he under investigation?"

"No, no, not at all. I mean. I told Washington...Earle that I wanted to mentor, and I know he was a board member there for many years. He mentioned you needed help in the morning and that's when I had free."

"Strange coincidence," Liz said.

"I didn't think it was the same Jordan. That's totally fine that it is, right?" She continued speaking, without allowing Liz a moment to respond. "But no, he's not under investigation or anything at all. He's not even an eyewitness. He arrived just as we were leaving. I know it's hard to lose someone when you're so young. I lost someone when I was around that age."

"Oh, I'm so sorry to hear about that. Alright, I'll speak with him to be sure he's comfortable with the arrangement. Jordan is usually at our center a few minutes right before seven."

"Sure, of course. I completely understand. I'll be on time," Lauren walked back over to the thermostat. The kitchen still felt as iced as it did when she came inside. "Can you tell me more about him?" She returned to the chair and crossed her legs beneath her, hoping to get warm soon.

"Sure. He's a senior at DePaul College Prep. Smart but needs direction sometimes. His home life is pretty quiet. He lives with his mother, and his father is deployed in the Army right now. His mother works a lot. So, he's really on his own most of the time. He's talented, and we're just hoping to keep him focused. We hope that his mentor, you, can help him with his writing because that seems like an important outlet for him."

"Writing?"

Elizabeth must have heard the hesitation in Lauren's voice. "I'm so sorry. Is this too much too soon? Earle mentioned your father. I'm sorry. Are you sure this is what you want to do? We can always do this at a later time. Winter session or spring session? Another student?"

No, neither would work. She needed to get close to Jordan, to know why he panicked when he saw the graffiti.

"No, this will be good," Lauren said. "I can do this. I can help tutor. I mean, mentor."

"I'm sure he'll be pleased. Life has been hard for him. All of us, it sounds like. I'm sure he will be happy to have you."

Lauren really hoped so.

They agreed that Liz would speak with Jordan, and if all was well with him, their first meeting would be at the center just after 7 a.m. this morning.

After she hung up, Lauren heard the familiar tone indicating an email had come through. When she checked, she found a message from the funeral director at Rosehill Cemetery. Everyone seemed to be getting to work early this morning. He started the email by saying this is the second time he had emailed her, and he needed instructions soon. He asked if she could call this morning because that would prevent any potential delays. Armando's tombstone would be ready in the next few weeks. He needed to know how the epitaph for the tombstone should read. In the email, he provided Lauren with an example, the text inscribed on Diana's headstone.

Diana Medina
Wife. Mother. Musician.

Her father's could include the Chicago Police insignia and read:

Armando Rodriguez Medina
Husband to Diana

Father of Lauren and Marie

She did not reply. Why did he have to use Diana as the example?

Lauren stood up abruptly, her chair nearly falling onto the hardwood floor. The temperature in the house had quickly grown warm as hot air howled through the vents. She poured herself more water from the tap. When she'd lived with Bobby at least she had been away from this house. This place rattled things in her memory that she hoped had been resolved long ago. Even from the spot of where bodies are buried grass and flowers grow, showing that buried things were still connected to the surface somehow. Long, jagged shadows stretched across the white walls of the kitchen. Lauren did not believe in hauntings as much as she did in regret, and in this house, she felt nothing but regret, and nothing but loss. This house was infested with sorrow.

This house was not haunted. She had known that for some time. She was the one who was haunted by her own actions…inactions—all of which converged here in this house. Things were good, for a while. Her father's death, however, had rattled the locks on what should have remained forgotten. There was nowhere to go. There was no one to text, message, call or email. There was nothing to preoccupy the time with except the dead.

Lauren looked at her phone again, willing for someone to come to her mind to call. She needed to distract herself, but there was no one to talk to who was not involved in this. It was her own fault. She had pushed everyone who came too close away until they fell off and disappeared from her life. Yes, Bobby still lingered here or there, but he kept his distance. Her most treasured friendships were with the dead. Whispered questions: asking who took them, killed them, and sometimes they answered. Sometimes there was a hint, a call, a witness who came forward, and sometimes there was justice, but many times over the years there was nothing. Silence in life as in death. No one to confess. No one to arrest. No one to prosecute leaving a murderer to kill again, and a family forever asking how.

Lauren looked at the time. There was no one to turn to for help. There was nothing to do but get ready and meet with Jordan. Just as she rose from the kitchen table to head to her bedroom, she heard it. A hiss. It was intense and then it was gone. Lauren rubbed her eyes. She was not going to do this to herself again. She was not going to allow the anxiety of being back here drive her into seeing and hearing things again.

"That was nothing," she whispered under her breath. "Your father's dead. You're tired. You didn't sleep well. You have to get ready, and you have to go. That was nothing."

The sound erupted again. A flash of light from the hallway. A hiss. Then gone.

Rats. That's all she could think of. It was just rats. Pests who crawled into the walls, scratching at boards, sniffling blind in the darkness, searching for something to eat.

She would call an exterminator. They would come. They would take care of her problem.

"Rats," she said and then laughed to herself. Rats had always been the core of her problem. Her stomach cramped. Her feet were stone. She did not want to move. The noise was coming from the first floor bathroom a few feet away. The sound quickened.

Snap.

Hiss.

Snap.

Hiss.

Lauren's nostrils tingled. There was a sharp scent in the air. Something pungent, burning. With dread, she moved toward the door. Another snap and hiss, and now a crack.

Snap, and hiss. Hiss and crack. Snap and hiss. Hiss and crack.

Lauren took hold of the doorknob and pressed her forehead against the door.

A rat. It was just a rat.

Snap. Hiss. Crack.

"Just stop. Please. Just stop," she pleaded with herself, willing herself to stop hearing the sounds. Pleading with this house to just lie still. She thought maybe she should call the exterminator *now*. The person was more skilled than she would ever be in catching rats. A rat-catcher. The smell of something burning hung in the air.

Snap. Hiss. Crack.

She turned the doorknob.

Snap. Hiss. Crack.

She pushed the door open slowly.

The bulb burst on, glowing bright, brighter, bathing the room in white, and then it flickered out. Darkness.

Snap.

The light behind her in the hallway cast enough glow for her to see something in the mirror. A hand in the mirror displaying a single matchstick.

Snap.

The tip burst into a flame.

Hiss.

The hand moved closer to the mirror's surface.

Crack.

Etched into the mirror's surface was the name, that name that pained her. The name that cursed her.

Pied Piper.

When she looked into the now distorted glass she saw herself, but years younger, snapping a matchstick, the crack as chemical erupted to flame, and the soft fiery hiss as it was extinguished once a single white taper candle wick was lit.

Her younger self's lips moved in the glow of candlelight, but there was no sound.

CHAPTER 14

She flashed her lights, blared her horn, and hit the gas as she took the red light. Lauren sped down Central Park. It was just before rush hour, and so the major streets were not congested. They would be in the next hour as people pulled out of their neighborhoods heading either east towards downtown to work in one of the city's many ivory towers, many of which with open-spaced industrial seating, endless snacks and luxury coffee to attract a younger workforce. While others drove north, south or west for a reverse commute to a suburb with corporate campuses with gray offices lined with cubicles.

Once Lauren hit Fullerton Avenue, she made a sharp turn, heading east. Tires screeched. No one dared honk at her, because no one honked at the police. The car lunged forward, ignoring another red light. She was almost there, and if she needed to park in a tow-away zone, she would. She was late, very late, but Liz had not called telling her that Jordan did not want to work with her. That was at least a positive sign. Now, would Jordan even talk to her? Would he even know anything?

She approached the building. She had passed it multiple times, but never been inside. She parked a half block away, in the only available spot. She turned off the car and then glanced up in the rearview mirror. She regretted doing that as soon as she did it. Deep, purple-black bags beneath her eyes indicated she no longer had a relationship with sleep. Her skin was pale and dry. She was not eating well. Her hair was pulled back in a wet ponytail. She'd had no time to dry it. Her body needed better sleep, better food, but she needed to be here right now.

Lauren readjusted her ponytail, and then leaned over and reached for the glove compartment. She found a breath mint and crunched down on it as she drank back black sour coffee from her tumbler.

Once inside, she found Liz who greeted her and took her to a large room that looked like a classroom. There was a whiteboard and a wooden desk in front of it. Bulletin boards decorated in bright colors, inspirational quotes and a daily, weekly and monthly schedule lined the walls. Long conference tables were arranged in three large squares, and scattered throughout the space were adults with students, laptops in front of them, or books, or sheets of paper. Everyone working on their own assignment.

In the far back corner were several large bookshelves that created a private reading nook, shut off from the rest of the activity in the center.

"This is the space," Liz announced. "If you need anything just let me know. We have laptops in back. We have a small library. We're slowly building it up with the help of volunteers."

Lauren saw Jordan seated in the corner across from the library, away from the conference tables, at a private table for two. He gave Lauren an annoyed look, then looked to Liz as if to say, "Now what?" Liz shook her head in that gentle way that said, "Stop it."

"There's Jordan," she said in a sing-song way. Every time Lauren spoke to Liz the woman seemed to be in an exceptionally bright mood, cheery, and optimistic. All of the things Lauren was not.

"You're late," Jordan said without looking up from writing in a notebook. "I've got to be at school by nine."

"We're done here at eight then?" Lauren looked to Liz who nodded enthusiastically.

"Jordan is very happy you are here."

Jordan looked up, his face twisted in a look of confusion. "Not really, but you said it'd be hard to find a replacement this term, so here we are."

Liz' eyes widened. "Jordan, you are very funny."

"Ms. Liz, are you serious right now?" Jordan said as he tapped on his smartphone, glancing at a text that had just come through. "My mentor's a cop. She's late, and honestly, how do I know this doesn't have anything to do with Hadiya?"

Liz gave a nervous laugh. "It doesn't, Jordan. Right, Detective Medina?"

"Lauren..." Lauren interrupted. "Just Lauren is fine." Lauren figured this should have been part of Liz's job, introducing Lauren just as a regular adult, one with a passion for education and mentoring inner-city youth. Lauren herself grew up in the city, learned to be street smart at a very young age, and while she saw many young people fall through the cracks, or worse, she continued moving forward through college and into a career in law enforcement. Yes, fine, she was Detective Medina. Yet, it was Liz's job to solidify Lauren into this role, the role of a mentor. This slip-up, of calling her Detective Medina in front of Jordan could make him nervous and so uncomfortable with the situation that he could cancel the entire arrangement.

"Right, Lauren. Sorry. Let's make that clear. She is Lauren, your mentor when she is here." Liz directed the conversation elsewhere. "Lauren is a great writer."

Lauren did not know where Liz got that idea from. Jordan was staring at Liz, with his mouth wide open, and right as he was about to say something Liz cut in.

"Earle Washington, one of our board members who just retired, told us about your literary studies, Lauren. An English honors graduate from Loyola University and a Master of Arts in Literature from Northwestern University. That's very impressive."

"Yup," Jordan cut in. "Impressive. Look at what she's doing with those degrees now."

"Exactly, Jordan," Liz said. "She is here right now with us."

"Really?" Jordan mouthed to Liz.

With a smile Liz said, "I'll leave you both to it." She leaned in close to Lauren and said, "Thank you again." Then, she was gone. It felt like Lauren was here alone in this room, with this boy who had just lost his best friend, and who did not trust her at all. It was as though the chatter among the tutors and mentors with their students faded.

"Do you mind?" She motioned to the chair across from him.

"You're here already," he said as he held onto the headphones that were wrapped around his neck.

"Looking forward to working with you," Lauren said as she took a seat.

Jordan did not look up from his phone. She could see he was selecting music. He tapped on play and sound flowed from his headphones.

"You're not really going to put those on now?"

Jordan lifted the headphones up over his head and set them on his ears. He increased the volume. He looked away from her, probably as upset as she was that they were both tangled in this arrangement. She looked around the room, and everyone else seemed engaged enough in what they were working on that no one seemed to notice that they were not working on anything together.

She took her phone out and sent Washington a message.

"This tutoring thing is working out great. Life changing."

He replied.

"Anyone ever tell you that you have an attitude problem?"

Jordan reached down for his blue backpack, a quote written across it in marker. It took a moment for Lauren to take in all of the words as they stretched across the fabric.

"That's the ideal meeting...once upon a time, only once, unexpectedly then never again." —Helen Oyeyemi

"You read a lot?"

Jordan shot her a look and shook his head. “Shocking, isn’t it?” The music level increased.

It was a stupid question, she knew it as soon as she asked it, but that is not what she meant. She was just trying to learn something about him, establish trust, rapport, to connect on some level. She wanted to tell him that she too would wake early before school to read, study, and practice. That she too would take the bus, and then the train to get to school. After Marie and then Diana, she would sometimes spend hours on the bus or trains, discovering new stations and routes, checking off each one as they passed. There were one hundred and forty-five train stations in Chicago and seven suburbs that bordered the city, and she had visited them all. Founded in 1947, the Chicago Transit Authority—CTA—felt like a safe place for her to be, because there she was constantly moving. And if she was moving she believed that her life could not catch up to her.

Chicago had operated some sort of urban transit system as far back as 1859, but then it was operated by a combination of horse, cable and electric streetcars. The various lines had all been consolidated throughout the years, many of the routes were eliminated but still, many of those old age routes remained and Lauren thought of that each time she rode the bus or train. Sometimes a pothole would open up in the city revealing cobblestones and the steel line remnants that streetcars transported people along. When Lauren would come across one of those spots in the street, even if it was damp with rain, or sprinkled over with frost, she would kneel down and touch the cobblestones or steel line, thinking that somehow she could be transported within that moment to a time when this city bustled with such vibrant energy as it grew. She never did complete her goal of traveling all of the bus routes, but one day she would complete her intent, checking off each of the 12,000 bus stops.

Jordan swapped out the notebook he was working in for one with a green cover. He flipped through pages of carefully handwritten text.

His penmanship was precise, all of the letters written in neat capital letters resting not on the ruled line, but within the white space center. Lauren had only ever seen text so carefully arranged on a printed page. Jordan found a blank sheet and proceeded to write in his careful print. When the music cut out, that moment in between the end of one song and the beginning of another Lauren asked loud enough so he would hear: "What are you writing?"

Without looking up, he said "Words. In English."

"He hates me." She typed furiously to Washington.

He responded.

"You should be used to people hating you."

After a moment Washington followed up his text with;

"That's a joke, you know?"

Washington was not helping.

Before she texted him back saying, 'You don't have to be an asshole' she slammed her phone face down on the table.

"There it goes," Jordan pulled the right headphone off his ear.

"There what goes?"

"Brutal honesty," he pointed to her phone on the table with his pen. "You don't want to be here, but you're here to ask me more questions because I didn't want to answer your stupid questions the other night. Nice to finally meet you."

"That's not fair. I do want to be here." Even to her, her words didn't sound believable.

"You're a horrible liar, Medina." He continued writing, but the right headphone was set just off of his ear. It was something. A small gesture that he would at least try to listen to her.

"Call me Lauren," she reminded.

"No way, Medina," he said. "You're here because you want something." He stopped writing and waved his pen at the people in the room. "You see all of these adults here? They don't want to be here either, but it makes them feel good...like, coming out and volunteering with some inner-city kids a handful of times a year places a bandage on the rest of the year when they just don't care what happens to us out here."

"You're wrong."

"Am I? Why are you here?" He crossed his arms and leaned back in the chair, waiting for an answer. "Go on..."

"Fine. I'm here because I want to know why when you saw that graffiti on the ground the other night you started shouting. Officer Guerrero said you looked terrified. Do you know who wrote it? Did you write it?"

His face did not give anything up. He sat back up, leaned toward his notebook, picked up his pen and continued writing. Lauren knew he could not be forced into answering what scared him that night. Maybe it was not the graffiti. Perhaps it was the shock of it all. After all, he did say he was running late that night. Lauren knew it was true. She checked out his story and verified with surveillance cameras along the route he took the train that night. Who knows? If he had been there, maybe he would not be here right now. Perhaps he would have gotten shot and killed instead of Hadiya? It was traumatic for so many reasons. Still, she needed to know what spooked him.

"And what do those words combine to say?" She distracted from the topic that hung overhead, and instead focused on what they were supposed to be doing, working on his writing.

Jordan ignored her.

"You know, those words that you're writing right there," she tapped the page. If he got aggravated, then so be it. It would at least force him to continue talking to her.

He pulled the notebook back away from her, set his headphones back carefully over his ears and the music increased in volume. He fell away into his world. For the next few minutes, he wrote furiously. Every now and again, in that space between one song and another she was able to edge in a question. Maybe he would shake his head or nod, or nothing. They went on like that for the rest of the time they had together, Lauren asking whatever snippet of a question she could manage within those seconds of silence.

At the hour mark, her phone vibrated.

Jordan lowered his headphones off his ears, setting them to rest around his neck. “Wow,” he said. “You really don’t want to be here, do you? You even got an alarm and everything to tell you when you’re done.”

“You’re wrong about me. You think you know me, and you don’t, and plus” she picked up her phone and waved it at him. “I’m a homicide detective. I can’t ignore my job, or more people die. I have to stay alert. That’s what being responsible is.”

Jordan ripped two pages out of his notebook and set them on the table. “What are you going to say next? That you understand me? That you’ve been in my shoes? All of that nonsense in order to build trust.”

Lauren could feel her nostrils flare then she closed her eyes and shook her head. “I do understand you.” She opened her eyes and glared at him. “My sister was killed when I was about your age.”

“Damn,” Jordan said. “Sorry.”

Lauren’s alarm sounded again, another reminder that their time was over.

“The alarm...”

“To remind me when to get back to work and for you to get to school.”

He gave her a look that said he did not believe her.

“What’s that look for?” She asked.

“You’re a cop.”

“And?”

“Cops don’t have a start or stop time. It’s like what you are. It’s like your identity. Hell, it should be added as a race option on the Census. White. Black. Cop.”

Jordan stood up and pushed his arms through the straps of his backpack. Lauren followed.

"Here," he shoved the sheets of paper that he wrote during the hour into her hand.

"What's this?"

"Words on a page."

She let out a breath. "I see that."

"A speech I need to give this Friday. Let me know what you think about it tomorrow."

He wanted to meet with her again? She thought this first meeting was a disaster.

"I'll help, with what I can." She scanned the pages "What class is this for..." She thought about what kind of classes people took in high school. "English, history, composition..."

"Hadiya's funeral."

Jordan gave her a nod and then walked past her. Without turning around, he said, "See you tomorrow."

"Just one question, Jordan," she called after him, soft enough so as not to distract the rest of the people who were ending their tutoring sessions.

He stopped. "Fine," and turned around to face her.

"Do you know who left the graffiti? Pied Piper?"

"I really wish I did," he shrugged, as he clutched the front straps of his backpack. "but I don't."

She believed him. Before he opened the door, he said without turning around: "If you want any more of your questions answered, tomorrow at least try to be on time."

CHAPTER 15

"Who is it you see in your room, Fin?"

Fin kicked her legs under her chair, swinging them back and forth. She was tired of being asked questions. She was tired of being here. She was just so very tired.

They were seated in a small white room. Fin on a cream-colored sofa chair directly across from Ruth. Ruth introduced herself as a doctor. Ruth asked a lot of questions.

"I don't see anything in my room," Fin muttered. Her hair was slick and oily.

Ruth leaned forward. Fin looked away from her to the small white table beside her. There were colored sheets of construction paper, markers, and crayons. She wanted to reach out and start drawing, but she did not want to be asked questions about what it was she was drawing and why. So, she just looked at the supplies and drew something in her head, something dark on green colored sheets of paper. A scene with looming trees. A tall man. A little girl being led away into the forest.

Something clattered in the hallway and then there was a scream. Ruth reached for her phone in her blazer pocket, but stopped herself from dialing when the noise ceased.

"You can ignore that," Ruth said. "Sometimes people get very upset being here."

"Then why should I even be here if it's an upsetting place?"

"Because we want to make sure people get better. We want to make sure people get the help that they need, and that's what we want to do for you. Sometimes though, it's hard getting help. It's hard to make changes that can make you better."

Fin looked back down at the paper and then to her hands, fighting the urge to pick up a black crayon and scrawl a picture of the man. In her mind, his arms were reaching out for her. She knew he was waiting for her, somewhere she could taste the earth in the wind, acidic and bitter, where she could hear the creaking of branches, and rustling, rooting, and scrabbling of critters among the leaves, and where she could breathe in deeply, wild mint and rotting wood. In the shade, or sun-dappled leaves, between the fallen twigs, and along the moss he was there. He was always there. If Mo had just moved a little faster, spoken a little less, then they could have met him, and everything would have gone on just like it should. Just like when she had met him the first time.

Fin wondered if she should tell Ruth everything, but then she quickly thought: why would she? Ruth should not be so lucky to know about the man. Fin knew he could get rid of anyone who was making life difficult for you—for a price of course. The price of a life. A life in exchange for peace. What Fin had recently learned, however, was that the man could come back, and if he came back, that meant he needed someone else, *another* price for continued peace. She did not know he would come back so soon. She did not tell Mo that he would come back. Mo came to her asking for help, asking for a way to kill the man who had robbed his father. So, she told him about the Pied Piper. She just did not tell Mo what he was getting himself into.

"Fin..." Ruth said to get her attention.

Fin looked away from the paper and the crayons. "Where is Mo?"

"He's safe."

"Where is he?" Fin could feel herself standing. Her arms shaking.

What did Ruth mean Mo was *safe*? Where was he?

Ruth raised a hand and motioned for her to sit down, and she did. "He's in a place, almost like this but not quite. He needs less help than you right now. He's safe. Trust me."

Fin scanned the walls in this room. She wondered how long she had been here. She had not paid much attention to the time, or to daylight, or to the hours she slept.

"How long have I been here?"

"Not long. Do you remember what happened? At Humboldt Park?"

"Can I see Mo?"

"No," Ruth said firmly. "Maybe you can tell me what you want to say to him?"

"And you'll send him my message?"

"No, I mean, instead of telling him you'll be telling me. Is that okay?"

Fin took a deep breath. She was not going to share anything with Ruth. She did not like Ruth. She did not trust Ruth.

"I'm hoping you can eventually tell me things. That's why I'm here, Fin. You can talk to me."

Fin stomped her feet on the floor.

"What's wrong?" Ruth asked.

"I have to turn in my paper for English class."

"You don't have to worry about that right now. Your parents know you're here and I'm sure your teachers have been notified."

"I don't have to turn in my paper?"

"No, you don't have to worry about that right now."

Out in the hallway, there was the sound of footsteps. They grew louder, and then just as she thought someone was going to enter their room the sound of the footsteps faded. Fin looked to the small window in the door. The man's face appeared, and just as she opened her mouth to call to him, to tell him she was sorry and to give her another chance, he disappeared.

Tears filled her eyes. “Why did he leave me?”

“Mo didn’t leave you,” Ruth said. “We need to keep you both safe, and we need to understand what happened.”

Fin cried into her arm.

“I heard you didn’t sleep well last night.”

Fin wiped away at tears.

“I’ve been told that voices were coming from your room last night,” Ruth said.

“Is it wrong to talk? We’re there in the room, and there’s nothing to do, and sometimes we can’t sleep, so we talk.”

“I thought you said you didn’t see anything in your room?”

“There’s nothing in my room!” Fin shot back. “There’s just my roommate.”

“What did you talk about?”

“Things. School. This place.”

“Did you talk about what happened at the park?”

“No,” Fin looked at her fingernails. “I don’t want to talk about that.”

“Why?”

“Nothing happened.”

Sounds returned to the hallway. A low, moaning screech. It sounded like an owl. Fin closed her eyes, listening, trying to make out what the man was trying to tell her.

“What do you think about that?”

She opened her eyes. “About what?”

“I asked about meeting again this evening?”

Was there any option to say no? This place was filled with doors, a door that closed in front of her, behind her, each of them clicking shut, an attendant on the other side making sure the handle did not budge. What was this place? She was never told. Just white walls, fluorescent lights, a thin pad that rested on a box that served as her mattress. A tray of cold food brought to her. In the hallway, she listened for life. She wondered if her room was the secret chamber in "Bluebeard," or the room in "Fitcher's Bird"? If someone opened it, would they find a bloody basin in its center with dismembered body parts within? Would those parts be hers?

"There's very little else for us to discuss," Ruth said. Perhaps it was a way to guilt Fin into providing more information, but she was not going to fall for this trick.

"Is there a bloody basin in my room?"

Ruth's mouth fell open. "I'm sorry. What do you mean?"

"Oh, nothing. It's just a fairy tale. Can I go to my room now? I need to talk to my roommate."

"Right." Ruth's eyes darted from side to side and she blinked rapidly, as if trying to spin the thoughts in her head together. "We're just about done here. We can get you back to your room. First, can you tell me what you and your roommate were talking about just as I approached the door earlier? It almost sounded like you were arguing about something."

"No..."

"No, you weren't arguing about anything? You sure? You don't want to talk about it?"

Fin did not answer Ruth. Ruth would just continue to ask another question and then another, an endless loop of silly questions. She only wondered how much longer she would be here; how many more minutes, hours and days. She missed her bedroom at home, her paintings and her artwork. She painted the forest around her and within her the forest lived.

"Can I have some art supplies for my room?"

"I can ask about that."

"When can I go back home?"

"I'm going to be honest, Fin. You may be here for some time. We want to make sure you are comfortable. I will ask about the art supplies. What is it that you like to draw?"

"Trees. People. Houses. I like to make dollhouses out of paper and place them in forests I create."

"I know it's scary to be here. It's a lot to take in. It's a strange place, but I can tell you that you are safe here."

"Is Mo safe?"

"Yes, he's safe. I promise you, you are both safe."

Fin knew that was not true, but Ruth could not possibly see the danger that Fin and Mo were in.

"Come on," Ruth said. "I can walk you back to your room, and we can talk tomorrow then since it sounds like that will work out better."

Ruth stood up and walked to the door. Beside it was a button she pressed. This alerted the attendant out at the big desk that their session was over. Ruth opened the door and asked Fin to follow her. Fin's room was down the hall. They walked in silence, Fin shuffling her feet along.

They passed the large desk. The woman seated behind it followed Fin with her eyes. The hallway was silent except for the sound of their footsteps along the laminate floor. The lights overhead were a sickly yellow that bathed the walls, floor, and ceiling in a muted beige light. They passed doors on their right, each with a three-digit number and a thin window.

"Here you are."

Fin took a peek in her room. There in the center was a basin, and piled and stacked up high and overflowing to the floor—small fingers and bones, detached little arms, and tiny feet, bloodied and bruised and putrifying.

"I guess we all wash ourselves in blood," Fin said.

Ruth's eyes darted from Fin to the window, pushing past the girl and looking inside, seeing nothing. "Everything alright?"

"Yeah, just tired."

Ruth unlocked the door, and Fin stepped inside and made her way over to her bed. She sat down on top of her bed. Crossed her legs and started speaking rapidly.

Ruth returned to her office, which was located three floors below Fin's room. It was time to call Fin's parents and provide them with an update. This was the part Ruth always dreaded. The phone rang several times, and then a breathless voice answered on the other line.

"Hello..." A deep inhale followed by an exhale.

"Yes, Mrs. Wills? This is Dr. Ruth Margraff. Do you have time to talk now? I've been working with your daughter."

"Right," she paused. "Lindsay, you can call me Lindsay."

In the background, Ruth could hear the movement of plastic bags. The jingle of car keys. A baby babbling.

"Is she okay?" Lindsay asked, and then she released a sob. "That's a stupid question. Everything's not okay. My step-daughter...what did she do?" Lindsay cried softly.

"Our session went well, but I was wondering if I could ask you a question. I know the last few hours have been traumatic for all of the families involved, but I need to know if Fin has been diagnosed in the past with any conditions. These are all things that we need to talk about and consider."

"I filled out a list for you all. Vaccines she got when she was smaller...broken arm when she was like ten. Pneumonia when she was eight or something. I'd have to go back and check. Her mother kept good records, but I'd have to check to be sure. My husband has them around here somewhere."

"And how old was Fin when her mother died?"

"Oh," Lindsay started. "That was just last year." The baby's babbling returned. The rustling of bags. The sounds of the phone being muffled, a mother on the other end trying to manage.

"I'm very sorry, I didn't know it was that recent."

"Her parents were separated for a few years, and her mother got swept up in a wave on North Avenue beach. It was hard for Fin," Lindsay blew her nose on the other end of the line and tried to calm the babbling baby. "I'll talk to her dad when he gets in from work."

"Thank you, and just to be clear, I just want to be sure we are not missing anything else that may be important..."

"Important?"

Ruth was not only making this phone call on a medical capacity. She was calling as a legal representative on Fin's behalf. "Is there a family history of illness that we should be considering?"

"Family history?"

"Is there anything else that we should consider? A history of any family members with mental illness? If Fin does not have any previous diagnoses, that is."

Quiet.

"Lindsay? Are you still there?"

"Her mother drowned. It was traumatic for her, and her dad... I know her dad remarrying again must be hard on Fin. That's stressful enough on a kid."

Fin had been through a lot in the past few years; her mother's death, a stepmother. The call ended and Ruth leaned back in her chair and stared at the ceiling. One of the fluorescent bulbs behind the plastic panel had burned out days ago, but she did not report it to the facilities' manager. She enjoyed sitting in the dim light with her thoughts.

Ruth's phone rang, and she sighed when she saw who it was.

"You've called like 100 times," she said after she answered.

"Exaggeration. Plus, I wanted to make sure you didn't forget about me. I need an update."

"This is so not legal, Lauren."

"I don't need to know anything about the case. I just need to know if Fin's been seeing things. If you think she's been seeing things or hearing things. Anything. I just need to rule out any other kids doing something like this."

"Have you ever heard of patient-doctor confidentiality? I could lose my license."

"There could be other people at risk. I need to know if she's been seeing anything...unusual."

"You are asking me to risk my job."

"Trust me, Ruth. I won't tell anyone we've talked."

Ruth picked up the pen that was on top of her notepad. She proceeded to tap the top sheet of paper with the pen.

"Just tell me something. Something that'll come out public anyway, something I could use."

"She's seeing things. She's hearing things. I can't rule out anything at this time, but hallucinations and a fixation with what so far seems to be a fictional boogeyman. I'm sure her lawyer will want to admit it to court for a possible insanity plea. Possible early onset of adolescent schizophrenia, but..."

"Okay, schizophrenia, what does that even mean?"

"I didn't say she *suffers* from schizophrenia, Medina. I'm saying it's possible. We'll need to formally evaluate her..."

"Ruth, come on. It's me, and what's with the Medina crap?"

"You ran off and got married...and you use people, Lauren. That's what you do. You use people to help you out with whatever case you're working on, and you used me. Hell, you are using me *right now*."

"I deserve that, and I didn't 'run off' and get married. We had been broken up, for a long time."

"Three months," Ruth corrected. "Three months, and you probably did to him what you did to me, because I heard about the divorce. People get close to you, and you just leave them or push them away. Tell yourself whatever it is you need to so you can get through your day, but you're a selfish and awful person sometimes."

"I'm not doing this for me, Ruth, believe me."

Ruth flung the pen across the room, because if there was anyone she could never say no to, it was Lauren. "If Fin does have adolescent schizophrenia, it would explain a lot. There's a range of issues it can pose. Problems with thinking and behavior, disconnected emotions. They have an inability to function as a normal person would, often because they are wracked with delusions, hallucinations..."

"Seeing things? Hearing things?"

"Yes, both visual and auditory hallucinations are possible."

"And Ramsen? Mo, I mean." Lauren asked.

"He's with the general population, in juvenile detention. I gather he went along with it, believing in all of it for her. There's shared delusion I'm seeing here. It's more common within a family, parents and children believing the same delusion, or siblings believing in the same delusions together. It does happen between those who are not related. It's rare, but it happens. Chicago has a strange history of children killing children. The Leopold and Loeb killing is one that pops into my mind. I was obsessed with that case in grad school."

"That was the 20s wasn't it?"

"Yeah, 1924, they were both University of Chicago graduates. They plotted to commit the perfect crime because they thought they were invincible. They thought they were literally supermen. They believed they were so brilliant they could outsmart everyone. They kidnapped and killed fourteen-year-old Bobby Franks and were sure they would get away with it. But they were sloppy. For how confident they were, they completely botched the crime scene, and they were caught."

"Bobby Franks," Lauren said. "That's the one gravesite I just can't seem to find."

"You always did like spending a lot of time at Rosehill Cemetery. By the way, I'm very sorry about your dad. I sent a card, but figured you were too busy—like always—to respond."

"Thank you...I've gotta go, Ruth, but thank you. Really. This helps tremendously."

"I miss you sometimes, and I did really love you once, Lauren. I hope you know."

"I loved you, too," Lauren said.

"Good luck, figuring this out, Detective."

As soon as the call ended, before Ruth could place the phone on her desk, it rang. It was the attending psychiatrist.

"Dr. Margraff here..."

"It's urgent. Fin said there's something that she wants to confess to you, and we need you here *now*."

CHAPTER 16

"I don't think I can do this," Lauren paced Liz' office. She had called her ex-girlfriend, Ruth, and then sat in her car and read the pages Jordan had handed her. As soon as she was done, she walked right back into the writing center.

"I know I said I would mentor him, but he hates me, and this kid needs more help than I can offer. I can't give him what he needs," she said. Lauren would figure out another way to do this, but right now she could not give this much of herself. So much of her had already been taken.

Liz sat calmly at her desk and spoke only when Lauren stopped talking. "What did he ask you to do, exactly?"

"Read this," she raised the sheets of paper in the air. "He's reading this Friday at Hadiya's funeral."

"Our kids go to funerals sometimes. You should know that, Lauren. Death is as much a part of their lives as school is. Some of these kids don't even have the option to be a kid. That's taken away from them. The reality of their life out there," she nodded towards the large window that looked outside onto the street. "I think you might know a little bit about that given what you do for a living. Do you realize that less than twenty percent of our children in Chicago Public Schools will go on to earn a bachelor's degree? What happens to our other kids? Many of them find meaningful work, yes, but many of them are underemployed or unemployed. These kids come here, and that's the first big step. They care. They are asking us, the adults, for help, and that's what we are supposed to do—help. Sometimes help is as simple as listening. I want you here, I really do, but you need to want it too."

Lauren rocked side to side on her feet, unsure of what else to say.

Liz pointed at an empty seat across from her. "Sit down, you officers make me all nervous when you're always standing the way you do."

Lauren gave a single dry laugh and sat down. It made her feel as though she had been called into the principal's office, seated across from Liz who was sitting behind a large wooden desk. It clashed with the rest of the clean, open space of the center.

"It was my mother's desk," Liz said, noticing where Lauren's eyes were drawn. "It's big, and the wood is chipped and scratched in places, but it was my mother's desk at the school she taught at for forty years. When she retired, she had the desk moved to her home. It sat in her basement until she died, and after she died, I brought it here. My mother couldn't leave me much, but she left me this desk, and this desk reminds me of what I need to do each day."

"And what is that?" Lauren asked.

"Show up. Be good to them. Make this a place they feel safe, full of people that want to help them. I have to save these kids," she leaned forward and interlaced her fingers in front of her on the desk. "If I don't save them, these streets are going to take them."

Lauren believed Jordan had nothing to do with the graffiti, and for that, she wondered what was the point in coming back. Maybe he knew something else that could point her in the right direction. She had not thought this mentorship through. She could not get close to people.

Liz opened her hands. Lauren passed the sheets of paper. "What did he want you to do exactly? Edit this?"

"Read it."

"He just wanted you to *read* it?"

Lauren lowered her face into her hands. "I'm tired. I didn't sleep well, and this is...much more than I can handle right now."

"Coffee?" Liz asked.

Lauren groaned "Yes, please," from behind her hands.

"Give me a minute. The coffee machine is in the break room. I'll be right back."

Lauren lowered her hands and looked down at those sheets of paper on that scratched, worn hardwood desk. It was a desk children had leaned on over the years, and where a teacher had graded papers late into the night. She looked at those white sheets of paper with black writing with dread. This is why she did not get close to people. When she got close to people bad things happened. She did not want anything bad happening to Jordan. He had already suffered enough. Lovers, and now a former husband, were abandoned before they could see the complications, and before they could fall down a hole they could not crawl out of. She had no real family, at least she avoided all of her cousins or distant aunts and uncles. Lauren needed to keep people at a comfortable distance, to protect them. Children were capable of such wicked things, but Lauren wholeheartedly believed Jordan was not involved in this like Evie or Mo. Jordan, she believed he was just a little boy whose friend had died.

So, she had read without expectation.

I promised you I'd meet you at the park that day. I was on my way, but the bus broke down. It seems like every time I depend on something it breaks down. I didn't call you because I figured you were with your cousins, and I just didn't want you to be upset with me, for being late. I'm always late. I don't mean to be.

There's so much that I want to say, but I feel like I'm drowning without you. You were my best friend. You were my only friend.

When you got your college acceptance to Northwestern University to study writing, I didn't tell you, but I cried. I've never been so happy for someone, and I was happy because you were going to get out. I wanted you to get out. I could see you, moving to New York or Los Angeles after college. You were going to write for TV, movies, magazines, games. You were going to live your dream, and I was so happy for you. I remember how excited you were for me when I got into UIC. I was sad I didn't get into some fancy private school, but you were so proud of me for getting into the University of Illinois at Chicago. You were really happy for me. You were always happy for me. You were always there for me when no one else seemed to be.

I texted last night to tell you I missed you. I don't know if your mom turned it off yet, but I just sat there with the phone in my hand, waiting for you to respond. Maybe, somehow, through the ether of time and space you could text out some letters and tell me you missed me too. I knew you couldn't. Still, I hoped somehow you could see the text I sent you, you can read this letter, and you can know how much I miss you.

There's this nursery rhyme—Humpty Dumpty sat on a wall. Humpty Dumpty had a big fall. I looked it up, and the first time it was recorded was in 1797. I like to think if I say it out loud I'm connected to everyone who has ever said it in time. Maybe you said it when you were a little girl in school. I'll say it out loud right now and hope I'm somehow with you. Funny, I feel like I'm him, Humpty Dumpty, broken and shattered, and I really don't know if I can ever pull back all of these pieces of myself together again and be whole without you.

I hate this. I hate that you're gone. I hate that the city you loved so much did this to you. I hate that your happiness has been taken away from me, from all of us. I hurt for you.

Lauren took a deep breath and let the soft whistle of her exhale wake her from out of the tragedy of those words. She had been exposed to the hurt, at the location of crimes, and at funerals, but those were mostly the words of adults. This was a child dealing with trauma, and she did not know how to properly process childhood trauma, because all she did with her own childhood trauma was to tuck it away, pretend it never happened and pretend it was not still here, festering.

"Here you go," Liz said handing her a mug of black coffee. Lauren took a sip and even though it was hot she could tell it had been brewed hours earlier. "I was thinking, maybe give it some time, or not. It's totally up to you. We'd love for you to work with Jordan, but I get it. Mentoring does come with its responsibilities, and one of those responsibilities is sometimes internalizing the hurt some of our kids carry."

"It's fine," Lauren said, downing as much of the harsh liquid she could. She set the mug on that big wooden table with the scrapes and scratches. Leaving another mark.

"I'll be here tomorrow morning," she said.

"Are you sure? I know there's been a lot going on for you, and I just want to make sure this is a positive experience for you—and more importantly for Jordan."

Lauren folded up Jordan's speech and tucked it into her jacket pocket. "Yes, it's just overwhelming." She thought of anything to say on the spot that might sound like the right thing to say. "I can handle it. He deserves someone."

"I'm glad, Lauren. I'm delighted. Remember, he just asked you to read it. While I know that it sounds like a lot and in many ways, it is a lot, just remember that he just needs someone. He just needs someone to listen, or in this case, read what he has to say."

"Right," she nodded and promised she would be back again. As she stepped outside, she called Van and asked if anyone had heard about Evie's condition. She was stable, he said, but her parents still did not want her to be interviewed. It was too soon. The surgeries had all been a success, but there had been many, and many more would come in the future.

"I need to know as soon as she can talk. It's important," she told him, but he questioned her when she said this. They did have their suspects in custody after all.

"Right, but what about motive?"

He laughed. "It's Chicago, take your pick. There isn't much to over analyze here."

"I don't care. I need to talk to her as soon as her parents say we can. I'm the lead on this." She hung up without saying anything else.

Outside, the sun was so bright she covered her eyes for a moment, allowing her vision to adjust. An old woman leaned against an empty storefront window that had long ago been a bakery. The glass of the storefront was covered in posters for concerts long ended. The woman's eyes were clouded over with milky cataracts, and memories. As soon as the woman noticed Lauren watching her, she grinned an open-mouthed toothless grin. Lauren turned her head down, shoved her hands into her trench coat pockets and kept walking.

"It's just an interview, Mom..."

Lauren looked up before she nearly collided with a girl who was on her phone.

The girl stopped, smiled and said "Sorry," before ducking into Logan Theater. Lauren felt like she'd run head-first into a brick wall. The girl looked just like Marie, but as a teenager—large green eyes, long dreamlike curls that cradled her face and cascaded down her back. Lauren stopped, pretended she was searching for something in her messenger bag as she watched the girl enter the chaos of renovation and was greeted by a man who led her away for that interview. Lauren and her father had been following the reconstruction of the Logan Theater carefully, how the theater that was originally built in 1915 was purchased by a controversial real estate developer, who many claimed would make this theater the center of Logan Square's gentrification. Lauren remembered visiting long ago, before they closed it, and it sat empty for nearly a decade. Even then, it had long ago lost its magnificence. The floors were sticky, the popcorn stale, and cigarette smoke lingered in the air and within the fabric of the frayed red velvet seats. Still, for just two dollars, this place had taken away all of her dad's hurt. He could laugh with deep joy at old showings of *Back to the Future*, *Once Bitten* or *Little Shop of Horrors*. Or, on Halloween—those were the best—when they would catch a marathon of black and white screen legends Frankenstein, the Wolfman, or their favorite, Dracula. Lauren was happy the movie theater she'd so loved as a child was being given new life.

Lauren continued walking, passing Intelligentsia Coffee and waiving hello to the familiar barista, a nail salon, before coming to the empty and closed Uncharted Bookstore, where she stopped. Her car was just a few feet away, but she heard something. It was a musical note. Like, when a band first hits the stage and the first chord of a guitar vibrates, announcing to the audience that music is coming. It was so soft, so subtle, but it was close, behind her right ear. Lauren spun around. There was no one. Perhaps it came from a passing car, or from an apartment window. She turned, and her foot caught something. She tripped and found her balance before falling forward.

The object she'd tripped over was a man's leg. She was sure she had not seen him moments before, but that was impossible from how settled in this space he was. His legs outstretched before him. The smell that emitted from him was rotten, sour and sickly sweet. He made no comment. He merely continued to sit there, eyes burning into Lauren.

"I'm sorry," she finally said, and with that he adjusted himself, pulling his legs away from the sidewalk and tucking them under himself. He sat on top of a collection of clothes and worn, soiled bedsheets. A dark green duffle bag against his back served as a pillow. A shaggy, brown dog slept beside him, not flinching once during this meeting.

He pointed to the empty storefront that once housed thousands of used books. “When you read all the books they are here,” he pointed to his temple. “You can’t unread what you’ve read. The words are seared on your brain. You might as well say them all aloud. Say the words. That’s all you have to do.”

He dug his hand in his torn coat pocket and produced a gold harmonica. It was the same type of harmonica Lauren had set inside Diana’s coffin at her funeral. Diana had treasured it so much Lauren thought she should take it with her. It was an 1847 L.E. Seydel—limited edition. Only 170 of them were made. German silver reed plates with stainless steel rivets. Each had its number 1-170 laser engraved to the left-hand side, and of course, they were gold coated.

Lauren could not move. Her feet were cement. He pressed the instrument to his lips and drew in a note, and then blew out a note, preparing. Lauren had her car keys in her hand now and moved carefully to her car, which was parked just a few feet away from the man. He removed the harmonica from his mouth when Lauren got to her car door.

“Say the words, Lauren. Payment is due,” he called out. “Payment is due, Lauren.”

Lauren forced her feet to move, breaking free from the binding that held her to the sidewalk. She walked backwards, watching the man as he played. She tripped, falling off the curb, catching herself before a bus blared its horn as it rushed past, ignoring the red light at the intersection. She pressed the unlock button on her key fob and pushed down on the handle. Nothing. It did not move. She pulled, pushed, and finally screamed for her car to open and it did. Inside, she locked the doors and started the car.

“Say the words!” The man shouted from the sidewalk. He stood up. The bunches of blankets falling off him like snakeskin. His arms down at his sides. His right hand clutching the gold harmonica.

Even from inside her car, she could hear him laughing. She closed her eyes for a moment and drew in a deep breath, and counted to four: *one*, *two*, *three*, *four*. Her arms shook on the steering wheel, her pulse racing. She held her breath, *two*, *three*, *four*, and then released, *two, three, four*. "This is nothing," she whispered.

When she opened her eyes, he was standing in front of her car, blocking her exit. He brought the harmonica to his lips again, that she could now see were dry, chapped and crusted over with dried blood. He closed his eyes and proceeded to play. It was a sweet, mournful, bluesy riff. One Diana liked to play.

The man continued to play, opening one eye, making sure she was there watching, listening, and he smiled. He raised a free hand to tip his hat. It was then that she saw his long, sharp, curled black fingernails against the fabric of the brim.

Lauren turned on the car. He stopped playing. The man held the harmonica overhead and shouted, "Pay the Piper!" He brought his hand down to his face with force, and in that quick motion, a blood fountain. Bright red blood sprayed out from his eye where he had lodged the gold harmonica now covered in crimson.

Lauren put the car in reverse. She pushed down hard on the gas. The car lurched forward. She pulled the wheel left, to avoid hitting the maniac who had now removed the dripping harmonica, a gaping hole where his eye had once been, and continued to play. Lips pressed against the blood-covered instrument, droplets and sprays splashing on her windshield.

A bloody ballad for her and only her.

She pressed on the gas further, passing streetlights. Cars beeping. She flicked her siren on. She sped. But no matter how fast she drove she knew he would catch up, to not just her, but to Jordan.

CHAPTER 17

Lauren found Detective Van leaning back in his chair, a pen dangling from the corner of his mouth. His fingers were interlaced behind his head, and he gazed at a fixed point on the ceiling.

"You were out early this morning."

"Early morning tutoring," she said, dropping her bag beside her desk and taking a seat in her chair.

"Kids voluntarily go to tutoring in the morning?"

"They do what they can to get ahead in this city.

She pulled out her tablet and looked over at the coffee pot in the corner and the Keurig machine next to it. She needed good coffee right now.

"I'm running out for coffee."

"It's all so bizarre," Van said, eyes still staring above.

"What?" She said, reaching for her wallet and car keys in her bag. "That some of us need caffeine to make it through the day?"

Van removed the pen from his mouth and sat up in his chair. "How's it being a mentor?"

"I've done it one morning. All the pros of being a parent, with most of the cons."

"What are the cons?"

"He's a senior in high school," she leaned against her desk. "He thinks he knows everything."

"Where's he at school?"

"DePaul College Prep," she said.

He stared at her for a moment. "Same school as these kids?"

"Yes."

He raised his eyebrows. "Does he know them?"

"Yes, and the entire school knows what happened. The principal sent a memo. Parents have been notified. Counselors were called in."

"Right. That's right," he said looking down at his hands and then asking. "But did he *personally* know any of these kids?"

"He knew of them…" She normally would ignore most of what was coming out of Van's mouth, but she wanted to know where he was going with this. So far it was clear, but she had to be sure, and she needed to be ten steps ahead of him so that he did not interfere.

"You sure you can trust this kid? This...what's his name?"

"Jordan," she crossed her arms in front of her chest. Jordan's name came out loud. Protective. She saw a lot of herself in Jordan. He was smart, lonely, untrusting, and detached from adults—because to children, adults were not always the protectors. Adults were the ones who brought about wickedness and regret.

"Jordan gotta last name?"

"Green."

"You sure you can trust this kid? Seems like there's a lot of strange things happening with kids at his school. One girl shot and killed. Two kids arrested, for murder and attempted murder, and now you're mentoring one of them? Strange week don't you think?"

It's been a strange life. Lauren did not like all of his questions, but she knew how Van operated. Van functioned at a baseline of paranoid.

"His mother works two jobs. She's never home but wants to be. His father is in the Army, deployed. He's a good kid. He's worked hard to get to where he is. Full scholarship to UIC to study creative writing and then his best friend is murdered. So yeah, strange week for a few people."

"He's raising himself, then?"

"Pretty much." That worried Lauren. They were children cast out, her and Jordan. And as time goes on, children who are pushed aside grow angrier and angrier, sometimes even plotting revenge against those that deprived them of happiness. Especially for children raised on fairy tales, because children raised on fairy tales are searching for their guaranteed happy ending, and they will do whatever it takes to live happily ever after.

"You worried about him?"

"No." Yet, she knew that Jordan walked past five gang territories on his way to school and back each day. These were not the days of singular gangs by city region; Northside Gang, Southside Gang. Chicago's gangs had splintered in the early 2000s when major gang leaders—who ran organized criminal operations like Fortune 500 companies—were arrested, jailed and imprisoned. This created less centralized and less hierarchical organizations, factions, crews, and a total over 2,300 of these groups. Each city block held its own crew, and just because you lived one block over did not mean you were safe. At least there were the Safe Passage crossing guards: city employees who stood out on street corners and helped kids cross the street. They were heavily present in feuding gang territories, which meant nearly every other block. Still, even Safe Passage crossing guards had been caught up in gang violence. One was recently arrested for shooting at a rival gang member. No one in Chicago, not even authority figures, could be trusted.

"He's a really good kid. I've read his writing. He's pretty good. I'm trying to keep him out of trouble, but trouble seems to find him. He texted me on my way here telling me his headphones were stolen from the bus. He just doesn't have many people to talk to."

"You're doing a good thing, Medina. You have the time. This kid needs someone with time. I'm sure he appreciates it, appreciates you. You know, when kids are young, teens and such, they do stupid things.

Most of the time they're forgiven for those stupid things..."

She did not like the direction this conversation was going. Before she could say something, Washington entered, pulling a dolly behind him with clear, empty plastic bins stacked on top. His desk was a heap and history of ephemera—scribbled notes on yellow notepads, stacks of them. The desk overflowed, struggling to hold onto folders, books, newspaper clippings, and magazines. Then there was the corkboard in front of his desk pinned with phone numbers written on napkins, as well as pictures of people and places that stretched back from even before her life. Everyone else's desk was bare: a laptop or tablet, a mug, maybe a picture frame.

"You can always push retirement away a few more weeks...or months," Lauren said as she left her car keys and wallet on her desk and moved to stand beside Washington's desk. A tower of books and old *Chicago Tribune* and *Chicago Sun-Times* newspapers teetered on the verge of collapse on the floor next to him.

"What are you going to do with those?" She asked of the papers.

"It just seems awful to throw them away. We're one of the last two newspaper towns. Before all this I used to work at the *Chicago Daily News*. Crime reporter."

"That, I didn't know, Washington. Look at you still keeping secrets."

"Reporters keep the best secrets," he said as he started setting the bins around him. "The Tribune is older. Been around since 1847. The Daily started in 1875 but closed in 1978. I was there on the last day. I became an officer not too long after. I needed a job, healthcare, pension. Nowadays, everyone gets their news from their pockets, but I really loved working with the newspaper and punching away at the keys of a typewriter. It felt like you were a part of the story, just that motion, being in a newsroom, cigarette smoke thick in the air, telephones blaring, people shouting. You never know what the good times are until they're gone. Before my time, to get breaking news you had to go down to Tribune Tower and read the bulletins posted on the windows. Just think of that, having to go down Michigan Avenue—which was a dirt road back then—all of those people crowded around that glass to understand what was happening in their world. Well, the original tower that is. The Great Chicago Fire took down the original tower. That Gothic skyscraper we have today was built in the 1920s. I'll miss looking at the top of that building. It looks like a castle."

He put his hands on his hips and inspected his legacy before him on the desk, plotting out where to start.

"Can I help?" Lauren asked.

Washington opened one of the bottom drawers. "These should all be organized and ready to put in a bin."

There were several large, stuffed manila envelopes. Each of them bore the same name written across in thick sharpie, BRADY, followed by a case number. Lauren picked up the first few folders and set them in a bin.

The Brady case was one singed on Chicago's memory. She had grown up hearing about it, and the warnings to not play in front of her house alone, wander off, or talk to strangers. Chicago had many known boogeymen: serial killer H.H. Holmes, who tortured and killed potentially hundreds in his murder castle, Richard Speck who murdered eight nursing students in a single night, The Ripper Crew, who kidnapped, ritualistically mutilated and killed over a dozen women, John Wayne Gacey who worked as a construction worker and a clown for children's parties and went on to murder and store the bodies of thirty-three boys and men beneath his floorboards, and today's Chicago Strangler who has killed over fifty girls and women in the South Side of Chicago, and is still operating.

"No one has ever heard from these girls?"

"No one. Lord knows I tried." Washington looked down into the container as Lauren set the envelopes inside. "Fifteen years is a long time for anything, for anyone."

Washington did not talk about the ten-year-old and three-year-old sisters much, but she knew they hung heavy on his conscience. Lauren opened one of the folders. It contained just two sheets of paper: missing person posters, one for each of the little girls. Lauren did the math quickly and realized the girls would be twenty-five and eighteen today.

When Washington wasn't in the office, Lauren knew she could find him walking the streets of Bronzeville, the city's historic center for African American culture dating back to the Great Migration. Washington went to Bronzeville trying to retrace those little girl's steps. It was his obsession: trying to figure out what happened to them. No one just disappears. He had gotten to know most of the residents of that community. He had even become a regular at some of the restaurants. He felt like he could almost reach out and grasp the girls by sitting in a place so close to where they were last seen. Washington had never worked a missing persons case before that. He did not work one after.

"No retirement party," Washington said, giving her side-eye.

"Do I seem like the type of person who would willingly organize a party, for anyone? Even for you?"

"Right," he gave her a sharp nod.

He shouted over to Van "No party, Van!"

"Already made the down payment at Revolution Brewery," Van said without looking up from scrolling through his phone.

"I don't like their beer," Washington said. "It's too bitter."

"What do you care? You're retiring anyway," Van said.

Lauren placed the remaining folders from the Bradley sister's case in the bin. "Apparently, it's his favorite place," she whispered.

"Look who's been making friends?" Washington smiled wide.

"Not making friends. He just won't shut up."

"Can you do me a favor?" Washington asked as he slowly removed the pushpins from a sun-faded picture of him and Mayor Richard M.

Daley, taken what must have been over a decade ago.

"No."

"Can you drive by Mina's place? Let her know...I've been busy, and I just didn't have time to stop in and say goodbye."

Lauren felt a sinking, cold feeling in the center of her chest, that feeling you got when you knew something you loved was coming to an end.

"You're not going to call her at least to say bye?"

"Things are just busy right now. Frank needs help fixing that old Hyundai of his. Still, lots to do around the house, and I'd like to go say goodbye to your dad at the cemetery just one more time."

Lauren closed the bottom drawer and reached for a framed picture of Washington and her dad that sat on his desk. On Lauren's first day she'd noticed a collection of dust on the top of that picture frame. Something about the dust being there made her feel as though Washington and her dad were no longer present, and so she'd reached in her pocket for a napkin, which she usually had from whichever cafe she had just been in that day. Then she lifted the frame and dusted the glass, removing those particles of time. The two of them, Washington and her dad, smiled at her.

"You know you're wiping away like two decades worth of dust there, right?" Washington had told her.

She set the frame back down. "It's weird for people who are alive to have dust accumulating on their photos."

He'd just shrugged her off, but she'd noticed that since that day he always kept the frame clean and dusted.

"You keep that." Washington held his hand out. "Your dad belongs here, in this place, and I don't mind being by his side."

"He didn't get the closure he wanted either, did he?" She said.

"No, he never got the answers he wanted. There were a lot of bad days, and then your mom, Marie and well..."

"Diana..." she sighed.

"It's been a long time," Washington said.

"I know...you're right," she said.

Washington pulled over a large garbage can. He sat down and proceeded to fill it with old restaurant menus and community alert flyers. "He had to move on, even though it was so horrible, and no one could really explain to him what happened." He paused. "I'm sorry. I know it was your life, too, shaken up by all of this. I'm happy you're here. I know he was very happy that you came here."

Her father and his partner bonded over the pain of the unknown. And that pain held their friendship together because not many other people could understand their suffering.

"I think I've got it from here," Washington said. "Don't forget, I'll need that ride to the airport early Friday morning."

She nodded, turned and walked back to her desk to grab her wallet and keys before her eyes could water. She was not going to cry, especially not here.

Van removed the pen from his mouth again. "How am I supposed to write this?" He said, staring down at a blank report form.

"The same way you do all of your other reports." Lauren reached inside her bag for her phone but it was already glowing. Another text had come in from Jordan.

"Can you drive me to the funeral Friday morning? My mom can't get out of work, and I don't know who else to ask."

She was becoming a chauffeur, and her Friday was already packed with things to do, but she was not going to tell him no. She would figure it out, somehow. "Sure, I'll pick you up and drop you off. I can't stay, though. You'll have to find a ride back on your own."

"Thanks," he responded.

Van grumbled under his breath, still struggling with the report.

"I'm not going to write it for you," Lauren snapped.

"It sounds like some drug-induced nightmare."

Lauren pulled in a deep breath. When she exhaled, she pressed her lips together, pulled her hair out from her ponytail and rewrapped it in a bun.

"Why'd they do it?" Van asked. It was not as if he were really asking her, just posing the question out there to the universe.

Lauren generally avoided wanting to diagnose the *why* of any crime. Many criminals were beyond logical comprehension. A case like this was beyond what she covered during her few years on the job. She had pretty much seen it all in Chicago, all manner of gunshots, and gun deaths stemming from gang retaliation shootings to mistaken identities. One time, a teenager shot and killed two other teens simply because they asked him how tall he was while they were standing in line at the corner store to buy soda and chips. She'd covered the range of sexual assault cases, from the known perpetrator to the unknown, child and elderly neglect cases, and there was even a death by chainsaw torture case she recalled vividly, but that was over drugs and money and cartels.

Much of the crime wave gripping this city was over drugs, who sold to who, who owed who what, and who could expand where. This city, with its glittering skyline and blue lake that hugged downtown, was the darkest place she had ever known. Any manner of crime was possible in Chicago. Still, what had happened out there in Humboldt Park had nothing to do with drugs.

"Your sister..." Van started, but Lauren cut him off.

"I was fourteen-years-old," she made a point to roll her eyes so that he could see her frustration for bringing it up yet again. "I can't remember anything. It was a very long time ago." It sounded scripted—and it was, in a way.

She'd never bothered asking Van where he heard about her case because everyone knew about her and about Marie. It had been everywhere, all of the local television stations - WGN, WLS, WMAQ, WBBM, newspapers *Chicago Tribune*, *Chicago Sun-Times*, and then the national news picked it up; a little girl lost, her father finds her, her sister located just a mile away, and a mother who later killed herself in her bathtub.

"I know," he waved his pen in the air. "I figured you could provide some insight into the mind of a teenager dealing with something like this. Hell, I haven't been a teen in like thirty years. I can't remember what it was like to be a freshman or sophomore in high school."

"I don't remember."

"Drugs, then?"

"You offering?" She laughed.

"Not this time," he said.

"Tests didn't show any."

"Yeah, but they've got all these weird drugs now," he said, scrunching up his face. "Like bath salts. What the hell is that even? Kids take this stuff and get all weird and eat people's faces off."

"Look, your girl wasn't on drugs. My guy wasn't on drugs. Maybe they're just bad kids," she said. "These two have never had a disciplinary issue in high school or any priors."

"Copycat?"

Lauren clenched her jaw. She knew he was going to say it eventually.

"There's no way. Those records only go back so far. There's no way anyone would find anything to do with that case unless they went specifically searching for it."

He stood up, stretched his back, palms pressing into his lower back. It cracked straight down, popping like the last few kernels of popcorn being microwaved. "You can't deny the book, *Grimm's Fairy Tales*, being out there wasn't odd."

"Kids read books. Sometimes they read *that* book. It's not odd."

He reached for his jacket. "Guess we should go grab that coffee then."

"I didn't invite you."

"Inviting myself," Van walked over to a coat stand beside the door.

"I hate you..." Lauren said.

"I don't care," Van shot back.

"Kids! Kids!" Washington called. "Be nice or I'll tell mom you can't go on your field trip." He pointed a thumb over to Commander McCarthy's office.

Lauren felt her phone vibrate. It was probably Jordan with another request. But the message was from Officer Guerrero. She unlocked her phone and looked at the image. Her face must have deceived her because Van could see from across the room that something was wrong.

"What's up? Everything alright?"

She shoved the phone back in her jacket pocket.

"Ex-husband." She dismissed.

"Husband..." Washington said beneath his breath.

"The divorce will be final in a few weeks."

"Mmmm hmmm," he rummaged through his desk. "Whatever you say."

What she did not tell Van was that another tribute to the Pied Piper had appeared, this time on a billboard overlooking the Kennedy Expressway, the major route into downtown. It now welcomed all who came into Chicago with "Pay the Piper," as the city's skyline glowed in the distance.

CHAPTER 18

After its introduction and through much of the 21st century, Humboldt Park had been seen as an escape from city life. Author L. Frank Baum was said to spend much time at the park while he lived in Chicago, enjoying the gardens and sitting beneath any one of the large trees near the horse stables, now converted into the National Museum of Puerto Rican Arts & Culture. Beneath one of those very trees Baum had written his most famous book, *The Wonderful Wizard of Oz*. He had lived right on Humboldt Boulevard. His original home was razed many years ago and only a modest marker honors Baum's time there. When he had lived here, Humboldt Boulevard had been a grand thoroughfare lined with majestic mansions. Lauren could only imagine how magical it must have looked like at night when Baum would leave his home and walk down the boulevard dotted with streetlamps. Was it here, where she walked now, that he'd dreamed up the yellow brick road? She liked to think so.

Lauren obsessively studied Baum, Hans Christian Andersen, Lewis Carroll, Charles Perrault and others in college. She wanted to know what they had done differently than the Grimms. She eventually realized that in Baum's tales the children overcome the greatest evil of all, the Wicked Witch. In Grimm's, the children never conquered the source of evil. Tossing the witch into her own fiery stove, killing the big, bad wolf and the wicked stepmother did not mean you had defeated all cruelty in the world. It was still there after you turned the last page.

Lauren had grown up in this park. She'd spent many summer nights here riding her bicycle as her parents picnicked nearby, because at one time there was no Marie. It was just her and her mom and her dad. They often walked the trails, brushing past prairie grass and knee-high bright orange butterfly milkweed, or vibrant purple cone flowers. Armando would park their car in front of the boathouse, and they'd find a shaded spot under a large tree. Lauren's favorite was a large hill where the city's skyline fanned out in front of them. Laying on a blanket, eating a guava and cheese tart, and drinking ice-cold coconut water as she looked over her city defined the feeling of her early childhood.

Slowly, their family picnics had become fewer. Armando's work schedule became erratic, and eventually, there was no line to distinguish when his workdays ended and began. Tension between her parents grew. It was like a rubber band being pulled apart. She knew one day it was going to snap. It had.

Lauren's phone rang. The call she had been avoiding.

"Detective Medina here."

The voice on the other end was soft and comforting. "Hello, this is Walter Dayton calling from Rosehill Cemetery..."

She covered her eyes with her other hand, somehow wishing she could hide. A car honked at her, possibly seeing the pain on her face, making sure she was okay. She removed her hand and raised up her middle finger.

"Yes, I'm sorry I didn't return your call. I've been busy."

"I know. I can only imagine. Know that we are a family here at Rosehill, and we are thinking of you. Our condolences and thoughts are with you and your family. We spoke with your husband..."

"Ex-"

"Apologies. We spoke with Robert and he said that you were

pleased with the service. That made me very happy to hear. I'm calling just so we can finalize the inscription on your father' headstone..."

She thought back to the funeral home's previous suggestion:

Armando Rodriguez Medina
Husband to Diana
Father of Lauren and Marie

"Yes, it can read:

Armando Rodriguez Medina.
Husband. Father.

You can include the Chicago Police insignia."

"Certainly, thank you so much, Lauren. I know this is a very difficult time."

"Umm...Walter..."

"Yes?"

Lauren rubbed her forehead. "Are there flowers? I had paid for flowers and I know her anniversary is coming up, and I just can't be there."

"I will check and make sure, but I believe there were flowers on all four of your family members' resting places when I checked this morning, but I will be sure, and I will call to let you know."

"No, it's okay. I just...thank you."

Now in the park, Lauren eyed each tree and wondered whether it was the one Baum had sat beneath to make his magic. Had she herself picnicked under that tree with her family? This park had been the center of her family's life. Yes, the entire city lived and breathed within her, but this park was special. This park had the power to create. It was here she had learned about good and bad. One day when they were here on a picnic after Armando had gotten home from work

Lauren had asked him what made someone so bad that they would have to go to the police station?

He'd answered, "It's not that people are bad. It's that sometimes, people do bad things."

That did not really answer Lauren's question, and so she asked instead, "But aren't there some people who are just meant to be bad?" Because even from a young age Lauren had known what the fairy tales had taught her, that some were born to cause suffering.

Armando did not answer that question.

The good days spent at Humboldt Park faded altogether. Armando became his job. Diana grew tired and frustrated, and then there was Marie. Marie was everything Lauren was not: kind and patient. Lauren was like her father, but instead of being consumed with work she was consumed with school —always focusing on her assignments and deadlines and studying.

One evening, Lauren had been studying for one of Mr. Sylvan's intense English exams. When Diana had called her down for dinner, Lauren shouted from her room that she was busy.

"You're like your father, you know," Diana had snapped back. "It's always work. Maybe it will be better if Marie and I were gone, then both of you could work yourselves to death!"

It was as if Diana had cast a spell with her own words of things to come.

Lauren came to the bridge on Humboldt Boulevard. She stopped and looked east, at the one-hundred and ten floor Sears Tower (Lauren refused to call it Willis Tower or any other name), the one-hundred floor John Hancock Center, and the dozens of other dark gray, black and blue skyscrapers that punched into the blue sky. Chicago had invented the skyscraper. The first steel-framed building to reach into the sky was the Home Insurance Building completed in 1885, and at ten stories it had been a global engineering feat at the time. She was just six miles from downtown but still, every time she saw those towering buildings, they looked like dark robed guardians of this city. Her angels in this purgatory.

This park had been dedicated in 1869, before any of those skyscrapers stood watch.

Lauren dug in her jacket pocket before crossing the bridge, and laughed to herself, because of a story that was told to her so long ago she could not remember how exactly it went. What she did remember being told was that trolls lived under bridges and would eat anyone who would not pay the toll. She found a penny and tossed it over the bridge and into the water as she crossed.

She looked west, to the empty beach, and saw a man standing there with a small dog on a leash, staring at the water. She recognized him from her morning runs through the park. On boiling summer days, she sometimes would stop and buy a raspado de coco—coconut shaved ice—from the vendor who stood on the sidewalk watching the men play dominoes. Ramon stood out to her because while he was older, he was still younger than most of the white-haired retirees who played. He was easy to spot in that crowd, younger, scruffy dark goatee, and he always wore a clean, bright red Chicago Bulls cap. Ramon also still bore one of the signs of his past gang affiliated life, a cross-shaped tattoo on his hand, beneath the crease where his pointer finger and thumb met.

Lauren greeted him. He smiled wide, shook her hand and told her he was very happy to help.

"Show me exactly where you were standing and tell me what you saw."

"There," he pointed. "She made it to the beach. I saw her as soon as I turned the path. She was laying there in the sand. Her feet were still in the water. Logan pulled my arm real bad when he saw her. I let the leash go. I couldn't hold on to him anymore because of the pain in my shoulder, and he just took off running. It took a minute for me to realize what I was looking at. The girl was just there, not moving..."

Ramon let out a sob. "How's she doing? It's so messed up what those kids did. It's all over the news."

Lauren directed him over to a bench. His dog Logan jumped on his lap, and Ramon cradled him in his arms, kissing him on the top of his head. Logan returned with licking his hands.

"At first, I thought maybe, I don't know...maybe it was some homeless dude's stuff. Sometimes people forget towels and shirts and things here. People leave weird shit around here sometimes. I found a tire right there, once," he pointed close to where the girl had been discovered. "Why would someone wheel a tire *here*? The street's, like, all the way over there."

"Did she say anything? Call out to you?"

"No. She was quiet." His eyes widened. "It was so messed up. I didn't expect to see something like that, ever."

"And then what?"

"Logan just started barking. He was scared. Shit, *I* was scared. I went to grab my phone, and then I dropped it. I picked it up and then I called 9-1-1."

"But then you hung up?"

Ramon drew out his phone from his back pocket. "Yes, I was shaking so bad my phone fell again. I called 9-1-1 back and said to hurry, that I was at the lagoon and there was a girl, and she was really messed up. I stayed on the phone with them. The lady, she asked me questions, but honestly, I couldn't tell you what she asked or what I said. It felt like it took so long."

"Did you see anyone nearby? Car go past?"

"I don't know."

"The dispatcher said she heard your dog growling and barking, and you started shouting."

"Yeah, but there was no one there. Logan just started losing it. It was just a lot. The girl…the sirens coming closer."

"But the dispatcher heard you say," Lauren looked down at her phone, at a series of notes from that night. 'There's nothing there.' Who did you say that to?"

"No one. Myself."

"What did you think you saw?"

Ramon placed his phone back in his pocket. He pressed his lips together and then said. "I was scared. I guess I thought I saw something, but I'm getting old, and my eyes aren't so good."

"What do you think you didn't see?" She pressed.

"It was off at the balcony, across the lagoon." He pointed. "I thought I saw someone standing there. It was dark, but I thought I saw someone."

"What did they look like?"

Lauren watched his face. It was as if he were struggling to come to terms with something.

"There was a person there," he pointed again and then rested his hand on the top of Logan's head. "But, it just didn't seem right. It was over there, standing on the little bridge there behind the lagoon. A little girl. She was in a school uniform, khaki skirt. Polo shirt. Curly, curly dark hair." He turned to Lauren. His face looked pained. "She didn't have a coat on. It was cold. I knew then I was seeing things. Why would a little girl be out alone like that at night? Especially without a jacket or coat? And she...I don't know, her face looked bad, really not right...blue. When I called out, Logan started barking. I bent down to pick him up. When I looked up, she was gone." He scratched his goatee and then lowered the brim of his hat over his eyes a little further. "Forget it. I'm tired. Old. Maybe crazy."

Lauren thanked Ramon for his statement, and then she watched as he walked across the park with his dog towards home. She looked over at the lagoon. It was still.

"What do you want, Marie?" Lauren shouted at the water, but it did not offer a response.

She felt her phone vibrating in her jacket pocket. She looked at the familiar number and answered.

"Hey, Ruth."

"Lauren..."

Lauren stood up and started jogging to her car. She knew that tone.

"What's going on, Ruth? I'm on my way."

"Fin confessed."

"I'll be there in ten minutes."

"No," Ruth stopped her. "She's sedated. She had an episode in her sleep, almost like she was reliving an attack, going through the same motions, jabbing motions, flailing her arms like she was in water..."

"Ruth, are you okay?"

Lauren leaned on the other side of the bridge railing, feeling cold. She had forgotten to leave another offering to the troll.

"Yes, I'm okay. I just wanted you to know."

"I can interview her as soon as she wakes. I can wait."

"I'm sorry. I can't allow that right now. She just needs time. I just thought you should know."

Ruth did not understand. Neither Lauren nor Fin had any time left.

CHAPTER 19

Mo grabbed his tray and made his way toward the table in the far back corner, away from stares. It did not matter how far he went, though. He was always being watched.

"Did you really think you were going to kill her?" Tyler asked a little too loud, and it seemed like everyone in the cafeteria line turned to look at them.

Calling it a cafeteria was a compliment.

Tyler was the first person who'd introduced himself to Mo when Mo had arrived late that night. Tyler was seated in the common room watching the evening news and did a double take when he saw Mo shuffling in, restrained at the hands and ankles. The news did not show or name the perpetrators in the Humboldt Park killing, but that did not stop Tyler from running up to Mo as he was being escorted by two officers and shouting, "You're *that* guy!" As if Mo were a celebrity.

Tyler was in detention for armed robbery and carjacking. He had been here once before, for robbery. He'd grabbed a phone out of a girl's hand on the train.

He'd ran.

The girl had ran after him.

She'd slipped.

She'd fallen.

Her head had split open on Clark Street. Her body convulsed.

Foam spilled from her lips and deep red stained the concrete. She did not die, but her lawyer said she could have. Tyler was only twelve at the time. He got a short stay in detention. The armed robbery and carjacking were likely going to give him a longer sentence, but as he said, it was not going to be as long as Mo had coming.

Tyler liked to talk, a lot. He also liked to ask a lot of questions. He wanted details, but Mo just said that he could not remember what happened. It had been dark. There was a lot of shouting. Water.

"You're the one that stabbed her first then? What'd it feel like?" He nudged Mo in the rib with his elbow.

"I don't know," Mo pushed him off. "I didn't do anything. I don't know!"

Tyler's mouth hung open. "What do you mean you don't know?"

Mo shook his head. The lawyer had told him not to discuss his case with anyone, that it could harm his prospects. Mo wondered what prospects. He did not know what any of this meant. He did not mean to do any of this. He just wanted to help Fin. He also just wanted the person who robbed his father's store dead and she'd told him this was the only way to make that happen. That he would not get caught. But here he was.

The cafeteria felt almost like high school, except for the numerous heavily armed officers who paced and walked about the room. The young men being held here knew they could not get too loud. Otherwise, security assumed a fight was brewing, and if a fight happened, they'd be secured in their rooms with something that barely passed as food for their meal.

Leo was already seated and waiting for them. He was only a year older than Mo, but Leo was six-feet-plus, wide, and was here for allegedly running over a police officer with a stolen car. Mo was surprised by this as Leo was so quiet, whenever he spoke it was practically a whisper.

Tyler slammed down his tray. "You're starting to bore me. Tell us what happened."

"You're nuts," Mo said as he sat across from Leo, who had not even looked up from his neon-green peas.

"I mean, if you're going to kill someone, you make sure you kill them dead," Tyler said. "Your problem is that girl sitting up in her hospital bed. Once she starts talking, then you and your friend are done. Life sentences. You're lucky Illinois no longer has the death penalty."

Leo took a long drink of water and set his cup down.

Mo looked at his tray. The food was as limp and processed as the food served at DePaul. He picked up a roll and sunk his teeth into it. It was stale. When he looked again, he saw a patch of fuzzy green. Mold. He spit it out as Tyler laughed.

"Guess they have other ways of killing murderers. You're going to be spending a long time in places like this, with food like that," Tyler said pointing his fork at Mo.

Tyler had been one month from turning fifteen when he committed his last crime. He had made sure to tell people that at every chance when they brought up his case.

"I'm only fifteen," Mo said.

With a mouthful of French fries, Tyler shook a finger in Mo's face. "Doesn't matter." He reached for a cup of water and washed it back. "Minors age fifteen and over are tried as adults in Illinois if they are charged with any of the five serious crimes: first-degree murder, aggravated criminal sexual assault, aggravated battery with a firearm, armed robbery with a firearm, or aggravated vehicular hijacking with a firearm."

Mo pushed his tray away. "I didn't kill anyone," he said.

Both Tyler and Leo looked at Mo with wide eyes.

"*Someone* killed him," Tyler said.

Mo looked down at the tray in front of him, trying to instead see back to that night.

Evie had arrived with Daniel by her side.

"Hey, you guys!" Fin had thrown her arms over Daniel and Evie's shoulders. They walked, the three of them, like that for a few feet, Fin in between, chatting about school, Mr. Sylvan, whatever, just to lead them up toward the lagoon. Daniel thanking Fin and especially Evie for inviting him. Mo had walked closely behind listening.

They all took a seat on the ground in front of the lagoon. The weather had been cool. The sky clear and purple, and for a moment it had not felt as though they were in a city, but in a kingdom far away.

Fin had turned to Mo and smiled. She was so excited, eyes bright, talking rapidly, hands waving in the air. Her energy was electric.

Before they'd got there, Fin had told Mo how she was able to lure Evie to the park. Evie's motivation was simply Daniel, and the promise to be rid of him. While Daniel was distracted taking a picture of the lagoon with his phone Mo heard as Evie leaned in and asked Fin, "How does the Pied Piper do this?"

Fin had raised her voice and clapped her hands. "Alright everyone. It's time! Daniel, leave your phone right here and follow me." Fin kicked off her shoes and slipped off her socks and set them on the bench.

"We're going in the water?" Evie asked.

"Just our feet," Fin reassured with a doll-like smile.

"It's freezing," Daniel added.

"Nothing good can be easy," Fin gave him a smirk. She motioned them to follow her. Her feet, then ankles and then knees disappearing under the water.

"Hurry up!" She turned around and walked backwards. "It's not going to get any warmer!"

Mo allowed Evie and Daniel to enter first, and then he followed.

Daniel laughed. "The crazy things we do for our friends, right?"

No one answered him.

"When the Pied Piper arrived, the mayor agreed to pay him generously...with gold coins"

"What?" Daniel asked, confused.

Fin continued. "As the Pied Piper played his flute, the rats came out from hiding, hundreds of them, and then followed him into the harbor."

Mo turned to Daniel. Daniel's face was twisted up, puzzled, over what it was Fin was talking about.

Fin reached out and placed each of her hands on Evie's shoulders. Fin bounced on her heels once, twice and said:

"Where they fell into the water and drowned."

Fin pushed back with both of her hands as hard as she could, forcing Evie to lose balance and fall into the cold lagoon. It was not a playful push. It was violence. An attack, and at the moment, Evie did not even scream she was so surprised.

Daniel rushed towards Evie, reaching his arms out to try to catch her, but it was too late. Evie was submerged. Her arms flailed, splashing, fighting to get up.

Fin screamed. "Mo! Get him!"

Mo dove for Daniel. He reached for Daniel's waistband. His fingers slipped. He fell. Water filled his nostrils. Stung his eyes. He gagged. He swallowed some of the putrid liquid back, feeling as some of the grains of sand cut down his throat. When he emerged again, his eyes burning, he saw Evie hanging onto Daniel. Fin held a knife high overhead and then it came down.

Daniel raised a hand, but Fin brought the knife down, lopping off his fingers. With his other hand, he clutched the stump and cried. Fin rammed the knife into him again, and again. Shocked and panicked, he stumbled back and fell again in the water. Splashing wildly.

Fin aimed the knife into Evie's shoulder.

Evie's mouth fell open, and her screams carried across the sky.

Fin yanked the knife out and stabbed.

Again.

Blood flowed.

Again.

Blood sprayed.

The knife went in, again, and again, Evie holding her hands in front of her, protecting her face. The knife aimed for Evie's face, but Evie turned. Her arms shaking, her pleas ignored. Fin brought the knife down and sliced off Evie's right ear where it plopped and sank into the water.

"Mo!" Fin shouted. "Help me."

Mo rushed forward, trudging through the murk beneath his feet. Fin shoved the handle of the knife into his hands. "Kill her!"

With the knife in his hands, Mo closed his eyes and stabbed at the air and then hit something, someone. He heard Evie scream. A wild, animal scream. He opened his eyes and saw movement through the corner of his eye. He looked out onto the bridge overlooking the lagoon, and he saw a man. A man in a black suit.

He turned back.

Evie roared with shock and pain, her entire body trembling. Her hands grasped the hole in her head. Blood seeped in between her fingers and dripped down her arms, and then Evie sank.

Daniel emerged and reached for his friend. He pulled, put Evie's arm around his neck, supporting her.

Daniel and Mo's eyes met across the water.

Mo reached for Fin. "We have to go," he shouted, as he looked back and saw the man in the black suit watching them. Water splashed in his face, and he wiped away at his eyes.

"We have to go!" Mo shouted.

Fin wiped her eyes. "We have to be sure they're dead!"

"Someone saw us. We have to go." Mo pulled her back before she could return to Evie and Daniel.

"They won't make it out of here. We have to go. Now!" He ordered. "We are being watched."

They moved out of the lagoon quickly, covered in blood and sand and dirt. Mo tripped, knife in hand and it struck his foot. He screamed in agony but continued moving, for fear of the unknown man. They slipped on their socks and shoes and ran. Freezing. Mo leading her away as she screamed that they were not done. He assured her they were done as he watched the man on the bridge fade into the distance.

"Have you heard from your girlfriend?" Tyler leaned forward, his elbows resting on the table, his chin in his hands.

"She wasn't my girlfriend."

"This is sure a lot of trouble to be in for someone that wasn't your girlfriend."

"No, I don't know where she is. I just figured they had her in another juvenile detention, to keep us separated."

Leo frowned. Tyler nodded.

"What was that?" Mo pointed to each of them. "That look you gave each other?"

"We've got an idea where she might be," Tyler said. "You said that this was all her idea, and so, maybe she's just insane, and they locked her up in psychiatric somewhere. Just popping some pills into her to keep her all drowsy, so she can plead guilty."

"No, Fin's not crazy." he said.

"And neither are you? Have you listened to yourself tell your side of the story? It sounds pretty wild to me," Tyler said.

Mo remained quiet. Fin understood him. She was one of the few, if only, people who did. He missed her, and he wondered if she missed him. He suspected that they kept them apart like this on purpose, perhaps to sow discord, so that each would lay blame on the other. Maybe this was all part of the process of proving themselves worthy to the Pied Piper. Perhaps he would still arrive and solve their problems.

Talking about this with other people, in many ways, was pointless. He and Fin were committed to getting the kind of life that they deserved, the kind of life that they wanted, without worry, without fear, and the only person that could make that happen was the Pied Piper.

It was supposed to be simple. As simple as reciting a fairy tale, saying a nursery rhyme.

A loud buzzer rang.

It was not like the kind at school. Harsher. Mo got up as quickly as he could, dumping out the stale and moldy food on his tray. Tyler and Leo followed closely behind. They did not have the same urgency. This was their sentence, this place for however many months. Mo's clock had not even begun to start ticking. Mo needed to get out of here, to be with Fin again, to tell Fin he was sorry and that he would set things right.

He should have finished them. He should have made sure they were dead.

Tyler separated from them, and Leo went to his room. As Mo walked, he heard someone shout his name. He turned.

"Heard your friend killed herself," a security guard he had never seen before said with a smile, all sharp jagged teeth. "You have a nice day."

"That's not true!" Mo shouted. The security guard laughed, a deep, guttural laugh, and walked down the hallway away from him.

Mo hurried to his room.

"Shit, they're coming," his roommate said as he ran into the room and faced the door. Mo was panting, standing straight, his shoulders back.

The officer stopped in front of the door and asked them to confirm their identities. The officer held a clipboard that had their number, image, and offense. Mo knew this only because one of them had accidentally set down the clipboard on the ground when he had run to break up a fight.

"Ramsen, your lawyer's here to see you," another guard called from the hallway.

The officer with the clipboard pointed at Mo with his pen. "Get going, Mohammed."

He and the guard walked down the hallway, which seemed darker now. It also seemed exceptionally quiet. Had everyone gotten to their rooms so quickly? What were they all doing that they were so silent? There were usually shouts and laughter, curses of boredom and the words that narrate a game of cards being played.

"I have to go to the bathroom," Mo said as they approached the men's room. He really did not have to use the restroom. He just wanted to splash cold water on his face. He had no idea what the lawyer was going to say or ask, and he was beginning to panic.

The guard stopped and smiled, displaying the canines of a wolf. "You have two minutes."

Mo rushed into the bathroom, unsure of what it was he had seen. He was tired. He was scared. He fought the urge to kick the door to a stall or to scream. Instead, he punched the concrete wall beside the mirror, hard. The skin on his knuckles split. Warm blood dripped down his fingers. He looked in the mirror. He tried to find himself in this reflection, but who he saw was haggard and defeated. He wondered where Fin was. Why would anyone joke about her killing herself? It was awful. It was sick. She would never hurt herself. But others, others she certainly would hurt, and had hurt, to have her way.

"What the hell did we do?" He asked his reflection.

His reflection smiled, and the teeth of a werewolf looked back at him, dripping blood and saliva.

"No," the word slipped out of Mo's mouth as he took a step back.

A door creaked behind him. He had not known anyone else was here in the bathroom with him.

"You have one more minute," the guard said in a singsong way.

Mo looked back to the mirror. The teeth were gone, but now he heard...whistling.

The door to a stall opened. Mo stepped back, nearly falling against the sink. He was seeing things. This was not happening. This was not here.

The figure, taller than the stall door, taller than any man Mo had ever seen, stepped out from the stall and glared down at him. Its eyes fire. A gangling man in a suit of pied: one half of his suit black, and the other half of his suit bright red. Blood-red. He wore a black woodsman's hat, a large red feather protruding from the side. The skull of a small bird pinned the feather in place.

The man did not say anything as he lumbered toward Mo. He stood on tall, thin legs, moving as if he were walking on stilts, stiff, long strides. He was so tall that the feather of his hat grazed the ceiling, and as it did, the points left trails of red against the wall.

Mo flashed back to the water, to the lagoon, and to the man he'd seen watching them. It had been him all along, the Pied Piper, watching, waiting for them.

Mo backed into the sink, striking his hipbone, a sharp pain shot down his leg. He fell to the floor. He whimpered.

The Pied Piper turned his head. The monster of magic and myth extended his long, ghoulish hand. His face never changed expression; wide-eyed, unblinking, jaw slack. Mo opened his mouth to shout for help. His body convulsed. He banged his head against the tiled wall. He began to choke, gag, and then, the water came.

Dark, murky water erupted from his mouth, and ran down his face, soaking his clothes and pooling around him, filling the restroom. The Pied Piper's eyes flickered.

Mo's eyes bulged. He grasped at his neck. Pulled down at his lips to try to force his mouth shut, to stop this. To end this. There was no breath. There was just water.

Water gushed. Water sprayed. The veins in his neck and under his eyes bulged.

Through tears, Mo looked at the Pied Piper's extended hand. A thin layer of flesh hung on his bones. Mo looked up at his face, gaunt and translucent, the color of ash. The bird skull turned and looked back at him. Its beak open wide. It chirped. A ragged deathly chirp. A funeral bell.

The Pied Piper's hand hung there as Mo fought to control his shaking body against the onslaught. It was in those last moments, those last moments of knowing, that Mo could see he was drowning, falling, slipping beneath the folds of the lagoon on that night. The dark water. The forest surrounding him. The man in black before him.

The guard sang, "Your time is up."

Mo tried to raise an arm and strike the sink, to make noise, anything to call attention to himself, to alert that he needed help, but he could not feel his limbs. All he could feel was cold, tears, and blood-consuming him. He was fixed there, drowning in his failed debt.

Words outside of the bathroom calling him meant nothing. His life before meant nothing, and he knew that.

The Pied Piper grinned. "Payment is due."

It was as if Mo's body was no longer his. He reached out his arm and took hold of the Pied Piper's hand. It was so cold it burned. His body erupted in shock and pain like he had never known. A paralyzing chill raced through his veins. He had lost control.

He had no choice but to follow the Pied Piper away.

He knew then that Fin really was gone, and he did not want to be without her. Maybe this was the way to reunite with her, perhaps this was the way it always needed to be. Maybe the torture of the water rushing out of his throat would stop. Maybe the feeling of ice and chill charging through his veins would fade, but it did not. The pain stung and pulsed and throbbed. It was as if he were out there again in that lagoon struggling, but this time fighting to come up, to break through the surface. He found himself sinking. Falling below, his feet touching the bottom of the lagoon. And then he opened his mouth to scream but only more water rushed out.

His lungs filled with the rank liquid, and just as his eyesight faded from the awful vision before him, just as the sound of rushing water quieted around him he heard it.

A flute playing.

CHAPTER 20

They had married a year ago at City Hall. This is not how she had expected to spend her first wedding anniversary, working. Or, maybe it was the only way she could spend it? Working. She took Washington's advice—stay away from the office and work from home for a few hours in the morning. It was the most rest she would allow herself. Still, she worked. She could make calls from home, and did. She called Evie's mother who insisted her daughter was still in no position to talk. Then she called Mohammed's father. The man cried uncontrollably on the phone. When she offered to come to his house and speak with him there, the man proceeded to wail. She said she would call again later. Fin's stepmother said she could not talk. The baby was teething and upset, and it would be best to speak with Fin's father, not her.

Now, Lauren was here alone in her living room reading witness statements and drinking strong Puerto Rican espresso. Lauren had remembered the call to her father the day she got married. Yes, it was a silly, spontaneous thing, but she loved Bobby. She'd known she would fall in love with him the day they met at the zoo when he told her about magic, wonder, fairy tales, and the Dream Lady. Up until then, she was the only person she knew who was obsessed with such things. He called her Lore, and he knew that fairy tales could bring both happiness and destruction, the same as she had come to discover in her life. When Lauren had shared the news that she and Bobby had gotten married, eloped at City Hall, her father had said, "Your mother wouldn't consider it valid, it wasn't in a church."

Angry, Lauren had hung up and when Bobby asked what her dad had said she'd lied.

The morning after they married, work called. A two-year-old had been shot in the head. The boy had been in an alley with an eighteen-year-old relative. They had just gotten home. A dispute at a party a few houses down spilled into the alley. There were shouts, then shots. Bleary-eyed, and with stomach acid climbing up her esophagus she crawled out of bed, but his hand had caught hers.

"You just went to bed a couple hours ago."

One hand reached for a pair of black jeans on the chair while she scrolled through the message on her phone with the other. "I have to check this out."

Bobby sighed and laid his head back on the pillow.

"A little kid's been killed. I don't really have much of a choice." She was annoyed that he would even question if work could wait. No, work could not wait.

Work could never wait. This is what she did. This is who she was.

In some ways, she thought of herself as some variation of Charon, the ferryman who carries souls of the newly deceased across the River Styx. In Greek mythology, Charon is given a coin for safe passage, but those who could not pay the fee, or were left unburied, had to wander for a hundred years, aimlessly. Lauren felt if she could not bring these people justice then they would be left to wander alone in the darkness.

Bobby kicked the sheets off and got out of bed.

"Where are you going?" She asked, pulling on her jeans.

"Figure you'd need coffee or something." He said as he moved towards the kitchen.

No one had ever done that for her, bothered with her, that is. He could have stayed in bed. He could have gone back to sleep, but he did not. He went and troubled himself over her.

It was that same night when she'd realized the end was coming soon for her father. On her drive to work he had called—to tell her Marie wanted to speak with her.

Marie had been dead more than half of Lauren's life. She had told him to get some sleep, and she would check in on him in the morning. Driving towards the police station, thinking of her father and her long-dead sister, in silence, is when she'd heard it—a sound so faint, so light. She'd known it was not coming from a nearby car. No cars were driving alongside her. There was just her, the dark streets, and the sound of music filling her car.

It was like that now. This morning, sitting in her living room, going through her notes after speaking with Ramon Castro yesterday—she heard music. It was soft, a steady hum. She closed her eyes, and a flash of memory came into view, and it was like she had always known.

He was getting closer.

Her phone vibrated on the table. She looked down at the message.

Hope you're doing well.

How do you respond to your ex-husband on what should have been your first wedding anniversary?

The marriage failed. Bobby could not accept her love affair with her job, so he left. Well, she'd told him to go. She was surprised he sent her a message. Yes, he'd been at her father's funeral. Yes, he'd helped with some of the arrangements, but she thought he did that as a courtesy—for her father, and not necessarily for her.

She stared at the screen.

When Lauren tapped the darkened screen the message from Bobby appeared again, begging for a response:

Hope you're doing well.

No, Lauren was not doing well. She tapped letters.

"I'm fine. Thanks."

Her phone proceeded to blink and buzz and vibrate: the alarm indicating it was time to go.

In the garage, before she turned her car on she shut her phone off. Just in case Bobby messaged again. He did not need to come back into her life right now, but she regretted feeling that she needed him, even with danger brewing. Something was stirring in the city. There was a soft anger that reverberated in the streets. She could feel it. It was not the pressure and charge of the changing of the seasons, from summer to fall to winter. Electricity hung in the air. There was a sense of dread and doom so pronounced she could feel it getting closer, brushing against her skin. It was the same terrible power she had felt in her father's house ever since the deaths of Marie and Diana. The house had never been the same, nor this city, nor her.

She found a parking spot right in front this time, and as she walked to the center, she turned her phone back on. Another message from Bobby appeared on the screen as she entered the room. He asked if she needed anything. This time she would not answer.

"Look at you being on time," Jordan said as she took a seat.

"Told you I wasn't going to be late."

He removed his earbuds and placed them on the desk.

"Look at you being unproblematic and living up to your responsibilities."

"Do you know who stole your last pair of headphones?"

He laughed. "Some dude on the bus yanked them off and ran. Whatever. I'm fine, Medina. I don't need a security guard."

"You tell me if you're ever in trouble, okay?"

"Yeah, you're the first person I'd call." He gave a dry laugh and then set a notebook down on the table.

"Is that sarcasm?" She asked.

"I can't help you through life, Medina. You've gotta figure it out for yourself."

Lauren fought back a smile. Jordan was a lot like her at that age, independent and unapologetic. She and Marie had been different, for so many reasons. Maybe if Marie had been a little bit more like Jordan things would have turned out differently, better. Lauren brushed the thought from her mind. It was Diana's fault. It had always been Diana's fault.

Jordan turned the pages, passing page after page of text until landing on a clean sheet. "You know," he said "You're kinda not that bad...for a cop."

Lauren laughed.

"Why'd you want to be a cop anyway? They're all bad," he said as he pressed pencil to page.

"My father was an officer for a long time, then detective. He died just a few months after retiring."

"That's messed up. And your mom?"

"My real mom...she left one night when I was seven. Just walked out the front door and never came back. My dad assumed she'd gone to her favorite jazz club, Rosa's. I have pictures of her just sitting there at the bar, just water in hand because she didn't drink. She said alcohol didn't allow her to feel the music right. She wanted to feel the music completely. She never called. We never found her car. We never found her. My dad married Diana a few years later. A musician."

Jordan scratched his forehead with the eraser of his pencil. "Nothing, no phone call. Nothing?"

"She just disappeared."

"I'm so sorry," Jordan placed his pencil down, stood up and walked around to her and threw his arms around her neck. Fairy tales always told you about the stepmother, how evil and cruel they were, but what they never told you was what happened to the real mothers and that was the cruelest thing of all.

Jordan pulled away and gave her a smile, a smile somewhere between a baby face and a grown man, and she felt in that moment that he would be okay, whether in this city or beyond.

"What do you remember about her?"

Lauren smiled. "She was absolutely beautiful. She smelled like cinnamon and I remember we ate a lot of cookies. She always tried making them from scratch and they always burned. So, she kept packaged cookies on hand and would pretend those were the ones she baked. We read a lot, well, she read to me. She would read to me after school, and every night, and it was always fairy tales. She loved the beautiful ones, the happily ever after ones. She was just...so kind and so sweet and everything that my father and I weren't."

"Your stepmother..." Jordan began.

The very word conjured a badge of cruelty pinned on the figure that took place of the real mother. Stepmothers in fairy tales were cannibals or wicked witches, and more often than not they were cursed with the ability to weave damaging spells. And it was always their stepdaughters who were the quiet sufferers and patient martyrs of their cruelty. There were no *good* stepmothers in fairy tales, Lauren knew, she'd checked. Biological mothers rarely played a central role in fairy tales. It was with their death or disappearance that caused the darkness to swallow up everything, leaving children lost in the wilderness and open to assault.

"What are your plans for college?" She asked, changing the subject.

He frowned. "Go, for one. UIC. I'll need a job to help pay for books and stuff. I've got some scholarships and some small loans to help. I'll be good. I'll be living at home and taking the bus to the blue line, and the train will leave me right on campus. It'll be a lot of work, but I can do it."

She believed he could, and he would. He had worked so hard to get here all by himself.

Before Jordan slipped his headphones on Medina stopped him.

"There's something I need to tell you."

"Okay..."

"There's a news conference planned for later this afternoon. We have a suspect in custody."

Jordan's head bowed. He remained silent, listening. "Who is it?"

"Your classmate."

He raised his head. "What? Who?"

"Finley Wills confessed yesterday to her doctor."

"Fin? How? That's impossible. The girl's like five feet nothing."

"You don't need to be that much more in order to pull a trigger."

"But…why?"

"Her doctor spoke with her yesterday. She's not well. It's admissible in court, and it'll take time, but I believe her. She says she shot and killed Hadiya." Lauren took a deep breath, because she already knew this was a lot for anyone to hear. "Jordan, she says she also participated in the attack on Evie and Daniel with the help of Mo."

She allowed the reality to settle for a moment, that a classmate had killed his best friend, and that same classmate had participated in the killing and attack of another. Then finally, she added. "Jordan, there's something I need to ask you." She handed him her phone. "Do you know anything about this?"

She showed him an image of the graffiti sprayed across the school doors.

He rubbed his eyes, they were pink and puffy. "I already told you, I don't know anything."

"I think you're lying."

Lauren could see Jordan shift in his seat.

"If there's any time to tell me what you know, it's now. You're not in trouble. Not at all. I just need you to tell me what you know."

"I'm not going to do your job for you," his voice cracked, and he reached for his headphones.

Lauren grabbed them first.

"Seriously?"

"You've seen it before? Lauren tapped on the screen of her phone.

"This name? This marker?"

"Why?"

"Because," she said slowly "I just need to know." She pulled the phone back. "No one wants to talk to me about it. No one. Not even my confidential informants. They say they don't know anything, but *someone* has to know *something*. I've seen this at your school. At Hadiya's shooting, and at the stabbing at Humboldt Park. If I don't figure it out then more people will die."

"No one's going to tell you who's doing this because no one knows who it is. It's there one day, then it's gone. That's it."

That was true. The graffiti did not stay up long. She did not mention this to Jordan, he obviously knew enough. The words appeared and in a couple of days—maybe even the next day—they were gone. Disappeared. She'd checked with the Department of Streets & Sanitation. No one had called in the graffiti for it to be cleared away. Homeowners did not want to see it scrawled across their houses, garages or community. The Graffiti Removal Program employs "blast" trucks that have a solution of baking soda under high pressure, and with hoses, they wash away unwanted and unsightly graffiti from brick, stone, and other mineral surfaces. Yet, at each of these places, the graffiti was not removed. It was as if it had never been there.

"Pretty big coincidence that it's showing up where people have been killed."

"No one thinks it's a coincidence. Everyone thinks it's there exactly for the same reason you do."

"Why's that?"

"The Pied Piper, whoever he is. He's making sure he's letting everyone know that payment is due. The spray paint shows up where someone's going to get killed. There. That's what I know. That's what everyone knows, but we're all too damn scared to even talk about it, Medina. Do you want him coming after me next?"

Lauren could feel her jaw tightening. She looked directly into Jordan's eyes, leaned in closer and said, "You're not going to get hurt. I promise."

He opened his hand, motioning her to give him his headphones back. She shook her head, refusing.

Pain shot down Lauren's jawline. "Is that why Hadiya died? She was talking about him?"

"Hadiya died because she wanted to believe in him."

"What else do you know, Jordan?" She slammed her hand on the table and pulled it away quickly. She did not mean to do that. She did not expect to get excited, but she needed to know more.

He placed his pen down on the table and stared at her for a moment. "There's this rhyme Fin found in a book. She somehow put it together that it went with the game on the NeverSleep website. That was the missing piece, the rhyme, and she found it and copied it. She thought it was just some stupid game. Like Bloody Mary, or Candyman. Stand in front of a mirror in a dark room and say Candyman's name five times. He shows up and..."

"Kills you."

Lauren wanted to know why a high school senior would go along with a freshman in this game.

"Exactly. But thinking of it now. It's pretty stupid for anyone to try to summon anything that's supposed to kill you. Hadiya and I were leaving school when she stopped in the restroom. She was taking a long time, and I didn't think anything of it. Then, she came running out screaming and crying. I asked her what happened, but she said she just wanted to get out of there. When we were a couple of blocks away, she told me Fin and Mo had been in the bathroom with the lights off. They had lit a candle, and they were both standing in front of the mirror. Fin was reading some words from a page. When Hadiya'd walked in Fin told her it was a game, just some stupid superstitious game: say the nursery rhyme and the Pied Piper appears. Hadiya said fine, go ahead, and she stood back and watched as they did it. They said the nursery rhyme, and…" he paused, lowering his eyes. "A man appeared in the mirror. She screamed and ran out of there."

"What did she see exactly?"

"A man. Dressed in black clothes. A black hat." Jordan shook his head as if shaking off the memory of what he had been told. "It's stupid. They just scared themselves. And Fin's obviously crazy because look what she did."

Jordan held out his hand, motioning for his earbuds again.

Lauren dropped them in his open palm.

"Do you believe Fin is crazy?" Lauren asked.

Jordan placed one earbud in his ear, and he paused before placing the other one in his other ear. "Does it really matter? Hadiya is dead. Maybe we're all a little crazy if we believe a nursery rhyme has something to do with it."

This still did not answer all of her questions. Yes, the Pied Piper was back—there was no doubt about that. She needed to get hold of that book, that was certain, and she needed to talk to the only person who could help her get to it.

CHAPTER 21

Fin screamed for hours. It sounded like an animal, raw, and in pain, and when the guards could no longer take it they begged Ruth to give Fin what she wanted. Fin had been given a small collection of art supplies. Ruth had delivered them personally. Now Fin had ruled paper, construction paper, markers, colored pencils, crayons and a couple of glue sticks. What she would have liked were a pair of scissors, but she was told that was not possible. When she tried to reason with Ruth that she would even take the dull plastic kind, the kind kindergartners used, Ruth had said that she would not be able to fulfill that request. When Fin asked why, Ruth had said they were a hazard.

How were dull plastic kindergartner scissors a hazard? At home, she often used scissors to cut out shapes. When she needed to be more precise, she reached for an X-ACTO knife. Since she had neither available, she did what she could. Fin carefully folded the paper along the edges where she would typically cut. She folded forward and folded back; again, and again until the crease was so embedded into the fibers of the paper that she could then lay that fold against an edge of the small desk in her room, tug, pull and then rip along the line. It took time, but it was effective. Fin preferred to cut her shapes, then, once they were all prepared, she would paint them. Painting the pieces after they had been cut out was easier because if she painted them and then cut them away—or tore them apart—their color would rub off.

This evening she was working on her dollhouse. It was a project she'd started working on at home. Since she was no longer at home, she'd started all over again from memory. The image was imprinted on her mind, burned behind her eyelids so that each time she closed her eyes there it was: the perfect home, and within the ideal family.

It was a relatively simple design. A miniature house with miniature occupants. It was modeled after her own home; a two-level bungalow with a finished basement. She had created each level but did not yet attempt to stack them on top of each other. For now, the levels were separated, she liked it that way, compartmentalized.

The basement was mostly an open space except for a bathroom and the laundry room. Then there was the first floor with kitchen, living room, dining room, a bathroom, a small den off the dining room and two bedrooms; hers and her baby brother's room. Upstairs there was the main bedroom and bathroom. There was still a lot to shape and cut: beds, dressers, nightstands, sofas. She wanted it to feel as much like her home as possible.

She took her time drawing the windows in her house. There were precisely seventeen. She had counted them, over and over before, just as she had the doors, walls, floors, and rooms. As she finished drawing the window to her room, it did not yet feel finished. She sat there a moment, looking at the window and knowing what it was missing.

She reached for her black pencil and slowly proceeded to draw a dark figure that would loom over where she would place the dollhouse bed.

He was always there. He would always be there.

Even here, in this dollhouse, he belonged. He was as much a part of her, her home, and her life as anything else in that house. With her real mother dead, her father uninvolved, and her stepmother uncaring and busy with a new baby, he was more reliable than all of them. The silent member of her family who cared more for her than her own blood. He cared. He listened.

Just like he had taken care of her real mother...

Fin realized she was crying and wiped her eyes. She wanted to scream again, but she did not think she had any screams left, her throat was so raw. She had failed, and there was no going back now.

There were footsteps outside of her room. She glanced up to the window in the door. It was just the evening attendant making their rounds. That is what they called them, "attendants," but Fin knew they were armed correctional officers. Fin also knew she was not in an ordinary youth correctional facility. There were doctors here, psychiatrists here. In the morning, screams came.

Fin called out to the woman, "I want to talk to Ruth."

"Is it an emergency?" Two eyes asked from behind the small glass.

"No, but she said she was going to check on my friend."

"Dr. Margraff will be in tomorrow, and you can speak to her during your scheduled session."

Ruth had promised her that she was going to check in on Mo. That seemed like hours ago. She knew because she had written it down. Time here was becoming thick, like clotted cream. Fin stood up, abandoning her dollhouse pieces. The house would never be perfect, she suspected. Not now, anyway. She proceeded to pace the room, back and forth, back and forth. The room was small enough that she knew how many steps exactly she needed to take in each direction.

One, two, three, four, five, six, seven, eight. Turn.

She paced, and paced, her footsteps took her faster back and forth across the room, creating a breeze, rustling the tiny pieces of paper she had constructed.

One, two, three, four, five, six, seven, eight. Turn.

"Why are you doing that?" Her roommate broke her silence.

"Because I'm thinking."

"You can't sit and think?" The girl said from a seated position on the middle of Fin's bed.

"No."

"That's a lie. You were just sitting there with your dollhouse, and you were thinking."

"No, I wasn't," Fin said.

"What do you call sitting there and toying around for hours with paper?"

"A distraction from this place," Fin said.

"It's also thinking. You were thinking about things. You can sit down and think."

"Fine," Fin plopped down on the edge of her unsteady foam mattress. "What should I think about?"

"You don't have to be rude," the girl pushed strands of brown, greasy hair away from her eyes. "You can start off by thinking about why you were so upset that you had to stomp across our room so loud that you woke me up."

"I didn't wake you up. It was time for you to wake up. You have been asleep all day. What are you planning on doing? Sleeping all night too?"

A grin spread across her roommate's face. "Maybe."

"I hate you."

"Keep saying those things. I'm the only person you've got."

"I've got Mo."

"Really? Do you even know where Mo is? Have you seen him around here? Heard his name? I bet he's not even in this building. I bet he's in another building altogether."

Her roommate leaned in closer. "You know what would be really messed up? If he wasn't even being held anywhere. What if he placed all of the blame on you, and what if because of that, he was sent back home? Free, and you are here in your bloody chamber."

Fin stood up and covered her ears. "Shut up! Shut up! Shut up!"

The girl giggled a musical giggle. "Tell me to shut up all you want, but you know what you did. You know what you did to Hadiya.

You know what you did to Evie and Daniel and your mother. Maybe not all mothers from fairy tales die of sickness or go missing. Maybe some are killed by their own children."

Fin stopped. Looked to the stranger seated on her bed and shouted. "You don't know anything!"

The girl stood up, and moved close to Fin. Their noses nearly touching. "I don't?" Her breath smelled of moss and dead flowers. The girl laughed, a loud, obscene, hurtful laugh. "You asked the Pied Piper to take your real mother. He did..."

"And he kept coming back!" Fin cried, dropping to her knees. Mouth open, sobbing hard and heavy. Her shoulders shook. Her hands shook. Her body convulsed in the knowing. Tears ran down her face. Saliva rolled down the corners of her mouth. She did it. She'd had her mother killed, and for what? What did she get in exchange? A dismissive stepmother and a curse.

"You don't know anything," Fin spat. "You're here with me."

"I know everything."

Pound. Pound. Pound. Pound. Pound.

Fin heard them on the other side of the door, trying to unlock the door but it would not open. The door shook in its frame as they pounded on steel.

"I know about the mirror. The candle. I know who you called. The Pied Piper came back to town and told you to do your job," the girl growled. "He asked for his payment."

"I'd already paid!"

"No," the girl grabbed Fin's chin with sharp black fingernails digging into her skin. The veins in her face throbbed thick and black like worms swimming beneath her skin. "He gave you what you wanted. He got rid of your mother."

"But he came back and told me to kill someone else, or he'd kill me," she fought through tears. "I didn't know. I didn't know this was a deal with the devil."

The girl laughed. "He's not a devil! He's a *god*!"

In the background, Fin could hear shouting. An alarm, a high-pitched whirling squeal. All sounds grew distant. Muffled cries followed.

"*You all right in there!?*"

"*I'm trying to open the door.*"

"*Where'd she get those scissors?*"

"*I can't open the door.*"

"*Who gave her those goddamn scissors?*"

"*Call Dr. Margraff now.*"

"*Fin, open the door!*"

Her roommate covered her mouth. Silent giggles now.

Where *did* these scissors come from, Fin wondered. Firm in her hand, the pivoted blades fully open, and carefully, carefully, one long blade slid down her throat.

Pound. Pound. Pound. Pound. Pound.

Time blurred. Time became water.

The last thing Fin remembered was the screaming and blood. It felt like razor blades sliding down her throat. When she awoke, she was on her back in a different room, smaller, with a dim light in the center of the ceiling. She turned, looked and found she was on the floor. It was soft. She tried to call out but could not. Her throat was sore, aching, sharp from the screaming, or something else? It took a moment, but she was able to sit up, and eventually stand, uneasy on two legs—a new fawn learning to walk. She pressed her face against the door, and she welcomed the cold from the metal against her cheek. She was too tired to pound on the door, but she tried. First, she tried hitting it with her fist, but it barely made a noise. Then, she just kept hitting her palm against the door, slowly, steadily until she could hear and feel the metal thud beneath her hand.

A different attendant appeared in the window. This person was a man in a white coat. "I'll call your doctor."

Fin turned around, pressing her back against the door, taking in the soft padding of the room, the soft light made the surface of the walls, ceiling and floor look gray. She slid down on her back until she sat down.

A few minutes passed, and then she heard echoed footsteps approach.

"Move away from the door. I don't want you to get hit," Ruth said. She must have looked down and seen Fin sitting there against the door.

The door opened, and Ruth crouched down to where Fin was seated. Ruth held out a cup of water to her. "How are you feeling?"

"My mouth, throat, it stings. I taste blood."

"You had an accident, but we were able to catch you in time before there was any major damage. It's just a cut, but the physician who checked you out while you were out said it will heal. Drink the water slowly. That should help."

Fin winced as the water splashed back in her throat. "I don't want it." She held the cup back out to Ruth.

"I understand. Are you ready to go back to your room?"

Fin nodded her head.

The door was opened, and they were back in the sickly yellow hallway.

"Can you tell me what happened?" Ruth asked as they walked.

"Why haven't you told me anything about Mo?"

"This is difficult for you, and I understand. But right now, you are getting the care that you need."

"Where is he?"

"Let's get you to your room where you can get some rest."

When they arrived at the door of Fin's room, the attendant was standing beside it, glaring at her.

"I'd first like for you to walk over to the window and look into your room and tell me what you see," Ruth instructed.

Fin approached the door and looked through the glass. She studied the room for a moment. Without turning her eyes away, she said, "A bed. A desk. A writing chair." She turned around. "Where did she go?"

"Fin, this is how the room has always been set up, just for one person. You've been in this room alone since you arrived."

The attendant motioned for Fin to step away from the door. The door was unlocked, and Fin entered without being told.

"Your stepmother will be here in the morning for a visit, and afterward, you'll be meeting with your lawyers."

"Stepmother," she said. Her eyes widened. "Lawyers? Why?"

"Fin, someone died. Don't you remember? Daniel died. Daniel drowned. Evie was stabbed repeatedly, and she's at a hospital recovering. You and Mo were arrested for involvement in that killing and attack. You're seeing things, talking to people who are not there. That's why you're here while Mo is being held in a juvenile correctional facility."

Fin nodded silently as she sat down on her bed. She looked at the torn pieces of her dollhouse scattered across the floor.

There were more words said, but she tuned them out, and after a while, she heard the door shut with a metallic clang. Ruth was gone.

Fin bent down and gathered the pieces of the dollhouse, and as she did, she heard a giggle behind her.

She turned around. He was there. He did not look happy.

Tears welled up in her eyes. She could taste the blood more now in the back of her throat, thick and syrupy as the bleeding started again.

"I'm sorry," She stammered, coughing up blood, her teeth staining red. "I tried to tell Mo what we needed to do. That we had to commit. We can fix it. It won't happen again. Let me try again."

Fin was trembling now.

She had failed. She'd called the Pied Piper to take her mother, which he did. She did not know then that he would come back seeking further payment, another death—Hadiya. Then, when he was not satisfied with Hadiya, he demanded payment, yet again. And that is why she called Evie and Daniel out to the lagoon that day. If she killed them both at once then maybe the Pied Piper would leave her alone. Mo wanted the Pied Piper to kill the man who had robbed his family's store. Mo did not need to know about the complicated terms: that he may be demanded to kill more in order to keep the life he wanted.

He had gone willingly with her into the bathroom at school. He had lit the candle. He had recited the words, those words so secret and archaic. Hadiya had entered the bathroom. Hadiya wanted to see what they were doing, and Hadiya saw the man too. She'd screamed. She fled, while Fin and Mo smiled knowing they had succeeded. They'd summoned him. They had given him names, and he'd tipped his cap in agreement.

When the man demanded more death Fin had known who to bring him.

Now, however, the words were difficult. She opened her mouth again to try to apologize. Black blood spurted out. She continued to try to talk, spurting, spraying black and red. "I'll do better next time. It will go right." She coughed more blood, trying to clear out her throat, but the more she coughed the more it flowed. Liquid rolled down her nostrils. Her vision blurred. She wiped and looked, more bleeding.

The more she strained to speak, the closer it came. The only sound in the room was her gasping and gurgling for breath, and the clicking of its two hooves.

Click, click, click, click.

Like the tapping of nails on a chalkboard, its hooves clicked sharply on the hard floor. Its yellow eyes drilled into Fin.

Click, click, click, click,

It was neither from this world or any other. It was both beast and man. Wild and rustic. Black curly hair, and two curved pointed horns which sprouted from his head. A deeply lined face, framed by thick hair. A bare torso, dusted with dirt and dry leaves rested on hindquarters. Two black, cloven hoofs moved forward again. Half man. Half goat.

This was the man in his true form.

Click, click, click, click,

The walls fell away and they were surrounded by green. Trees that crashed against each other, straining for space. The sun struggled to fight through branches and leaves, leaving shadows dancing across her body. She looked up and saw that canopy strangled the sky. Blood flowed down her orifices, eyes, mouth, nose, ears and pooled on new fallen leaves around her feet.

Its hooves shuffled across the forest floor. Closer.

Nothing more needed to be said, and nothing more could be said as she fought the onslaught of liquid flowing out of her body.

It reached out its hand towards her, caked in dirt and leaves. Its hands were red, covered in liquid. Long, sharp black fingernails were inches from her eyes. It reached further, the nails resting against the skin of her forehead, and then hot pain as its nails bore down into flesh, puncturing through scalp. The crack of breaking bone. Splitting the spongy folds of her brain. Breath became liquid, swallowing salty, bitter iron.

It lifted her up to meet its eyes. Deep black pools.

Sight lost to a curtain of red.

Tremors shot through her arms. Legs shook violently.

Her hands were no longer hers as they shook and waved. Her body fought to stay connected.

She could not scream.

She could not see.

Breath became lost to blood and water.

And at that moment, right before the here and now, much like that space in between sleep and awake she thought she heard music—vibrating, wafting, bright, then shrill and penetrating.

Her trembling stopped.

The beast released its hold, knelt down and placed a gold coin in her mouth.

CHAPTER 22

Early in the morning was the only time of day Lauren felt she could get a hold of this city. After her session with Jordan ended she came here, to this too familiar place—Humboldt Park. Lauren felt like she knew each and every piece of this place. She knew the trails, the prairie gardens, multiple baseball diamonds, and playgrounds.

Lauren had buried her father just days ago, but in a way, it felt like he had been gone for months. While she found Rosehill Cemetery beautiful, she felt like Humboldt Park was the place she could connect to him, the old him, and really talk to him. She drove to Cafe Colao for a cortadito, a double espresso with milk. There, she left her car and walked down to Humboldt Boulevard. As she did, she passed one of the large, steel sixty-foot Puerto Rican flags that stretched across Division Street. One at the corner of Division and Western and the other at the corner of Division and California. Installed in 1995, they were made to look like they were blowing in the wind. At the time, the neighborhood had been about eighty-percent Puerto Rican, but many of them had left. Some died. Some moved to Florida, and others moved back to the island, fulfilling their dream of returning to their home, to Borinquen — the name originally given to it by the indigenous Tainos before Christopher Columbus came and took everything, including their name, away. Those flags that stretch across this major street, weigh fifty tons, can withstand winds up to seventy miles per hour, and on cold, silent winter days provide some warmth of the memory of those who came before her, like the first wave of Puerto Ricans who came to this city in the 1940s to work in the steel mills in Chicago, to whom the flags are dedicated.

She crossed the street toward the Humboldt Park Formal Gardens. Humboldt Park was part of great Chicago architect Daniel Burnham's boulevard park system plan, Lauren had learned. Before the Puerto Ricans, there were the Polish and then Germans and Italians, and then Norwegian, Swedish and Danish. This neighborhood was a living, breathing thing, and Burnham knew this city lived and so it was part of his of his 1909 Plan of Chicago. She had studied this park, its history and the history of the people who brought it to its present condition. For his plan, Burnham envisioned several large green spaces that would decorate the city like a necklace, and Humboldt Park was one of the most magnificent parks in the city.

The park is home to several historic structures, the Boat House, the Field House, the Horse Stables, and of course, the formal gardens where the bronze buffalos stand, a place she often visited with her family. The gardens were created by famed landscape architect Jens Jensen in 1908, just a short walk down from where Humboldt's statue stands watch.

At the entrance of the gardens, Lauren approached the two large bronze buffalos, replicas of buffalo statues that were displayed during the World's Columbian Exhibition in 1893. The event was meant to celebrate Columbus' arrival in the New World in 1492. The fair was so spectacular that people still talk about it today, the fourteen great buildings constructed by famous architects. There were fairgrounds of wonder and mystery, science and invention, but almost all of it was temporary, temporary buildings, canals and lagoons. Over twenty-seven million people visited Chicago in those six months during the fair and took with them to their small rural towns, cities across America and country's far away the stories of a great city on a prairie, a great people, and all of the magic that lives there.

Lauren later heard a rumor that the buffalos were not replicas but were the actual statues from the World's Fair. While all of the buildings at the World's Fair burned in a massive fire, it is believed by some the buffalos survived. Their plaster bodies were then covered in a coat of bronze, or at least that is what the rumors say.

Lauren wanted to believe they were real, and so each time she visited the gardens, she would place her hand on one of the bronze statues, feeling in a way that it could connect her to this city's past, so many years ago to 1893. That this park, Humboldt Park, somehow served as a portal back to a past when the fantastic was possible. Right around the same time, a rare and unique copy of the *German Popular Stories* made its way to the city, eventually finding a permanent home at Newberry Library. Within that book, there was a page that contained a passage in error. What was it? A spell? A ritual? Whatever it was, it was a way to summon something ancient and evil. A source.

"I hate that every few years the questions seem to come up, and from a different person too." She spoke to the cool breeze and then took a sip of her drink. "It's bad this time. I feel it. The house isn't right. The city isn't right. It's like there's this odd vibration everywhere, and I can't turn it off."

She looked around to the dying and dried flowers. In just a few weeks the formal garden would fade under heavy blankets of snow. Chicago's winters had a way of hiding things, if only temporarily.

"I have to call Bobby," she said. "I'm sure you'll like that. It's the right thing to do. This is all so convoluted, Dad. The graffiti. These deaths. The Pied Piper. Fin called him, but he's not leaving until he gets what's owed to him, and I'm not exactly sure what's owed to him, but...." She inhaled deeply. Tension tightening in her jaw. "He's coming, and I'm scared because I don't know if I can do what I'm supposed to do. No officer should have to discharge their weapon."

She looked at the time. It was nearing the time to start driving towards the South Side, but there was someplace she needed to stop at first. As she raised her coffee cup to her lips she heard it, that hypnotic, penetrating, wind-like music. She stood up and moved to the pergola, drawn to the sound—even though she knew she could not be harmed by it, it was always a threat. She walked past the crumbling concrete columns, heading towards the sound, but in many ways moving away from it.

When the music stopped, she stopped. She knew it was time to go.

A scattering of people stood on the sidewalk in front of the abandoned lot, waiting for the blue van to park. The man inside was careful, making sure the van pulled up as close to the curb as possible. He put the car in park and turned it off. He reached over to the passenger seat and grabbed a gray hat he placed on his round head. He stepped out of the car with a smile, approaching those on the sidewalk. They stood with arms crossed, harsh stares and scowls.

"We're not going to let you put that thing out there," one woman in the crowd spat. A man standing behind her repeated her words.

An older woman spoke softly. "It just...it's not what we want people to think of us. All of this death. Here."

"Right? It's depressing," a man agreed. "Don't nobody want to be reminded of all that every time they walk past here."

The man with the gray hat moved slowly. He had been doing this many years, but for some reason, the anger seemed more intense this year. The crowd continued their protestations, even as the man made his way to the trunk of his car.

A news reporter positioned himself away from the curb. It was a better shot. The crowd would make their way to the empty lot in between two crumbling buildings.

Lauren leaned on the hood of her car just a few yards down. She had taken to spending a lot of time here. An empty lot surrounded by empty, dilapidated brownstone buildings. Their broken windows boarded up with plywood, but just a few lots down were newer townhomes. Chicago knew gentrification intimately; old and abused mixed in with the new. One day there would be more dumpsters parked on the street, plaster, drywall and detailed woodwork and hand molded stone destroyed, collected, and discarded away in favor of steel, glass and harsh, cold lines.

Unlike a cemetery that closed at sunset, this place was always accessible. It was like a cemetery because of all of the crosses. A field of white-painted wooden crosses, each bearing the handwritten name of a person who had been murdered in Chicago this year.

Lauren wondered, when she died would the city ring out in a chorus of gunshots and police sirens welcoming her death? Would her death be celebrated with fireworks at Navy Pier? Colored sparks firing off from the waterfront, hovering over the great Ferris wheel? She wondered if she was now part of that great Chicago plan.

The man in the gray hat saw her and gave her a wave and a warm smile. They had run into each other a few times out here. Everyday strangers. They exchanged pleasantries, the kind that seemed second nature in a smaller community or suburb, but that jarred out here in the city.

Good morning. Good afternoon. How are you? Good to see you again.

People did not talk to each other out here. Typically when someone said, “Good morning,” she cringed, already reaching for her weapon in her mind. “Good morning” was never good morning in the city, nor was “Good evening,” “Hello,” or “How are you?” Any greeting from a stranger in the city could be an animalistic strategy, a predator inadvertently alerting prey to his presence. What most predators failed to realize was that in Chicago you could never be too sure if another predator was present.

A tall man came out of the crowd and tried to push the gray hatted man's trunk closed.

"Leave it alone," Lauren shouted.

The man inspected Lauren and nodded once. It did not take long to register that she was law enforcement.

"How's that fair?" A young woman in a pink puffer jacket squealed. "This isn't his neighborhood. He doesn't live around here. He doesn't own this lot. How come he can do this?"

Lauren crossed the street. "Take your opinions to the city, your alderman. For now, move aside," Lauren ordered. "Go ahead," Lauren told the man in the gray hat. It was time to set this cross in the ground so that the city could see a new name.

The man in the gray hat slipped on a pair of workman gloves and pulled a large wooden white painted cross out of the van. He rested it on his shoulder, leaving the trunk open. The crowd on the sidewalk grew. The television reporter spoke quietly, directing his cameraman where to point the camera, following the man in the gray hat as he made his way to the field of crosses. The man in the gray hat carefully placed the cross in the ground. The name of Chicago's latest victim written across in black lettering: Hadiya Santos.

The reporter descended on the man in the gray hat, asking questions, nodding his head, asking another question, and giving an actor's look of concern. This was the first time Lauren had actually been on the field when a crossed was placed. She normally watched from across the street.

"Why Garfield Park?" Lauren heard a young man ask. "Why not somewhere else?"

No one answered. It's not like Garfield Park was the only city neighborhood that experienced homicide. Last year he'd made 780 crosses. Lauren had read about Mr. Gerald Zanis and how he had been making these wooden crosses to commemorate tragic loss for over twenty years. His crosses have stood at Columbine, in Boston, Orlando and many other places where tragedy struck. This was his city, so he spent the most time here, and he had committed to creating a cross for each person killed by violence in his hometown.

"It smells like death, don't you think?" An old woman said as she positioned herself beside Lauren.

"They're just displays. All it smells like is an empty lot that needs tending."

"Do you think the crosses do anything?" The old woman asked.

"Maybe, for some people," Lauren shoved her hands in the pockets of her jacket.

"Does it do anything for you?"

Lauren turned, looking the woman over carefully. She had never seen her before. She was small and wore a red knit sweater and a heavy coat over it, unzipped.

"They're just crosses, and nothing can be done or felt by a collection of names in a lot."

Lauren took a step forward to head back to her car.

"Get the golden key and open the door. You can't ignore it, Lauren," the old woman said. "You owe him another death."

"Excuse me?"

The woman smiled a toothless smile. "I am the Old Woman in the Woods. Open the door and reveal the splendid things." The whites of her eyes had grown black. "Don't worry Lauren, they're your children, too. Call them, summon them, all of your children of Chicago, born of the prairie, and skyscraper steel and forged in the Chicago Fire."

"Momma!"

A man ran up and put his hands on the small woman's shoulders. He caught his breath, "Momma, I told you not to leave the house without me." He looked to Lauren. "Sorry if she bothered you. She's been wandering off lately."

The old woman took her grown son's hand. "I'm tired. Take me home."

As they walked away, Lauren noticed some people holding up

their cellphones, recording and taking pictures. After Mr. Zanis was done, he stood there a moment, took off his hat and said something quietly to himself. As there was nothing left to see, the crowd began to thin. This memorial to the dead would not be removed today.

Lauren gave Zanis a nod goodbye. They would see each other again, she was sure. Friends of the dead.

It was time to go ask for that favor. She crossed the street and opened her car door. As soon as she sat down and closed the door, her phone rang. She answered as soon as she saw who it was.

"Ruth..."

"Lauren," she sounded distraught. "We found Fin in her room. She's dead."

CHAPTER 23

He agreed to meet her on campus between classes. He chose Rockefeller Memorial Chapel. It was a cruel reminder, but Lauren agreed.

When she pulled open the heavy wooden door she did not know what to expect; perhaps a service in full swing? A baptism? Or worse, a wedding? She had not been in a church except for a funeral in so long she was unsure of the protocols.

The space was empty.

Sun poured in through the stained-glass windows. All of the interior lights were on as well. Lauren took a seat at a pew near the exit.

The chapel was named after the University of Chicago's founder, John D. Rockefeller. It was his final gift to the university, completed in 1928. Unlike most buildings of the time, no structural steel was used in its construction, rather it was made with concrete that drove down to the heart of the foundation. The modern Gothic architecture was still a premier example of ecclesiastical structures in the United States. Not only was it an immensely impressive building, it was also where Bobby had proposed.

She heard the door open, and footsteps. He did not say anything as he placed his backpack on the pew and sat down.

"I'm sorry." Perhaps she said it first because she could feel the anger radiating off of him. She had been so short, so curt with him for so long, and when she realized that he could very well be the only person that could help her, she'd panicked. She had to set this right between them.

Bobby did not say anything. He must be incredibly furious, she thought. He was always talking, it seemed, except for now. Lauren knew she could always depend on him to fill the silence in the room, fill the gaps in a conversation. The last time she'd seen him before the funeral was at the grocery store, with a woman who looked nothing like Lauren could ever look. Smoothed hair, not a strand out of place. Fitted, structured jacket. Makeup, gleaming teeth. He was clean-shaven, pressed black suit, shined shoes and a red pocket square. She could smell him, and he smelled of fresh cedar on a summer day.

She had not realized it, but in the time they had been apart his hair had grayed in bunches all over his head.

"Thank you for saying that." His acceptance seemed forced, and while he did not have to be here he was, and that alone meant he accepted whatever weak apology she would offer.

Although, she wondered now what he thought she was apologizing for. Being short in her text message responses? Or for letting their marriage fall apart?

"I need your help. With a case."

"It's always about work with you, Lauren." He laughed.

"This is important."

"It's always important. What about you? How are you? Are you at least sleeping because look at you, you're certainly not eating. When was the last time you ate? Showered?"

"I..." Lauren could not answer that question because she did not know the answer "had coffee..."

"Lore," he threw his head back. "You can't do this. You can't become what your father became after Marie and your mother..."

"Diana, was not my mother," she growled. "She was my

stepmother."

"I meant your real mother. Lore...I just...I'm here. To help. Always."

She wondered if she should just get up and go. This was already a disaster. The problem with Bobby, she thought, is that his life was too wrapped up in obsessing over the structure of the stories he loved so much. He felt like someone always needed saving, and in this case, it was her. Bobby's interest lay in the remythialization of fairy tales. She had heard him give his lecture on it several times. She remembered it vividly.

"We cannot live without mythology," he had said at a lecture at the University of Chicago shortly after they married. "It's the way we reason. The way we survey. The way we make sense of our world. It's just that the stories we've been using—mythic stories, fairy tales, legends—they're not working for us anymore. We need something new."

She looked down the aisle of the church, to the empty pulpit. It was an unusual but marvelously simple design, a hexagonal space visible from every seat.

"I don't want to fight," she said. "This doesn't need to be hard."

He exhaled, relaxing into himself.

Devotion to their careers had always been common ground.

"I really loved your dad," he said.

"He really loved you, too. I think he was happy to have someone else in the house. The house felt alive, less..."

"Depressing," he finished her sentence.

"I was going to say haunted, but yes, less depressing too. It made him happy while you were there." She looked at him, studying his face.

He reached his hand out toward her face, tucking a strand of her hair behind her ear. "It's not up in a bun," he commented.

All she felt was this intense warmth and sadness, knowing that she had isolated herself with her dead victims, shutting out the living. Bobby had made her tremendously happy. She sometimes wondered if she loved him because of who he was. Or, did she love him because of who she became when she was with him? He allowed her to release the tension of murder and mayhem, if only for a little while. He made her feel like someone else in those moments. When she was with him, her mind did not flash to the dead. Bobby taught her about fairy tales—literal fairy tales and about heroes, villains, and ghosts.

"I'm proud of you," she said, "You belong at University of Chicago."

"I'm glad the university hired me. It saved me the trouble of having to move."

She had heard about his tenure from her dad. Bobby was brilliant.

"Did you get any other offers?"

"A few out East, but Chicago, she never lets you go."

The idea that he even applied outside of Chicago made her chest ache.

"What do you need help with?"

"I'm doing some research and need some help with folklore..."

"Folklore?" Bobby raised his eyebrow. "*You* want to talk about folklore?" He stifled a laugh.

She understood the animosity. One night while they were still living together, Lauren was studying the placement of a body in relation to where it had been found in a red line station, just feet away from where it would have been crushed by the train otherwise. The murder did not occur there, that they knew, but why move the victim to the train station? That had been what troubled her. As she studied the image, the nude, limp body of a woman, Bobby broke her concentration.

"Duffy and the Devil!" Bobby shouted from behind his laptop screen. "That's the variant I was looking for and couldn't find."

"What?' Lauren was confused, ripped away from the dank smell of the cold subway, the roar of the passing train, and the slumped, bruised and battered woman's body at the foot of the escalator.

"Rumpelstiltskin. You know?"

No, she did not know and did not really care, because at that point in her life, her need for fairy tale knowledge had been store away.

He continued. "The devil in Duffy and the Devil plays essentially the same exact role that Rumpelstiltskin plays in his fairy tale, and I got images of one of the original copies. Look."

He lay down a manila folder right beside her laptop.

"Can you not right now?" She closed her eyes for a moment and told herself not to scream at him. When she opened her eyes again, he was standing there with a look of confusion on his face. He had no idea what he had done so very wrong. He interfered with her concentration. He interfered with her work. "I'm in the middle of something important, and I don't have time for...fairy tales," she snapped.

"Right, because no part of my work is important."

"It's fucking fairy tales, and I'm trying to catch a killer!" She did not even realize she had stood up and was shouting, inches from his face. "Fairy tales are not real. None of them are real. What you're doing...it's just pointless."

It was as if she had shattered a glass between them. Each stood still for fear something else would break, that something else they said would cut. Bobby quietly reached for his folder and moved to the door. "Do you remember what you told me on one of our very first dates?"

She rolled her eyes. She did not want to talk about this.

"You asked me if I believed in the possibility that any of these stories could be true. I said perhaps some aspects of them. There's a little bit of truth in some of the stories that the Grimms brothers collected. These stories were collected by word of mouth, sometimes across small, rural towns in Germany hundreds of years ago. Many of these people believed what they were talking about. These stories explained what dark things happened in the forest at night. These stories explained why some people left and never came back, why some people were jinxed, and others were blessed. And I think there's some part of you that's terrified talking about fairy tales, and I want to know why."

"I'm just tired," she said, hoping that would explain why she said what she said and that this argument would just end.

"Tell me why you asked me that?"

Lauren refused to answer.

He took his folder, closed the door, and it was then she knew this marriage had to end, especially before more questions arose and he got hurt.

Lauren looked up to the ribbed vaulted ceiling in the church. Within the ribs were medallions. Bobby had told her long ago that these medallions represented emblems of the universe, the object of human study. Repeated in the nave were images of the sun, moon, stars, air, water, fire, and then there were the angels with their musical instruments. There was an angel with a tambourine, one with a drum, another with triangles, one with a horn, and then one playing a pipe.

"If something doesn't involve saving someone's life or finding some bad guy, then it's not good enough for you," he shifted his position on the pew.

"I said I was sorry."

"But, you're not really. You're sorry that you have to do this. That you have to go through the motions, apologizing for something you're not really sorry about because you need information. You use people, and the problem is I don't know if I can even be mad at you because you do it to help other people. And now you want *my* help, and there's nothing I can do or say other than okay. I'll help." His voice cracked, and her cheeks felt hot, and she almost regretted calling him, but he was all that she still had. Washington would be gone forever in days, and Van, well, what kind of partner was he considering he did not trust her?

Lauren wanted to diffuse the anger, and so she asked him something she thought he might want to talk about. "Sorry, forgot to ask how your girlfriend was..."

"I don't have a girlfriend, I don't date my students. We were on our way to a department party, and I bumped into her at the grocery store. I offered to drive her to the event. You left so fast you didn't let me explain."

She nodded. She was happy about that but did not want to admit it. Before he could say anything else, she returned to her purpose. "Fairy tales..." she said.

"What do you want to know? It's a pretty broad subject. I teach four sections of it to undergraduates and graduate students."

"Is there any importance to their settings? And, are there any places in Chicago that are similar? If that makes any sense."

He nodded and then said, "While it's not an enchanted forest, our city parks are probably the closest you could get to one. An enchanted forest contains...well, enchantments. Daniel Burnham recognized the power of green spaces, which is why he spread our great parks across the city like a necklace. Walt Disney knew the power of magic, and he was born right here in Chicago. The man is responsible for packaging fairy tales to the masses. And forests are even a common feature in his animations. The dark places. They can be found in the oldest of fairy tales. They're a representation of things unknown, of transformation. Forests also bring about a sense of adventure, wonder, refuge, dread, and danger." He stopped. "Aren't you going to write any of this down?"

"Don't need to," she raised her phone. "I'm recording it."

"Isn't it illegal to record somebody without their consent?"

Lauren shrugged. “Maybe.”

“You’re just like him, you know. He did a lot of things that bent the law in his favor.”

“How’d you know?”

“When you were working, who do you think was with him? I spent a lot of time with your dad. He needed someone to tell all of his old stories to who hadn’t heard them dozens of times before.”

“He hated me. He blamed me for all of them...”

“No, he didn’t. None of it was your fault. Some people are cursed with more tragedy in their life, and I’m sorry that’s been the case for you...”

“But why a forest?” She placed her phone back in her jacket pocket. “Why there?”

“In many of these stories people don’t go to the forests because they necessarily want to. Strange things occur in these places. Odd people live in these areas. The forests are home to fairies, witches and monsters. They can sometimes be places of refuge. The hero in many of the Grimm’s tales goes into the forest. These places are sometimes considered beyond the realm of human experience, and so act as a place of transformation. The kids found in Humboldt Park, you could consider their location to be as close to a forest as possible.”

Lauren fought back a smile. “Nice, making that connection and all.”

“It’s been all over the news, and you’ve always gravitated toward bigger cases if you could.”

He started to speak again, but he closed his mouth and shook his head.

“What?”

“Lore,” he paused. “There are similarities. You can’t ignore that.”

“Coincidences.”

“Are you kidding me?”

She closed her eyes because for just a moment she did not want to believe there was a connection, an eerily similar connection.

When the memories would come to her, they would come to her in snapshots, vivid, unsettling snapshots. Her cherubic-faced sister, all curls and big eyes screaming, arms outstretched, her body physically begging for help.

No words.

No sound.

Just the image of her sister and...water.

"That was a long time ago."

"So. Some people still remember. For those that don't remember, I can't imagine it's too hard to find out at least some details about what happened to Marie."

"Most of those details were sealed, at least to the public so as not to taint the investigation with any fake leads."

"Lore, some people know you're a detective. Some people know you're working this new case."

"Bad things happen at that lagoon all the time," she said with finality. "And you're not allowed to do that. You're not allowed to pick apart my life."

"You're right. You asked me to help you, and I'm here to help you."

Lauren thought back to the notebook and then asked, "Monsters then...a lot of these stories have monsters?"

"You could say that. Monsters. Ghosts. Demons, Boogeymen. Tricksters." Bobby paused. "I don't see what fairy tales have to do with murder."

"This helps. Tons. Trust me."

Bobby lifted the cuff of his shirt, checking the time on his watch.

"If you have to go, go," she said.

"I have a few more minutes. What do you plan to do with the house?" He asked.

"Keep it, but somehow remove all memory from it. It's home. I just need to clean it. I haven't gotten to my dad's room yet."

"The offer stands. I can tackle that for you, so you don't have to. And…this case," Bobby said, "if it's too much, maybe you should move away from it."

"I'm fine."

"Really, Lore? The book? The lagoon? Maybe these kids dug up something about your sister, and I don't know, are copying it. People do sick things."

She gave a dry laugh. "You sound like my partner. It's not the same. Just a bunch of messed up kids."

"Your dad tried to protect you from all of this."

"*Tried?* Just because you were around for a short time doesn't mean he really tried. How hard did he really *try* looking for my mother?"

"Years went by," Bobby said. "He had to move on. He tried. He never forgot. He never stopped looking for her."

Lauren closed her eyes and shook her head, seeing her mother standing at the stove, staring at burned cookies and laughing. She would grab the packaged ones on the counter and laugh harder. She always fixed everything. Bobby did not really know what it was like those last few months, living with a father dying of Alzheimer's who blamed her for her missing mother, murdered sister and the death of his second wife. Every time she would walk past the door to his bedroom, which he always had to leave open, he would shout: "Get the golden key, Lauren! The golden key! You'll find her with the golden key!"

"This, right here, right now, this isn't about me. I would like for everyone to stop saying that. My questions are about a recent crime that took place, that we still don't have all the answers to."

Bobby's phone began to chirp. "Class calls. If you want to wait..."

"I can't."

"I can text you a list of things to look at. Some websites, stuff for you to read through. It may help, and I can call you and talk through them..."

She smiled and felt her cheeks grow warm. "I'd like that."

The book, she thought. She needed to ask him about the book.

They both rose from the pews, and as they walked out of the chapel, Bobby asked, "Was there a specific fairy tale you were researching?"

"The Pied Piper."

He looked stunned, blinking rapidly. "That's a coincidence."

"Why?"

"The Newberry Library, they just put together a small collection, an event really, on just that, the Pied Piper of Hamelin."

She pretended to sound surprised. "It seems like a really niche topic."

Lauren's throat felt dry. Memories came rushing back in a series of pictures, cut and pasted onto each other. It had been many years, and still, those pictures came flooding in. Children. School desks. A teacher standing in front of a yellow school bus. Images of neighborhoods folding past as they drove. A red brick building. Holding onto the iron railing as she walked up marble steps. Green carpet. Books on heavy wooden shelves. Oil paintings of people from another place and another time watching over their moves. And then, the book.

"That's what they do. It's a research library, and they often hold specialized events."

"Is it possible to get a look at it? You must know someone there that put it together."

"If you think it would help."

She smiled. "There's actually one specific book in the collection that I'd like to see. The oldest."

Bobby shook his head from side to side slowly. "That's the question you wanted to ask all along."

"Maybe."

"I'll make sure you get to it. I'll call a friend. She owes me a favor."

"*She*?" Lauren did not mean to do that. She did not mean to imply anything.

"Her name is Valery. She's lovely, and so is her wife. She teaches part-time in my department but is on leave this term. They're expecting a son."

"You didn't have to..."

"I did. I'm not with anyone. Haven't been, and I don't know if you don't realize this, or if you're ignoring it, but I left because that's what you wanted me to do. When you are ready for me, I'll be here."

They walked together in silence down the aisle. Together, but apart. He asked where she'd parked, and she pointed to her car. Without hesitation, he took her hand as they walked, and she let him. He stood next to the door for a moment, perhaps calculating what to say next.

She closed the car door and rolled her window down to say goodbye.

"I'll call you," she said, starting the engine.

"I'm sorry..."

She did not know what exactly he was sorry for. Maybe he was sorry for even meeting her and getting involved with her life that just seemed like a black pit, dragging everyone around her into a state of sadness and despair. She did not know what to say other than, "Don't be."

When she motioned to him that she was going to raise the window, she spotted the gold band on his finger. He still wore it. Hers had been tossed in a drawer, something she did not want to look at or acknowledge, but something she knew was there in case she needed it.

CHAPTER 24

"All cultures have boogeymen. We don't know where they originate. We like to think from stories." Bobby said as he paced back and forth behind the podium he rarely used in this class. He preferred to stand, walk about the front of the classroom, or sit behind the desk.

"We can only look back to the oldest recorded story. But then we have to ask ourselves, what is the oldest story? Because the written word did not come until later." He clicked the remote, but realized he had reached his last slide. He had been speaking for most of the lecture. Class was almost over, but he needed to stress these next few points.

"Stories were originally sang, or simply just told." He stood behind his chair, hands on the seat back. "Think about the troubadours, those loyal lyrical poets who went from town to town. Not all of their stories were centered around music and poetry. Many sang about real people and places, telling news from their travels. They also shared fantastic tales about adventure, heroes, princesses, knights, dragons, and magic. What, if any, of those stories the troubadours shared were too grim to be repeated? What, if any, of those stories were too horrific to share? What if some of those troubling tales remained in those towns because townspeople feared that the story was *too* evil?"

He looked about the room, feeling the energy deflate as eyes fell away from him.

"Because," he raised his voice "there was a belief that telling these horrific tales gave it power—motivation to morph into something more wicked—something beyond a story, beyond a thought: a virus."

"What is the oldest known fairy tale?" He asked the class, and a few people guessed names, but he picked out the correct answer from the audience.

"The Smith and the Devil," correct. It's a very simple premise. The iron smith sells his soul to the Devil in exchange for supernatural powers. The Smith eventually uses those same powers to trap the Devil, which I suppose the Devil should have seen coming. The Brothers Grimm are given much credit for the fairy tales they compiled in *Kinder-und Häusmarchen* in 1812, but fairy tales go farther back, thousands of years before that. "The Smith and the Devil" likely stretches back 6,000 years. Why have they remained with us so long, evolving, shifting, but still, the premise is the same? Because of the combination of the fantastic and the ordinary. "Beauty and the Beast" is a story about a man magically transformed into a monster. That's the fantastic. The ordinary part of that story is that it's just one about family and love."

Bobby scanned the faces of his students. Many hid behind their laptops and tablets. Others tried to hide that they were scrolling through their phones, their eyes drawn downward, here but not.

"Think about these things. Think about how these stories have influenced our thoughts and behavior around fear. How these tales of heroes, kings, princesses, brave children, devils and villains, of especially the boogeyman, which we concentrated on today, have influenced our culture. Quick," he raised a hand as a show of encouragement "Give me some examples of boogeymen..."

"The Pied Piper," someone shouted from the back of the room before anyone else could say anything.

Bobby took a step back and glanced at his seating chart. He did not recognize the boy in the blue hoodie. The room was dark as he had dimmed the lights for the presentation, but this boy was utterly cast in shadows. When he realized that there had been too much of a gap in between the boy's suggestion and his response and that the sounds of students rustling in their seats had increased, he spoke.

"That's interesting. I was just talking about the Pied Piper earlier today, but yes, he is an acceptable example of the boogeyman."

"I saw something about that online the other night," a girl in the front row said. "There's someone calling themselves the Pied Piper, killing people in the city."

"Let's keep the discussion relevant please," Bobby said.

Someone laughed. "It is relevant. Killer. Boogeyman."

"Serial killer," someone else said.

"I saw the graffiti. There was some over the Kennedy Expressway," another boy said. "It was right out there tagged on a billboard, 'Pied Piper.'"

Another student responded, "It's an internet game people play. Make a deal with the Piper, and he'll get rid of your pest. Just like he got rid of pests in the fairy tale, except here pests are people."

"How do you play?" A girl in the center aisle turned around and asked. "I've got more than enough people I want to get rid of."

"You call him three times like Candyman. Stand in front of a mirror with a candle and say a rhyme or his name or something, and he appears."

"Someone, text me those instructions," a student said as he was scrolling through his phone followed by laughs.

"Didn't he kill the town's kids because the mayor didn't pay him for getting rid of the rats?" A girl asked.

"Yes," the boy in the back responded again. "Professor." He looked in the direction of Bobby, but Bobby could not see his face from this distance, just the outline. His face was blurred by the shadows.

Bobby rubbed his eyes. He was tired, he reasoned, and his eyesight was worsening over time, all of those late nights in front of his computer screen.

"Yes..."

"You mentioned "The Smith and the Devil," but what about older stories? There are mythologies surrounding forests. What about the god Pan? He's much, much older than any fairy tale."

"You're right," Bobby said, walking over to the light switch. "But this is Comparative Folklore and Fairy Tale. Ancient Mythology is being taught by another professor." He flipped the light switch, but the lights did not turn on. He tried again. Nothing.

"Can someone explain this whole Pied Piper thing, because I'm lost. Who is using his name to kill people?" A male student said from the middle row.

Bobby returned to the podium. "Okay, fine, then let's deconstruct this," Bobby said. "If there is someone killing people using the Pied Piper's name, then why? Why use *that* character's name?"

The class remained silent. Bobby pressed. "Think about everything we discussed today. What is the Pied Piper?"

"He's a villain?" A boy in the middle of the room said as he yawned.

"Yes, and what else?"

"He's a boogeyman," a girl said as she tied her dark hair back in a ponytail. "There's no specific reason why. He's a villain and a boogeyman, and it's all about chaos for the sake of chaos and what better place to bring chaos then to Chicago where a bunch of young people are already suffering high rates of crime."

"Interesting," Bobby said, nodding his head. "Chicago is a city, but it does have many parks. So, the setting is there. Most people associate fairy tales with enchanted forests. Sometimes they can be places of refuge. Snow White found refuge there with the dwarves from her stepmother. But other times, the forests are places where there are monsters. One of the oldest tales, the *Epic of Gilgamesh* has the hero going to the forest to defeat monsters."

"So, you're saying stay away from trees?" A boy asked, followed by laughter.

"Maybe," Bobby said jokingly. "In all seriousness, if we can talk about fairy tales with real reason, most people associate the forests in fairy tales as a scary place, a place where the unknown lives, and the unexplained happens. There are some woods so dark that no one dares enter. Our heroes are often warned beforehand, but they still charge forward."

The boy in the back of the room with the hoodie leaned forward in his seat. He raised his hand, and Bobby called on him.

"It likes those dim places, where the light barely penetrates. Those sunless places welcome suffering. Chicago makes a good temporary home. There's suffering enough here which is why that symbolism could work in this city. This is the home of the once largest stockyards on the planet. The World's Hog Butcher they called Chicago. Where millions of animals were slaughtered. Millions of pounds of animal innards, skin and waste, were dumped in the Chicago River. The river forever turned a murky green. Bubbly Creek, it was called then and now, because the decomposition of the animal remains left there produced gases that bubbled to the surface, producing a stench that stretched across the city. The sick smell of death infected everything and everyone from that river and still does. There's something about that, about Chicago, about this infection, about it being a consistent host to horrible things that it just continues to breed horrible things. The Fort Dearborn Massacre, Chicago Fire. Eastland Disaster, Camp Dearborn, the Saint Valentine's Day Massacre. Numerous serial killers. It's as if Chicago is the perfect setting for a dark fairy tale."

The mystery student's words made Bobby's face grow cold. He felt as if he were in a trance, and he broke free only when the boy stopped speaking. Bobby pressed the home button on his phone. They had gone two minutes past the hour.

"We can pick this back up next week," he said dismissing the class. Students stuffed their bags with their devices, notebooks and pens and streamed out of the room. On passing the switch, one of them flipped it and the lights turned on.

Bobby made sure the projector was off and reached for his bag when a student approached.

"Professor Garcia, I have a question about the boogeyman. Can he be equated with humanity's depiction of death?"

While he would be willing to discuss this during class hours, so the rest of the class could hear, he was too tired to go on about this to a single student, he felt drained of all energy.

"That's a good question, and we can discuss it next week."

The student gave a weak smile, turned, and exited the room.

Bobby erased his notes from the whiteboard and placed the eraser back on the ledge. He walked towards the door and then turned around to give the room a quick look to make sure it was in the same condition he found it in.

It was at the door that he noticed something, a sheet of paper on top of one of the far back tables. He looked at it for a moment from afar and then searched the room again, making sure there was no one there because he was certain there had been nothing there moments before. He approached the table slowly and looked down. It was a single sheet of ruled notebook paper. On it, the following words were written:

In the year 1284 on the day of Saints John and Paul on 26th June. One hundred and thirty children born in Hamelin were led away by a piper clothed in many colours to their Calvary near the Koppen, and lost.

Bobby balled up the sheet of paper and looked around the room again. He felt an icy shiver up his spine. He rushed to the door and threw the crumpled mass in the trash on his way out.

He ran, cheeks red, and chest burning straight to his office to call Newberry Library. He felt the urgency of Lore's request now. He would get her access to that book *now*.

CHAPTER 25

Lauren stood on the corner. She counted the number of cars that went by in ten minutes. There were thirty.

Someone must have seen something, even if it had been so many years ago.

She walked to the end of the block and counted the number of houses on either side. This was the same time of day when the Brady sisters had gone missing long ago.

People went missing in Chicago. It happened.

It was a city, and, in a city, things moved. People moved. But more than often they would return. Of course, sometimes things didn't end happily. An elderly family member would leave their house, get on a bus, and never been seen from again. In those cases, Lauren assumed they wound up homeless and helpless under a viaduct either in this cold city or another, or something worse. It's the something worse that she could not think about, particularly in the same thought as her real mother.

One day her mother was there and the next she was not.

Sometimes Lauren thought those very early years were a dream, a fantasy, a perfect family on a perfect summer day. Then came the stepmother who had a child, loved that child more than her, and Lauren was pushed away and left alone, all the while obsessing over where her real mother had gone. Fairy tales never told you the real mother's name or what happened to her. They only ever told you what happened to their suffering children, tortured by stepmothers and their cruel offspring.

Lauren sympathized with the dead, and especially with the missing like Chaunti Bryla, Rio Renee, Mercedes Matthew Keyser, Crumpton. Lizette Mata, Ciaro Rios, Saeid Rahidian, Brian Becker, and so many more. So many with eerie stories like Kiara Colson, a young, pregnant postal worker missing for over a year. Surveillance video captured her walking past her car. She was in her US Postal Service uniform, even though she had called her job and told them she was not coming. A case like that, a person who had completely vanished pained Lauren to her core. Where had they gone? Where were they? Had they fallen down a rabbit hole? Were any of them with her mother? Chicago was plagued with hundreds and hundreds of unsolved murders and missing persons cases. Lauren knew this was her purgatory, her reason for living to find them and set this right.

The case of the missing Brady sisters was as unusual. One hundred detectives had been assigned to their case at its height. All those detectives, Washington included, had walked this sidewalk, up and down, up and down, at all hours. Lauren wondered how many hours Washington had spent at this corner.

Washington talked a lot about this case. It haunted him. Each week when he came out here to walk up and down the block, to meet with whoever remained from the old neighborhood, he reopened the wound, sprinkled salt on it and plunged a rusty knife in it. And that's what a homicide detective did in many ways working on these cold cases; driving themselves into such utter consuming madness that they could only think about the cases they were working on in hopes that they could put something unseen together, to make out the image of the puzzle even though some pieces were missing. When they revisited the material over and over again, the pain of the loss of that person was punched again into the fabric of reality.

Washington had told her how he'd interviewed and re-interviewed Brady family members and suspects. He was younger then, and had been one of the first to don a protective suit and dive into the Humboldt Park lagoon searching for anything that could lead to where the girls may have gone. Washington jumped into dumpsters, sifted through garbage, and interviewed anyone in jail and out of jail who could have possibly known anything. He told Lauren how he had personally coordinated the interviews of a hundred sex offenders in the area. He had followed tips personally for years, even driving down to a small central Illinois town where a tipster stated the girls were being held. Nothing came from it. Still, everyone was a suspect, and yet no one was a suspect.

"Hey Detective Lauren," a high-pitched female voice called out, followed by a cackle. "Woman, you need you an umbrella, it's about to pour."

Chicago could not decide if she wanted to allow winter in or the fall to linger. Snow flurries had turned to cold rain. The skies had darkened, and the city was scheduled to endure thunderstorms through the morning.

"I'm good," Lauren gave a weak smile. "Cold November rain is to be expected." She had stood out in the rain during so many cases the cold did not bother her anymore.

"Get up here on this porch and give me a hug."

"How are you, Wilhelmina?"

"Detective, stop, it's Mina." She motioned for Lauren to hurry up the steps of the house. "I'm doing better than you, honey." Mina gave Lauren a full, deep hug. The kind your mother or aunt would give you after not seeing you for a time. "You're fading away. You need to get some good food in you."

"Just coffee's good."

Mina gave her a wave. "Food too," her eyes widened. "Now, come inside."

Mina had come outside plenty of nights to give Washington a hot cup of coffee and a few minutes of pleasant conversation. Lauren had met Mina several times, and immediately felt like the woman was family.

Mina tugged Lauren inside and over to her living room table. "I made breakfast."

"Apple juice and miniature muffins?" Lauren noticed the spread on the table.

"Ha, that's for the kids. Not us."

Mina ran an at home daycare out of her house. She cared for kids from the neighborhood. After the Brady sisters had gone missing, her house had been one of the first places Washington had visited, hoping that the little girls would go someplace with other children.

"I've got some scrambled eggs and French toast in the kitchen," she said, taking a seat at one of the large wooden chairs in the living room. "Coffee's hot, too."

A plate appeared before Lauren could protest. One of Mina's aides had placed it down and walked away.

Mina took a long gulp from her coffee mug and said, "Another anniversary is coming up."

"You haven't asked me where he is," Lauren picked up a fork and took a bite of eggs. It was the best thing she had tasted in days, and now she realized her diet had mostly consisted of dry cereal at home.

"I know where he is, packing up his life and heading off to where a lot of people go to when they leave this city." She leaned forward, "A better place. Don't get me wrong. I want him to find peace from this. These girls. This city stole a lot from him. It's good that he finds a place that hopefully will give him some love before his time ends. Until then," Mina set her cup down and slapped the tops of her thighs with her hands "There'll be the rest of us to sit here and make sure our own are protected."

Lauren swallowed back fresh homemade French toast and her

stomach thanked her. "I thought about these girls..." Lauren started.

"Don't you start, too, Detective Lauren. This case will hurt you as much as it hurt him, and I know you've got enough heartache behind you and ahead of you."

"Mina, do you remember that graffiti that was painted on the building across the way after the girls went missing? You reported it sprawled across the wall of the corner store right next door."

"Yeah, I remember. Only because when the police went back to check call logs, including those service calls to 3-1-1, they asked me about it. It was fresh. I remember that."

"This was it, correct?" Lauren pulled up an image on her phone and showed it to her. The word "Pied" sat above the word "Piper."

"I found this looking through old crime scene photos, and this is the best one I could find that showed this graffiti."

Mina tapped the screen. "That's it."

"Who do you think was involved with the disappearance of those girls?"

"Same person I told Washington. Their father."

"Do you think their father killed them?"

"I'm convinced. But there was just nothing. No evidence. Nothing at all."

"And if you had to bet the father did it..."

"He did *something* to those girls. Again, Washington tried everything, but there was just no evidence. He was a young father. He didn't want to have two little girls. He was at work that whole day. There was clear proof of that, but Washington could never connect it to their dad no matter what he checked out or who he talked to. But Washington tried. He gave those girls so many years of his life, trying to find them justice. It's nice to know that he was around to think about those girls, worry for them."

Mina sighed, and just then, the doorbell rang. One of her students had arrived early to start their day.

Lauren thanked Mina for the coffee and meal. She gave Mina a hug and felt saddened because, in a way, the Brady sisters would be forgotten without Washington, their sentinel who had carefully kept watch over their case for so long.

When Lauren got in her car, she pressed her head on the steering wheel and closed her eyes. She felt a moan rising in her throat. It finally clicked. Washington had never noticed the graffiti. Plus, he would not make anything out of it if he had seen it. This was not just another random act of vandalism. Lauren knew now that the case that had plagued Washington for so many years could be answered simply—the Pied Piper had murdered those girls, and likely at their own father's request.

He was out of the story, out of the book, because he had been summoned so long ago. Lauren needed to get to that book and rip out that page and destroy those words so that he could never be petitioned again.

Would he know she was coming to stop him?

CHAPTER 26

Lauren had been to Newberry Library just once, a long time ago. During that field trip for Mr. Sylvan's class her first year of high school.

"Newberry is an independent research library with an extensive non-circulating collection of rare books, maps, music, manuscripts, and other printed material spanning over six centuries," Mr. Sylvan had said.

As they walked up the stairway to the second floor, Mr. Sylvan had told his class that the library's collection included over 1.5 million books. Just as Lauren felt skeptical that all of the books could not possibly be held here in this building, Mr. Sylvan had clarified that some books were kept in a facility next door.

"The majority of the Newberry's collections are stored in the stacks building, which is not open to the public. When you request a book, manuscript, or a map, a staff member goes to the stacks building and retrieves that specific item. They are then brought to the reader in one of the reading rooms. And as you noticed, there are a few rules that need to be followed in the reading room."

He led the class up two more flight of stairs to a large room with emerald green carpeting and long dark wood tables and chairs.

"Thank you for leaving your items on the bus. Just to reiterate, no food or beverages are allowed here, nor are backpacks, book bags, scotch tape, glue, post-it notes, highlighters or markers." Mr. Sylvan bounced on his heels as he inspected his class as they entered the room. He held a handout, directing them over to the large wooden tables at the far end.

"A few other items to note. Pencils—not pens—must be used. You'll find white sheets of paper and pencils in front of you. Again, we are in the Special Collections Reading Room. This room has a specially regulated temperature for some of the books we're going to be viewing today to protect the material."

He motioned to the items in front of each pair of chairs that were covered in a black cloth. He looked around the room. Lauren could see that everyone seemed disinterested.

"Gently remove the cloth from the top of your pieces," he'd said.

There were a few sounds of 'What's this?' and a few gasps as people unveiled the antique books they would be handling today.

"I made this exercise easy for you. There's an envelope next to your book and within that is a card that gives you the title, year published, author, and the significance of that work. Take five minutes, review, and then we'll go around the room, and you can share what you have."

The big brown book in front of Lauren looked weather-worn and damaged. It smelled like their basement after it flooded, and she hesitated to even touch its binding.

"Time's up," Mr. Sylvan said, his tone just below a shout. "Let's start over here." He pointed to the girl seated next to Lauren. "What do you have?""

This is a first edition *Frankenstein* by Mary Shelley Wollstonecraft, which is pretty cool."

"It *is* pretty cool," Mr. Sylvan said. "We'll be reading that in the coming weeks."

Lauren clumsily took hold of her card. It slipped and fell out of her hands and onto the table. She took hold of it again, her cheeks flushing pink. "This is a really old book."

She looked to Mr. Sylvan, who smiled encouraging. "Just read the card," he said.

"Right, it's the *German Popular Stories* by...umm...the Brothers Grimm from 1823."

"Very good. That's their second edition. We're reading some of the Grimm's works in the coming weeks."

"Fairy tales?" She asked.

"Yes," Mr. Sylvan said and then moved to the next person.

As people continued to present, Lauren stared at the plain cover. She wondered how many hands had touched the binding. The book was over a hundred years old. Had seen so much. Had traveled so far. She turned the cover. The leather binding feeling almost like human skin between her fingertips. She looked at the elaborate ink stamped image from a publisher long gone. She turned the page and found a table of contents in a language she could not read: German.

She continued turning pages, fascinated by intricate script. She turned pages in chunks of twenty or thirty pages until she landed on a page with the title "Rattenfanger von Hamelin." It was not the title that made her pause, it was the single black page with golden script written in English which she could read.

As Mr. Sylvan continued going around the room. He did not notice her, and so Lauren read:

Pied Piper of Hamelin
Please remove my worry
Payment will be in blood
To get the deed done
If I fail to meet my obligation
I'll offer the ultimate item for confiscation

Before Lauren knew it, she was saying the words softly under her breath. When she finished, she looked around the room. No one had noticed what she had been doing. Mr. Sylvan was talking to the last student about the book in front of him. It was a first edition Agatha Christie novel, *The Murder of Roger Ackroyd.*

Mr. Sylvan told them all how Agatha Christie was the "grande dame" of mystery and suspense. Lauren had learned very early on in the class how to tune out Mr. Sylvan, and so she did. She scanned the room, noting the large windows, and the large bookshelves. She looked back to the doorway they had entered through.

She gasped when she saw him. A tall, pale, gaunt man stood in the doorway wearing a dark suit. Something about him made him look not like a man, not like from this era, or even human, but she could not tell what it was that made him so strange. He raised a hand and waved, just to her.

No one else seemed to notice him.

The girl seated next to her gave her a dirty look and moved her chair an inch away. Mr. Sylvan glanced in her direction but was now remarking how *The Murder of Roger Ackroyd* was not only one of Christie's best works but one of the best crime novels of all time because of the twist at the end.

When Lauren looked back to the doorway, the strange man was gone.

"Where's the bathroom?" Lauren had asked as she stood up. Mr. Sylvan continued speaking and only pointed out the doorway they had entered.

Lauren rushed to the door. She found herself in the room that was taken up by old card catalog cabinets. Mr. Sylvan had mentioned that the library was in the process of phasing out the old card catalog system. People were moving their research online. They could all very soon be able to request books online from their home, and when they visited the library, the books would be waiting for them here.

Lauren passed the aisles of large, gray metal filing cabinets. Searching. She approached the final aisle. Then she'd heard it. A low, soft, airy tone. It was just a few notes, but it was full of melancholy.

He had been standing at the far end of the aisle, leaning against the wall. A flute in his hands, his lips pressed against the instrument. When he saw her, he dropped it. It fell to his chest, hanging there by a black string. His clothes were black. A black wide brim boater hat rested on his head. His eyes were black marbles. His skin a sickly gray.

He smiled a sharp smile.

He removed his hat and gave a bow.

"I am at your service," he said.

Today, they entered an empty reading room.

"I get a private room?" Lauren mused. The emerald green carpeting was still there.

"It's better that way so that the patrons don't get nervous…with the gun and all," Sara said, looking down to Lauren's holster.

"Sorry, should've worn a longer jacket," she said as she took a seat.

On the table behind where Sara had brought her, there was a massive book that had taken up nearly half the table.

"Maps?" Lauren asked.

Sara smiled. "The *Malleus Maleficarum*. It translates into roughly the Hammer of Witches. It was written by Catholic clergyman, first published in Germany in 1487. It endorsed the extermination of witches. It was also the second most sold book behind the Bible for 200 years."

"Witches?" Lauren arched an eyebrow.

"These people weren't real witches, in the supernatural sense."

"But that's what the authors believed?"

Sara nodded.

"I don't believe in the supernatural," Lauren offered, even though that was false. If she did not really believe, she would not be here right now.

“You *are* here to look at a book of fairy tales,” Sara motioned to a covered book at a nearby table. Sara instructed Lauren to wear white cotton gloves provided and to turn the pages slowly. Also, she was not to lift the book up from its bed.

“Make sure it rests well there...like Sleeping Beauty.”

“Funny.” Lauren was not amused by the joke, but Sara did not seem to care.

Before Sara left Lauren asked, “Could you let me know who else has requested to see this book...for the past I don’t know, ten or twenty years?”

“I’m assuming you don’t have a warrant and you’re hoping that I’ll just show it to you because I’m that kind?’

“A lot of being a cop is really asking people for things and hoping they are kind enough to do it.”

“I’ll do it in the hopes that you catch the criminal that you’re looking for.”

The book did not look spectacular. Its cover did not have gold lettering. It looked old, much older than an old library book perched high up on a shelf no one would ever reach for.

Carefully, she turned the cover. Then, even more precisely, she turned the next page, feeling the sensation of the paper beneath the glove. She stopped at the table of contents. The list of stories within the book ran down the length of the page on the left and right. She proceeded to turn pages as she had so many years ago, turning, turning, searching, but finding nothing. It was then that she found a gap where the book opened naturally to where a page had been ripped out. The black page with golden script was gone.

“Here you go.” Sara reappeared and took a seat beside Lauren.

Lauren closed the book.

Sara handed her a printed page. “I can’t stand very long these days,” Sara said. “I’m retiring in three weeks. I’ll be back here volunteering, but it's time I take a very long trip. Germany's on my list," she nodded over to the book.

Lauren gave her a questioning look, all the while her heart raced wondering, who had torn out that page. Who had the rhyme? And worst of all, with the rhyme out of the book, how many people could now call him? She looked at the request sheet, Mr. Sylvan from DePaul College Prep once this year, once last year, and then there was a large gap with her year being the last time the book was requested, over ten years ago when Lauren had reviewed it, but then once yearly before that.

"Wilhelm and Jacob Grimm were German, and that's where they collected nearly all of their tales, Germany."

The Brothers Grimm. When Lauren first heard their name, she could not help associating it with the adjective grim, forbidding or uninviting. It was odd, in a way, for a name associated with children's literature to be a homonym with a word that was related to dangerous and harsh things.

"Do you know a lot about Chicago history?"

Sara laughed. "What do you mean by 'a lot'? This city has a long, complicated history."

"It was settled by a diverse group of immigrants, including Germans?"

Sara nodded and crossed her right leg over her left, rubbing her knee. "Germans, Czechs, Italians, Poles, yes."

"And I imagine a lot of them brought their...stories with them?"

Sara tilted her head. "You mean, superstitions?"

"Yes."

"Does this in part, explain the interest in fairy tales?"

"A little bit." It was then that Lauren could only assume that this cursed book had traveled here with someone from Germany long ago. Maybe it was a bookseller. Perhaps it was a regular citizen. Or, perhaps it was someone who had to unload this damned thing somewhere.

"I hope you enjoy your retirement and your trip. I won't keep you any longer, but thank you," Lauren said.

"Will we see a dramatic capture on the news, soon?"

"You'll be seeing something on the news, I'm sure." Lauren slipped off the gloves, set them on the table, thanked Sara, and walked out of the building.

Once she got to her car, she felt as if she had allowed a bomb to detonate in the world. She should have returned years ago, she had known that. Others had called him, and she should have set fire to that book or that building in order to stop him before he had collected more people.

CHAPTER 27

Today was Washington's last day in Chicago. After this, he would be a permanent retiree. Washington had made it clear he did not want a party. "I'm just a man who cares about the law," he said as he held up a glass of champagne at his forced send-off at the precinct. His desk had finally been cleared. There were tears, from nearly everyone except Washington. He did not have any more tears to cry, he'd once said.

Washington was strangely quiet on the drive to the airport. Perhaps it was the shock of knowing that this was the last time he was leaving this city as a Chicagoan. Yes, he would return for his son's graduation at Northwestern, but beyond that, how often would he be back?

Lauren exited at the O'Hare International Airport exit off the Kennedy Expressway. She drove steadily towards Terminal 5, International Departures.

Washington had his hand on his right knee. His leg shook the entire drive.

Lauren pulled up to the curb, placing the car's hazard lights on.

"If you get a ticket, just blame Van," Washington said.

"I don't mind getting a ticket. I just don't want to get towed," she said.

Washington released his seat belt and opened the door. Standing on the curb, he stretched. Lauren opened the trunk of the car and carried his bag over to him.

"Stop, you didn't have to do that."

"Please, you're an official retired senior citizen. Your goal should be to live an easy life."

Washington's voice cracked. "I miss your dad, and I'm going to miss you, kid."

Before she could step in and give him a hug, he started crying.

"No, Washington, don't." She hugged her former partner, one of her only friends.

He released his hold. "There's something I need to tell you." He took both of her hands in his.

"I promise to take it easy on coffee, and I promise to eat and sleep."

He laughed. "This is serious." He pressed his lips together, looked up to the sky, and then finally met her eyes. "I know," he said, and that was all that he needed to say.

"I..." She did not know what to say. There really was nothing left to say.

He nodded as if telling her she did not need to speak. "At your dad's funeral, I let myself into his office. He was trying to put something together right before he died. He didn't finish it, but I was able to. It's on his desk. You're welcome to look at it. Do whatever you think is right. I put the key back in the cupboard."

Washington gave her one final hug. He promised to call. To email. To text.

Lauren leaned against the car and watched as he walked through the automatic doors and out of her world.

Playing chauffeur all morning, first driving Washington to the airport and then Jordan to Hadiya's funeral almost made her late.

To another funeral.

She had not been to this church since Diana was alive. The part of this church that left the biggest impression on her was the chapel in the basement. The old deacon had told her and Diana after one Easter mass in the chapel that the stone that made up the altar was transported from the southwestern French town of Lourdes. Diana's mouth had dropped. Lauren did not understand her immediate excitement. Lauren later learned that in the foothills of the Pyrenees mountains, the Virgin Mary had appeared to a young woman,Bernadette Soubirous, on nearly twenty occasions. The Catholic church went on to confirm the authenticity of the sightings as well as meeting Bernadette's demands of building a chapel at the location of her sightings. Dozens of people had claimed to have been miraculously healed by the spring water that runs through that mountain. Lauren did not understand what the big deal was. How could people just blindly believe a young girl had seen a supernatural being?

"Couldn't she have been lying? She was just fourteen years old. Maybe she was doing it to get attention?" Lauren had later asked Diana who was going through a book of songs on her desk.

"At first no one believed her. I'm sure it was investigated thoroughly, for that time. She's a saint now."

"But..." Lauren stammered. "There's no way to prove you're seeing something the person next to you cannot see."

Diana looked up from the book and crossed her arms. "There's nothing I can tell you other than you're right. Maybe she made it all up. Maybe she didn't see the Virgin, but I guess that's what faith is. Wholehearted belief in something. In this case, it's complete belief that challenges all of our laws of reality."

As the Father in the church spoke, Lauren was struck with an overwhelming sense of nostalgia, the smell of frankincense, the light streaming in through the stained-glass windows on either side casting colored shadows, and the steady hum that vibrated in this place.

A man approached her and asked if she would be interested in doing one of the readings. She hesitated but then looked around and realized very few people were capable of separating themselves from their grief today, fixated on the closed white coffin in front of them. The boy inside who would never graduate high school, who would never go to college, who would never smile and laugh and love again. Daniel.

"Corinthians 15:50-57," she began, and the words just tumbled out.

"Where, O death, is your victory? Where, O death, is your sting?

The sting of death is sin, and the power of sin is the law.

But thanks be to God. He gives us the victory through our Lord Jesus Christ."

Lauren looked out over the congregants. "The word of the Lord," she concluded. The congregation responded, "Praise to you, Lord Jesus Christ," in unison.

Lauren closed the book and placed it on the lectern and then carefully walked down the marble steps. She returned to her seat in a pew in the back.

As the father stood and approached the lectern to give his homily, Lauren thought of Diana and Marie and how she hated both so much. Diana came in and tried to be her mother, but Lauren had already had a mother out there in the world somewhere. And then there was Marie who one day said, "You don't have a real mother, Lauren. Your mother is dead. My mother said so because she's been gone so long she must be dead."

And Marie had laughed and laughed.

Lauren noticed the chipped and scratched wood back of the pew in front of her. The green linoleum floor with white and black swirls that were so old they were bubbling in areas. The floor had a permanent sheet of dust. As she worked her eyes upward, she noticed the names at the bottom of each stained-glass. "Donated by the Richmond's," "Donated by the Mularz's," and so on. The church was founded in 1910, and these were names of those families who had lived in this neighborhood long ago and who had contributed to this building.

None of those original families remained. She was sure of that. That was one of the many terrible things about Chicago. So, few people remained in this city of wind for long, blown away by hope or terror.

The father concluded his sermon. It was now time for the Lord's Prayer. Lauren stood, recited the prayer, and gave the sign of peace to those closest to her, a short woman with red hair and glasses and an elderly man who sat two rows in front of her. His clothes were old but clean and well-pressed. His thin blue jacket looked like it was something from the 1980s.

When she returned to her seat, she could not bring herself to kneel, so she just sat there, thinking about those long-lost families. She wondered how much they had paid to donate a window. Did that donation put a financial strain on their family? Would they be happy to know that this congregation had changed so much?

Her mind wandered back to her reading as two parishioners walked the bread and wine to the front of the church where they would eventually be changed into something else by the power of faith. There was even a word for it, transubstantiation, which was the actual change of the substance of bread to the flesh and wine to the blood of Jesus Christ.

As the father held the Eucharist up towards the congregation, Lauren moved to the edge of the pew, on the outside aisle. She stood quietly and proceeded to walk towards the exit. She was careful not to let the door slam behind her. Lauren could feel the stares. She had come here to pay her respects to Daniel and his family, and she had.

She pushed on the door, and the bright light from outside, stung her eyes. She kept them closed for a moment, and when she opened them, she felt disoriented and overwhelmed.

Her phone rang, but she hit ignore.

She did not want to talk. If she opened her mouth right this second, she would cry. As the phone rang again. Lauren clutched it tightly in her hand and answered.

"Detective Medina..."

"It's Evie's mother, Virginia."

Lauren ran her free hand down her face.

"How's your daughter doing?" Lauren asked.

"Good—well, better. We talked this morning. I came back home to get her some more t-shirts and pajama pants so that she could be comfortable."

"That's great." Before Lauren could ask, Virginia told her what she had wanted to hear.

"She's ready to talk..."

"I can come by right now."

"She's having some tests done this morning so afterward should be fine." Virginia covered the phone. Lauren could hear her muffled grief. "In a couple of hours should work."

"I'll see you then."

Before Lauren hung up, Virginia stopped her.

"Detective, do we know what happened to Daniel? Evie wanted me to ask if you knew *exactly* what happened to him."

That was an odd question. Evie had been there that night. If anyone knew what happened to Daniel, it would be Evie. Lauren did not want to tell the woman that the medical examiner had determined the boy died of drowning. Lauren also did not want to tell the woman that whoever had held him underwater had put enough force on his trachea to crush it. It had been an agonizing death.

"He died quickly," Lauren lied, as she often lied to mothers and fathers, easing whatever pain they would carry for the rest of their lives.

"He and Evie were such good friends."

"I'm sorry, for some reason I thought that he was friends with only Finley and Mohammed. I have been trying to understand the connection of the four of them meeting at the lagoon together."

"She's known Daniel since they were in kindergarten. We didn't even know that's where she was going. We didn't know the others."

"Does Humboldt Park hold any significance for Evie, for you or your family?"

"Why'd you ask?"

"I'm just trying to determine if it had a larger meaning, them going there that night."

Virginia hesitated for a moment. The silence on the other end of the line confirmed to Lauren that there was something else, something that connected that place to her daughter.

"My sister drowned there many, many years ago when she was about Evie's age."

"I'm so sorry," Lauren cut in. "I'm so sorry. I have to stop at home, but I'll see you soon."

Lauren leaned against her car, looking up at the outside of those stained-glass windows, thinking how they have stood there through time, through Chicago's harsh winter snowstorms, powerful spring wind gusts and rain, and scorching summers. For over a hundred years, those images remained there, embedded into that building, intact, never changing while the neighborhood changed around it.

Now it seemed that the Pied Piper had been making regular treks to this city, and she knew he was not done. She needed to go home and collect her thoughts first until Evie was ready to talk. Lauren also needed to make one more phone call.

CHAPTER 28

Every time Lauren entered her home, she felt as though she were disturbing someone. It was not really her house. At least, it had never felt like her house. It was her parents,' and she stayed, not because she liked the neighborhood, or because she adored the historic red-brick bungalow with stained-glass window accents in the style of famed Midwestern architect Frank Lloyd Wright. She stayed living here in this house, in this city, because she did not know what else to do.

Lauren unzipped her boots and dropped them on the rubber mat beside the front door. The floor creaked beneath her steps. Lauren made her way past the living room, dining room, and into the kitchen. Even though it was still daylight outside, the house felt blanketed in darkness.

She opened the refrigerator. She looked at the containers stacked on the shelves, leftovers from the funeral. Lauren swung the door fully open and then dragged the garbage can over. She grabbed containers and tossed them into the bin. She did not want any of this food. She did not want to eat anything prepared for her in pity. When everything was gone, the only things that remained from her last purchase were eggs and bread. Lunch would be scrambled eggs and toast. She set the plate down on her desk as well as a mug of black coffee.

Outside noises made their way inside, cars hitting the speed bump just feet from her door. Horns beeped at the major intersection outside only one street over. Her phone vibrated, rattling on the surface of her desk. An email alert came through, and then another asking for her to call. She dialed his number as she read the subject line.

"I don't read German, you know that right, Bobby?"

"Good time, I assume?" He asked.

"There's no such thing," she took a bite of her eggs and then moved the plate away. "But it's you, so why not?"

"Oh, this is something new, Lore, being mildly kind to me."

She smiled but moved on quickly.

"I don't have much time. What is it I'm looking at?"

"It's from the Lüneburg manuscript..."

"I have no idea what that means, and you're going to have to tell me why that's significant."

"Do I sense a little bit of attitude there?"

"Wasn't a little bit." She paused and then corrected herself. It was not Bobby's fault she was exhausted and eager. He was trying to help and honestly if she were him she would not even answer her calls.

"I'm tired."

"Figured. Did you eat?"

"Yes, but I don't want to talk about me right now," she wrapped a hand around the coffee mug and took a sip.

"I get it. This manuscript gives an early account of an event that corresponds to some text that can be found inscribed on an old house in the town of Hamelin in Germany. If you scroll down, I translated it for you."

Lauren found the place and followed along with Bobby as he read aloud.

"In the year 1284 on the day of Saints John and Paul on 26th June. One hundred and thirty children born in Hamelin were led away by a piper clothed in many colours to their Calvary near the Koppen and lost."

"Translate it again. Koppen? What does this all mean?"

"This is high German Kuppe, Koppen. It means a dome or a hill."

"You're telling me that 130 kids were lost at a hill? In Germany? In 1284? I don't understand how that helps me."

"I'm telling you that on June 26th, in the year 1284, 130 children from the town of Hamelin were reported to have gone missing and they were led away by a piper wearing a suit of pied."

She remained silent.

Please remove my worry.

"Don't you remember the fairy tale?" he asked.

"Humor me. It was a long time ago."

"The piper leads the children to a forest, and only two children managed to escape. One of them was blind. The other was deaf. So the full extent of what happened could not be clearly communicated."

"You're saying that the variation of the story we know today is not really complete, then? Because it originated from these two children who could not tell the full story?"

Bobby laughed on the other line. "It depends on how much of these fairy tales you want to believe. We know the Grimm brothers collected these tales by interviewing people who lived in small villages and in rural homes. Many of these people believed strongly in magic and superstition. It was a way to explain the unexplainable of the world."

Payment will be in blood
To get the deed done

"Is this real?" She asked. "About the children? Is there any way to cross-reference it with a historical event?"

"There are theories as to what happened to the children. Some believe they were sent off to war, to be a part of some child brigade, that they were killed. Others just believe it's just that: a fairy tale."

If I fail to meet my obligation
I'll offer the ultimate item for confiscation

"What is he then? A person? A ghost? Demon?"

"A villain, a boogeyman, *the* boogeyman. There have also been some comparisons between him and the god Pan."

Lauren lowered her head into her hand. Her head began to throb. "Explain."

Bobby continued. "In Ancient Greek culture there were major and minor gods, one of those minor gods was Pan. Pan's worship centered around nature. People went to worship him in caves, grottoes, pastures, and forests. We get the word panic from Pan. He's also associated with the pan flute. There are plenty of mythical stories about his antics. I'd need to give myself a refresher, but the Pied Piper isn't a man or a ghost or a devil. If I had to categorize him, he'd be more along the lines of a trickster god. He'd be Pan."

"What does Pan look like?"

"Half man. Half goat. Almost like a centaur."

Half and half, she thought. A suit of pied. Pied means having patches of two or more colors.

"What if his patches were two or more beings?" She questioned. "And not a suit of pied, or any other suit?"

"I suppose. He's a trickster. He can appear however he wants."

"And if he had gotten his payment, who's to say he wouldn't have led the children away anyway?"

"I'm not following..."

"What if he always intended on taking the children? What if he always intended to kill them? He wanted the children all along. What if he knew that they were never going to pay him money for this service? What if he had always intended on taking them as payment? Maybe that's why he showed up mysteriously, unexpectedly? Because someone wanted him there to get rid of the children? He did not want the gold, or whatever payment. He wanted the children."

"I don't know...maybe that's why the definition of a trickster god fits in best. He made a deal. Yes, the deal was broken, but he took it to another level. Something evil."

"Just hear me out," she was already slipping on her jacket. "What if there are people out there that believe if you summon the Pied Piper..."

"Summon? How?"

"What if I told you there was a rhyme that summoned him?"

"Wait. What?"

"Listen, what if you had a person who was a problem. What if you called upon the Pied Piper, and he showed up and got rid of the person that was being a problem for you?"

"Got *rid* of?"

"What if he tricked you, never really making clear what the payment was for getting rid of that person? Never really clearly stating the terms and conditions for this contract of sorts? So, he comes back and demands payment, but this time you had to kill a person for him, a sacrifice, and he comes back again and again, each time he comes to town. He can call upon you as many times as he wishes, and if you don't follow through, then he'll take you...?"

"Lauren...are you okay?"

She set her phone on the floor as she pulled on her boots.

"I'm fine Bobby," she shouted towards the direction of the phone. "Look, I've got to go. I'm fine." She picked up the phone and zippered her jacket. "I'll explain later. Thank you."

"Wait, where are you going? I'm worried."

"To Lurie's Hospital. I have to interview someone."

CHAPTER 29

Ann & Robert H. Lurie Children's Hospital was ranked at the top regionally in pediatric specialties, and Evie was lucky that she lived in a city with an advanced children's trauma hospital who could attend to her severe injuries. She had been stabbed multiple times in her arms, legs, and torso. She had already undergone several surgeries, and her doctors anticipated many more, over a lifetime, to come.

Lauren knocked on the door. There was no answer. She pushed it open and found Evie sitting up in bed, a laptop open on the tray table in front of her. The girl seemed so small to be attached to so many tubes connected to soft beeping machines. Dark red, blue, and purple bruises covered her pale face, hands, and arms.

"Yeah?" Evie said, slowly closing her laptop screen.

"I'm Detective Medina. Your mother said you were ready to talk." Lauren took a seat beside the window. "Weird, guess I'm early." A view of the lakefront spread out before them.

"My mom's not here yet. She's on her way."

Lauren ignored her.

"She'll be here soon," Evie urged as if that would make Lauren get up and leave the room. "You're not supposed to be here. My mom said I'm not supposed to talk to anyone unless she's here."

"Yeah, I don't care," Lauren said, looking out the window. She tapped on the glass. "This is a nice view you have."

"I'm going to call a nurse," Evie said.

Lauren turned to her and smiled. "No, you're not." She crossed her arms across her chest and leaned back in the seat. "I don't have much to say other than Fin is dead, but I have a feeling you might already know that." Lauren crossed her legs.

Evie nodded.

"And, really, there's only one question I'd like to ask you." Lauren interlaced her fingers and lay her hands on top of her right knee and leaned forward. "Why did you kill Daniel?"

For a brief second, the corner of Evie's mouth curled up. "I didn't kill him. It was Fin. She pushed him down in the water, and..."

"Yeah, that's bullshit, and you know it. I just need to know why. Why did you kill Daniel?"

"I didn't kill Daniel," Evie said her voice trembling. "He was my friend. I loved him."

The tears came, and with that, Lauren laughed. "That's a lie, and you and I both know it. When Fin and Mo left, your arms were still wrapped around Daniel's neck in the lagoon. You drowned him. Forcefully, too. You crushed his damn trachea. The Pied Piper was there. He would have done it for you, but you didn't care. You hated Daniel so much you were fine with killing him yourself."

Evie looked down at her closed laptop.

"What were you working on before I got here?"

"Just looking at pictures," Evie said.

"Nice, I love pictures." Lauren stood up and sat in a chair directly against Evie's bed. "Let's see."

Evie eyed the nurse call button.

"You can press it, but then I'm going to have to tell my commander that I have evidence that Daniel was not murdered by either Fin or Mo." Lauren bit her lip and then said, "Weird. That would leave you as the only suspect."

The tears stopped quickly, and Evie brushed the wetness off her cheeks.

"He'd be mad if he knew you were here," Evie said. "He's watching you, too, you know. You're ignoring him. You owe him. Payment is due, Lauren. Why do you keep ignoring him? It's never going to stop."

Lauren took a deep breath and closed her eyes. She pressed the palms of her hands against each eye, and she listened as the girl continued. She listened, but she could see now, bright, sharp flashes of memory bursting before her. Her head throbbed. Her stomach hardened.

"Where's the page you tore out of the book?"

"It's safe." Evie laughed. "Under my bed at home."

"I'm going to your house, and I'm going to destroy that damn thing," Lauren said through her teeth.

"I mean, you *can*, but I already took a picture of it," Evie turned her laptop screen towards Lauren. "I posted it online at NeverSleep." Evie's eyes beamed. "It's all over the internet."

Lauren's mouth dropped, horrified. "You have no idea what you've done."

Evie laughed. "He's everywhere now. He's never going to stop. It's never going to stop."

Lauren stood up. Her back was to Evie and before her was the big, blue Lake Michigan. It looked like it stretched out onto forever, but it did not. It ended somewhere.

There was no point in wondering if Evie knew what she had done, and the conditions of the deal that she had struck. Evie was no victim in this. Evie was lucid. Evie was complicit. Evie had conjured a thing from another world, and she was pleased with the results.

"I hope you realize your deal with him will never be over," Lauren said as she stood up.

There was nothing she could do to save this girl. Evie was like her, beyond the possibility of salvation.

"I hope that you know what you've agreed to by murdering Daniel."

***

"Where?" Van shouted. It was getting dark now. The sun had set over the city, and the last few minutes of light were fading. He pressed the gas, pulling the car into a U-Turn, flipping on the siren and accelerating. Lauren watched as he turned off a major street and sped into a residential neighborhood.

Van pressed on the horn as he approached a stop sign, warning others that he had no intention of slowing down.

The dispatcher repeated the address.

"The hell is going on in Humboldt Park?" He shook his head and then murmured to himself. "It's gotta be a gang war, something," he tried to reason, but there was no reasoning here. "This is just too much weirdness in too few days."

"CIs haven't mentioned anything about a gang war," Lauren said. And her confidential informants did not need to. She knew what was going on. It was like water starting to boil, you did not see the bubbles at the bottom, but you knew things were getting hot, and soon the surface would erupt.

"You hear anything from that Jordan kid you're tutoring? Maybe he knows something?"

She eyed him with that are-you-serious look. "Are we friends now, Van? Best friends? Do you really expect me to tell you everything about my personal life?"

Van laughed. "You've got a lot of secrets, Medina."

"What does that mean?"

He pressed on the gas, and she reached up and held onto her seatbelt.

"Look, you've got to be careful. That's all I'm saying."

"I'm a mentor. He's my mentee. He's not a gangbanger. He's a kid whose best friend was shot and killed on the swings in the park. He doesn't know anything about the mess going on in these streets. He's a good kid. He's going to be somebody. Better than me."

"Medina," he gave her a pointed look, taking his eyes away from the road. "People out here, don't forget."

"I don't remember what happened," she shouted.

He raised a hand. "I'm not talking about your sister. I'm talking about LaShaun Donahue. I'm talking about Edgar Cruz. I'm talking about Madeline Kline. I'm talking about Hugo Jones. You've been on the force a handful of years, and you've shot and killed four people, besides those you've beat up badly. There are officers out here who have been on the force decades and have never discharged their weapon."

"I've been cleared in all of those cases. I was undercover and attacked in most."

"It doesn't matter. It doesn't look right and people out here, they're angry, and they don't forget, and then your mother, your real mother, sister, and your dad being on the force at the time, it's just," he shook his head. "It looks bad. That's all I'm saying, and that's why people out here don't like you. It's why these guys on the force don't like you. It's suspicious."

"About Marie, I was a kid and did nothing. About my job, it's my *job* to take down the bad guys."

Lauren turned away from him, looking out of the window, watching the reflection of the pulsating blue and red lights. It was hypnotic in a way. There was no way she was going to take life advice from Van.

The car began to slow. A firetruck was already on the scene when they arrived. An officer was securing the area with tape. The smell of burnt plastic stung Lauren's nose when she opened the door.

Van stood in front of her. "Lauren, we are the good guys, and bad guys live for taking us down. Just be careful, that's all I'm saying."

Alderman Suarez was standing in front of one of the police cars blocking the entrance of the alley. His hands were at his sides. Hands balled in fists.

"He's the last person I want to be dealing with right now," Lauren reached back into the car and grabbed her coffee cup.

"Do you really have to bring coffee into every single call?"

"It's for your benefit, Van."

"How so?"

"If there's something in one hand I'll be less likely to punch Suarez in the face with the other when he comes charging at us. Doubt you want your partner out on suspension."

"Your hot head is going to get you in real trouble one of these days, Medina."

"Hasn't yet," she took a sip.

"What the hell, Detective!" Alderman Suarez raised his arms up, motioning over to where the fire department was packing up a hose. The alley was sprayed down with water.

"You tell me, Alderman." Van said. "It's your ward. You live here. I don't. I live on the North Side. You know, the safe neighborhood."

"That was pretty good, Van" Lauren added.

"I'm going to call McCarthy," Suarez yelled after them as they crossed over the police tape.

"I don't care," Lauren said without looking back.

She covered her face for a moment, shutting away the smell of chemical thick in the air. The house where her real mother had grown up was just a few doors down. This she did not mention to anyone. It was not relevant.

Lauren had fond memories of visiting her grandparents in that house. Their red and white sofas protected in clear vinyl, lace white curtains hung in the windows, and the constant, soft soundtrack of salsa music from another time.

She remembered spending summer nights in this very alley, her grandparent's garage door would be opened, their cars would be parked in front to make room for the tables and white lawn chairs. Hot dogs and hamburgers would be on the grill, and her grandpa's requisite bottle of Bacardi would be sitting next to a two-liter of Coca-Cola. Neighbors would stop by, grab a hot dog, trade frustrations over the Cubs' floundering season and then head out to other parties.

Today, the alley looked different. Many of the new owners had installed six-foot tall wooden privacy fences. "Beware of Dog" signs hung prominently on gates. Many of the garages looked worn, paint chipped and cracked with broken siding. For those houses that had not had an enclosed porch built in the last decade, old furniture, brooms, mops, and toys took up what little space their porch held. The neighborhood felt changed, and it had been so many years since Lauren had even driven down this block that she could not say if asked what the most significant change from the old neighborhood was. It just felt…different.

"Who's our victim?" Lauren asked, slipping on her plastic gloves.

Van watched as she maneuvered, holding her coffee cup while putting them on. "Impressive," he said.

"Male. Hispanic. Young adult." The officer handed Lauren a fabric wallet. "Found this behind the garbage can. Must have fallen off when he was placed inside."

"Do we have any idea if he was alive when he was placed inside?" She flipped open the wallet and found herself looking at a high school junior's ID. "DePaul College Prep. Fabian, Thomas."

A few neighbors appeared at their back gates. One of them opened their garage door to get a clearer look at the chaos. He was in a thin black jacket, pajama pants, and slippers.

"I called three times already," the man shuffled toward Officer Guerrero. "These kids keep writing crazy stuff all over our property. Gangs. That's what this is about. Those over there, they weren't set on fire at least." The neighbor pointed across the alley to a collection of garbage cans pushed together.

"I don't see any graffiti."

"Just turn them." He pointed, directing his finger back and forth.

"The neighbors have been turning them around, but if you turn them around, you'll see."

From where she stood, she could see that the old man was right. A letter "E" was written on the side of one. "Officer, can you help me?" Lauren shouted.

Two officers approached and proceeded to turn around the garbage cans, one by one, like tiles on *Wheel of Fortune*, they revealed the valued phrase, "Pied Piper."

This was a small detail that Lauren had kept hidden from Van, the recurring signature, but there was no hiding it anymore. Evie was right. He was everywhere now, and Lauren did not know how she was going to contain this monster.

"Same thing at my last case with Washington," she turned her back to the name, hoping to diminish its power. "Just some new tagger getting his name out there."

Van remained quiet.

Without him by her side, she proceeded to do her job. She ordered fingerprints be checked at the garage where the fire had been set. She took names of several people, and witness statements, and tried not to ask where Van was, or go looking for him. For some time, he stood there at those garbage cans, looking at the name, and then something on his phone. He disappeared someplace, she assumed it was to the car. When he returned, she had spoken to every neighbor who was outside.

In the car on the drive back to the station the light late evening traffic morphed into early morning traffic. The only words that had been shared since the alley was Lauren telling Van that she would drive.

"Driving over to Passion House Coffee," she told Van as she drove around the roundabout in Logan Square with its towering monument, the Illinois Centennial Monument that was installed in 1918. Just knowing that that structure had stood here, and seen the neighborhood shift, grow, and change, for over a hundred years made her feel as though people's stories who came and went, that their accounts were being witnessed by that eagle perched atop that Roman column.

"*Another* coffee shop?"

"This isn't just another coffee shop, it's the best coffee shop in Logan Square, and I'd argue the city."

"Why's that?"

"Small batch coffee. They source beans from around the world and roast the beans by hand on a vintage 1957 German Probat cast-iron roaster. They offer coffee blends, combining coffees with profiles that complement each other, single-origin coffee…it's fancy. Trust me."

A parking spot was open right in front. Directly across a CTA bus let off a mass of people who descended into the Logan Square Blue Line station.

"Don't need anything fancy. Just a cup, black, for me."

As Lauren unbuckled her seatbelt and reached for the door, Van finally told her what had been on his mind. Anxiety rose in her stomach, acid rising in her throat.

"Pied Piper, does that mean anything to you?"

"It appeared at my last call. I thought I told you that."

Van crossed his arms across his chest. "No, you didn't, but does it mean anything else to you? Further back?"

Before she could say no, he continued.

"I mean, I studied that case extensively. I was obsessed with that case. Your mother goes missing. Then your half-sister? How could a small kid go missing like that, especially when she was supposed to get picked up by her older sister after school? Her father being a pretty respected guy in the force and her stepmother being a stay at home mom who otherwise had an eye on her kids' each and every moment of each and every day. It was bizarre. Then, the little sister shows up floating in the lagoon. Her body unharmed otherwise. Drowning.

Accidental, they said. But I didn't think so, because that little girl, maybe she was with her older sister that day, and then all of a sudden, her older sister went missing too, found eventually by her father's partner in the same park. Remembering nothing. Nothing about how she got there. Nothing about being with her sister earlier that day. Nothing about the lagoon. Then your stepmother? Suicide. That's a lot of tragedy for such a small family. Very strange. All very strange."

Lauren clenched her jaw so tight she was sure she would crack a tooth. "You're sick, Van," she slammed her hand on the dashboard.

Van didn't move.

"You're crazy. You're obsessed and you need to stop! It's disgusting that you're bringing this up. It's insanity that you *keep* bringing up my family trauma like it's some kind of fucking fun case study for you. You studied it in the academy. Well, you're not in the academy anymore. These are real fucking people out here dealing with loss. Me, I'm a real fucking person dealing with loss."

She pushed open the car door, exited, and slammed it shut. Hard.

As she pulled the door open to enter the coffee shop, Van rolled the passenger window down. "I lied. Make it a latte."

"Go to hell, Van!"

"Already there, it's called Chicago."

Her phone rang as she stepped inside. She picked it up with a shout, "What?!"

Everyone in the cafe turned to look at her and Lauren closed in on herself, looking down and lowering her voice as she walked to the far back of the space. "Just a sec," she said to the caller whom she could not yet hear because of the music. A generic coffee house jazz record played in the background, but it was not loud enough to silence the espresso machine, which roared.

Lauren turned around and looked out of the windows, making sure Van could not see her. She didn't want him watching her, scrutinizing her body language. She moved to the furthest back corner and stood to look out a window that faced into an alley.

"Medina, it's Ruth. I don't know what's happening with these kids..."

"Is everything alright?"

"No, Medina. Everything's not alright. It's Mo. He's dead."

The music went quiet, and the buzzing of the espresso machine ceased. Lauren could feel eyes on her, and when she turned around, everyone was staring at her. Everyone was grinning wildly, madly at her.

"It's time, Lauren," the barista called from behind the counter. On the counter before him was Mo's head, split open and rotting. Curved horns jutted out from his eye sockets. His mouth hung wide open, a single gold coin lay on his black, swollen tongue.

As she opened her mouth to scream the door beeped. It was Van. Generic music once again filled the space and Van motioned he was going to the restroom.

The head was gone. The counter was clear.

"Lauren," Ruth said on the other line. "Are you alright?"

"Yes, I'm fine. What happened?"

"We just don't know yet. I wanted you to hear it from me."

Lauren thanked Ruth, placed her order, and returned to the car. Van was already back from the restroom. As she pulled her seatbelt on and looked back at the coffee shop as they pulled away, she saw a familiar person waving to her from the window. A man in a black suit and black hat. His face obscured, except for his grin.

CHAPTER 30

Children's Memorial was an old Chicago structure, and that gave her a sense of something she could hold on to, but this place, too, would soon be gone. The city was changing, and she was changing with it, and she was not sure how much of herself she would lose. Children's Memorial Hospital had saved a lot of kids, but also a lot of them died there as well. Lauren knew that Children's is where they had brought Marie when she was found.

Lauren had taken in heaving sobs of strangers as they watched on in horror; the white sheet, the slow-moving ambulance, the silence, and the finality of that door closing. She was too familiar with the reactions of mothers losing their children, but when it was her own father screaming and crying, begging for Marie to wake up, those cries disrupted something deep within her.

The first wrecking ball struck at 12:18 p.m. The ground rumbled beneath her, and it unlocked something she had long ago buried. Lauren let out a cry and furiously wiped at her eyes. She had not even cried at her father's funeral, and here she found herself sobbing, saying goodbye to the shell of a building where her father mourned his child—a child who maybe should have been Lauren.

In the case of Lauren's missing mother, dead sister, dead stepmother, and now her dead father, there was no reassurance that the bad guys, or the bad *guy*, in this case, would ever find themselves behind bars.

Her sister's murderer would never be caught. She was more than sure of that. As the wrecking ball struck again, Lauren turned. She gave the building one final look and watched as glass and steel and concrete crumbled. The ghosts of those who died at Children's no longer had a home to haunt. She watched as rubble from the top of the building filled a windowless room below.

She was not surprised to see him there.

He removed his hat again and bowed his head. Always in your service, she thought.

"Medina, some kid out there with his father says he wants to talk to you," Officer Bauer said.

"Me?" Lauren stood up from her desk. The precinct was especially loud today.

"That dad and his son are eyewitnesses from the shooting the other night. Kid says he wants to tell you something."

"I didn't think there was anything more to say, but yeah, let me talk to him."

Lauren approached the front desk in the lobby. The boy turned to his father to say something as soon as he saw her.

There was a quick heated exchange followed by, "I'll be okay, Dad."

"I'm not waiting in the car," the father said. "If it's just about your bike, I can stay right here."

Lauren looked from the boy to the father. "How are you both doing? You can just tell me right here what you need to tell me."

The boy looked at his father again. "My bike was stolen, and someone said I should talk to you."

At first, Lauren thought it was a joke. As she tried to make out the word 'What?' the boy pressed his dad to wait for him outside.

"Fine, I'll wait there." He pointed to the vestibule.

Lauren asked the boy to remind her of his name.

"Johnny," he said. "Sharkey, Jr. Just Junior's good." He shot a look over to his father in the vestibule.

"Stolen bicycle? I'm a homicide detective. What's really up?"

"It's the best thing I could think of from making sure he didn't freak out." The kid placed both hands on the counter, looking at his fingers. "It's different kids that be doing it."

"What?"

"The tagging, Pied Piper. It's never the same person. That's part of it. There are lots of kids thinking about doing it, about calling him, the Pied Piper. They don't realize how bad it can get."

"Why are you telling me all of this."

"Because I saw him that night." Junior turned around again to make sure his father was not watching. "I saw *you* the other day, at Young Chicago Writers, with Jordan. He's next..."

"What do you mean?"

"I saw him, up on the 606-trail tagging the piper's name. I thought you'd want to know. I think he's trying to call him."

"Johnny," the boy's father called out to him. "Everything alright?"

"Yeah, she said I need to make a police report for my bike, but it doesn't matter. It's not like I'm going to get it back anyway."

"Well, come on then, let's go!" His father said.

"Junior," she called after him. "Thank you."

Lauren ran back to her desk, grabbing her jacket and bag.

"Where you off to?" Van asked.

"Left my stove on."

"Funny," when he said that she was already halfway down the station.

"Medina?" Van called.

"Gotta take care of something," she shouted behind her.

She waited until she got to her car before she texted Jordan.

"Where are you?"

"Church."

"I'm serious."

"Bloomingdale and Lawndale. Why?"

"Stay there. Coming."

"?"

He was at the trail. So far, Junior's story checked out. Evening traffic had begun, cars blocked intersections. Medina drove her car right up onto the curb on Fullerton and Cicero Avenues. Car horns screamed. Tires screeched. Metal crushed into metal somewhere, but her car was fine.

She drove. Fast.

The car propelled her forward. At Fullerton and Pulaski, her foot pressed down on the gas.

Yellow light.

Press.

Red light.

Press.

In her jacket pocket, she felt her phone vibrate. It was Jordan. She knew what he was planning, plotting, wasting. She was not going to allow him to lose himself.

She parked at the hydrant. Night was lurking at the trail head. A former factory loomed behind. The large exhaust pipes that ran the length of the massive yellow brick building that was an abandoned factory made the structure look like a creature from another world. The black water tower on the roof of the building bore her threat's name in white and gold, for the entire neighborhood to see; Pied Piper.

The Pied Piper was here, and he was luring all of Chicago's children to him with promises of salvation. But what these kids did not realize was that the Pied Piper was a liar. Yes, things would be good, for a short time. Your problem would be taken care of. That horrible parent, sibling, teacher, friend, enemy—whoever would be killed by the Pied Piper. But what he did not tell you is that he would return, again and again, and if you did not kill someone else for him, then he would kill *you*.

When Lauren got to the Lawndale Avenue access point at the elevated trail, there was no one there. She walked down the ramp and looked up at the work the graffiti artists had been commissioned to do.

Lauren's breath stopped when she saw the incomplete image on a brick wall. Half man. Half goat. A horned beast. Pan. Panic.

She ran back up the ramp and ran down the trail. She knew where he would be. Lauren rushed down the boulevard, running as fast as she could as the sun began to set toward Humboldt Park.

When she got to the lagoon, it was already dark, but she saw Jordan standing there. Night had fallen over this place once again. There was no one here except for them, the cold water, and a creature hiding somewhere in the trees.

In the distance, she heard sirens.

"Jordan!" she called out to him. "Hadiya, her family, her friends, none of them would want this. Drop the gun and walk toward me, please," she pleaded.

Jordan let out a wail, the sound pierced her ears, his trauma and mourning ripping through her body.

"Jordan!" she shouted above the approaching siren. They were drawing close. "Don't do this. Put the gun down."

"This will stop it. I told him to take me, and he's coming. I can already hear the music. It's inside of me, Lauren. So, what'll happen if I just shoot myself when he gets here. Will he go away then? He had Fin kill Hadiya. Maybe I'll just kill him, kill the Pied Piper when he gets here."

Lauren's knees were weak. Her stomach cramped. Her eyes stung. "It doesn't matter, Jordan. He's been summoned. He's coming. It doesn't matter if you kill yourself. He's not going to stop. You can't kill him. Don't you think I've tried?!"

Blue lights flickered. The shock of a siren.

"Dammit, Jordan. Put the gun down, now! If another officer arrives and sees you with a weapon...I don't want anything bad to happen. Please, Jordan. Please don't do this. We'll figure out a way together to stop him. You and me. I promise!"

She shouted again for him to drop his weapon, to walk toward her. She did not want to prompt an accident. She had been known for firing too quickly, too soon, too early. Her own gunshots had killed suspects out in the streets, but there was a reason for her speed with the trigger.

He sobbed and wiped his eyes with his sleeves, with the same arm that held the gun.

Lauren held her hands out. "Please Jordan. It'll just be you and me. Let's go get coffee…"

He laughed.

"I'll drive you home. We'll meet at the center, and you can ignore me, and I'll laugh at your jokes, and I'll call your mom and her and I will take you to UIC on your first day of classes. I promise. We will get through this together."

"Lauren..." He cried. Finally saying her name. Finally, trusting her. "I just want my friend back."

A blast fired behind her.

Lauren screamed.

There was another shot, and then another, tearing through the air.

Gunfire erupted behind her.

She could not hear herself screaming, but she could feel the roar of panic and pain burning her throat.

The moments were clear, but then not. It was as if a family picture had been submerged in water. The image was there, but then distorted.

All hearing was lost in her right ear, and a low, ringing took the place of all city noises.

She screamed so hard, and so long she tasted blood. When the shooting stopped, she felt the heat across her face, arms, and chest.

It was a sad silence. It covered everything; the air, the trees, her breath. For a moment she hoped it was her, that she was injured, that she would be the one who would bleed out on asphalt. Perhaps that was the only way to end this. She had started this when she was a child so many years ago in that library when she opened that book, read those words, conjured a killer, and thus made herself one, and now he seemed to be everywhere.

Jordan's body was still at first, as if his entire being were placed on pause. He hung there, like a marionette, and then he collapsed to his knees, his hand slowly releasing its grip on the gun, dangling for a moment in his fingers before falling to the ground. He met her eyes, and while she wanted desperately to believe he was still there with her, she knew he was gone.

Across the lagoon, the man in the black suit appeared. He was always there, always watching. She screamed at him, damning him, cursing him, even though he was already cursed. Even though he had already accomplished panic. He *was* panic.

Lauren found herself sitting on the pavement, cross-legged, her head in her hands. Behind her, she heard a wet gurgle. Van.

She crawled towards him. He had been shot, multiple times. Jordan must have discharged his weapon out of fear and confusion.

"Call it in," Van spit out blood in a spray of gurgles. "Officer down."

Lauren looked back out toward the lagoon. She rocked herself back and forth. She dug her nails in her scalp and screamed. Her insides burned.

She screamed and rocked, one long scream that had been building in her core, not just right now, not just this week. For years.

"Once upon a time," she struggled and sucked in the cold air and rocked back and forth. "In a certain country..." She wiped away at cold tears. "A thousand years ago..." She punched the asphalt beneath her, again and again, breaking flesh and bleeding. "Once in an old castle in the midst of a large and dense forest..." All of it. All of those beginnings, those things were not supposed to pertain to the here or the now, but they did. The vagueness of the fairy tale beginning once symbolized that these dark caves, old castles, locked rooms, and dense, dark woods were not of our reality. But Lauren knew now and always they were. And her insides raged. Her screams shook the surrounding trees, and the night laughed as she grieved.

The man in the black suit removed his hat. He had come to her service so many years ago when she needed him. When she was filled with hate, jealousy, and fury. And so, she had called the Pied Piper to kill Marie. What Lauren did not know then was that he would come back again and again, asking her for other lives.

"Officer down," Van coughed, and wheezed, his words softer this time.

"I can't do that," Lauren sobbed, she looked down and saw Van's face growing pale. She looked back out across the lagoon, the gangly man took a bow. It was as if with that sweeping motion he was telling her I was at your service once, and now you're at mine.

Van killed Jordan. Jordan nearly killed Van, but Van was not yet dead.

"Payment is due," she said.

The Pied Piper's eyes flashed a brilliant yellow.

Van closed his eyes tight. "Why'd you kill your sister?"

"I didn't kill her. The Pied Piper killed her for me because I hated her. I brought her out here, and he dragged her into the lagoon."

After Van drew his last breath, Lauren looked up to find the Pied Piper waving goodbye. He would return again someday, as he had over the years, maybe sooner than normal now with his nursery rhyme posted online for all to see.

Now, anyone had a chance to make this deal.

"You promised me you'd tell me what happened to my mother! You promised me and I gave you Marie! What have you given me?"

The fluttering came from within, inside her chest, and then the music. The music called from within and out. His music.

"I gave you life," the monster spoke. "The life you wanted, of misery and regret. Your martyred life."

Lauren drew her weapon, aimed, and fired. She pulled the trigger again, and again. Each shot across the lagoon was reversed back by him and into her own legs. Lauren collapsed, and as warm blood soaked into her jeans she looked at the canvas of stars above her, points punching into eternity. Many of these lights sparkling above her now in the folds of darkness had been here a hundred years ago or more, had possibly been seen by the Grimm brothers themselves, men who spun tales of horrors and passed them on to children as warnings. But Lauren did not heed the warning, and so she called the ogre in the forest and the witch in the house, she drew the wolf near, and called the Devil.

He stood over her now, neither monster nor man. God of the wild.

"One hundred and thirty..." His golden eyes flared.

"Never!"

"One hundred and thirty children...and then you'll learn what happened to your mother."

"No!"

And just then the music erupted, and she was forced to stand on erect, bullet ridden legs. His puppet. The music pulled her to the water. One jagged movement of bone crushing against bone.

In the water thousands of dead rats bubbled to the surface. Her bloody, battered legs moved against her will. Cold shocking her wounds. Taking her further into the lagoon, the bodies of bloated and rotting rats brushed against her skin. Slimy, peeling, decomposing furry skin pressed against her face and lips. Lauren moved to the center of the lagoon. Her movements not her own, controlled by the music. She tried holding her breath, but the water lapped against her nostrils, and the taste of acrid water shot in the back of her throat, and just as she stretched her head up to gasp for one final breath, she was dragged below.

Their eyes looked at her with hate.

The missing and murdered children of this city, all lived here at the bottom of the lagoon. Hundreds of them. Thousands of them. These were his children. The true payment he sought, and the Pied Piper demanded more.

Their smiles stretched back wide.

Rotted arms reached out to her, their beaten and battered and swollen bodies.

Then, Marie appeared. Black curls floated around her pale face. Black veins as thick as millipedes bulged across her skin.

Her eyes were filled with violence. She kissed Lauren's cheek, and then raised a key to Lauren's eye, a golden key.

The key.

Lauren could no longer hold her breath. She grasped her neck. Eyes rolled back in her head. And just as she opened her mouth wide to allow death to consume her they arrived.

"Goddamnit, Detective!" Officer Bauer reached down and lifted Lauren to her feet. She was still on land. Dry. Her legs uninjured and unharmed.

"I'm fine, but, Van..." She motioned to her partner on the ground. Tears filled her eyes, and she did not know if those tears were for Van, Jordan, the children or herself.

"It's alright, Detective. You should go. Take a seat. Did you want some coffee? I've got some in the car."

Lauren stood there, trembling. He was in her mind. The Pied Piper invaded her thoughts long ago, and he was watching. She followed as the paramedics loaded another young person into their vehicle. The Pied Piper had taken from her another person who mattered, because something about Jordan made her feel less like the murderer she always knew she was.

When Lauren got home, she showered, changed into her academy pants and sweatshirt, and finally stood in front of the cupboard and retrieved the key. The golden key and opened her father's office. She had almost expected to see him there behind his desk, in that creaky, worn chair, coffee mug in hand. The room hummed with the sound of his computer, which she had never bothered turning off.

After he died, she had locked the door, hoping to forget this room even existed. She wished that the house would swallow up this space, sealing up the cracks along the door frame, taking this room and those memories to someplace where the heaviness of his life and job would not have to be tapped into again.

In his final days of cognition, her father spent a lot of time in this room, like always, but there was an absolute frenzy about his movements. He would reach for this, arrange that. He was preparing, and now she could see what he had been making, notes for Washington to leave behind for her.

A thick manila folder lay beside his computer where Washington said it would be. Her father's badge was on top of it.

When she opened it, it was as if all feeling in her legs had been lost. The chair caught her. In the manila folder there were evidence pictures, surely never seen by anyone besides her father, Washington, and now her. First of the lagoon, the trees, and then there was a picture of the *Grimm's Fairy Tales* book laying on the sidewalk, and then a picture of the first page within:

This book belongs to: Lauren Medina

Then, inside the folder there was the actual book, *her* book, her copy of the *Grimm's Fairy Tales* and the inside page her father had torn out before turning it into evidence.

Her father had known all this time that she was at the lagoon with her sister. He had known this entire time she had killed Marie. He had protected her all of these years. One daughter, the killer of his other.

Cain and Abel. Lauren and Marie. He even arranged Washington to train her, to shield her from what she had done as a child so long ago.

But still, she was a killer.

As long as the Pied Piper roamed the city, she would continue to be forced to kill, unless she stopped him, cursed by the loathsome hatred that had consumed her in her youth. The key on the desk reminded her that she had the power to open doors, the book to a new story, and to flip the page to the beginning of a tale that could save her; one in which the maiden destroys the creeping and detestable monster set at destroying her life.

About the Author

Cynthia "Cina" Pelayo is the author of *Loteria*, *Santa Muerte*, *The Missing*, and *Poems of My Night*, all of which have been nominated for International Latino Book Awards. *Poems of My Night* was also nominated for an Elgin Award. She holds a Bachelor of Arts in Journalism, a Master of Science in Marketing, a Master of Fine Arts in Writing, and is a Doctoral Candidate in Business Psychology. Cina was raised in inner city Chicago, where she lives with her husband and children. Find her online at www.cinapelayo.com and on Twitter @cinapelayo